SOMEONE TO LOVE

THE SKYLARK SERIES

MICHELLE MAJOR

Cover Design: Shanoff Designs

Cover Photography: Regina Wamba

Editing: Michelle Fewer

1

SADIE

I TAKE A DEEP BREATH, paste a smile on my face, and walk into the Cover to Cover bookstore in the heart of Skylark, Colorado.

Shelves brimming with books and assorted knick-knacks line the cozy space. The scent of old paper and fresh-baked cookies fills the air, the inviting combination encouraging a person to get comfortable and stay a while.

The conversation dies as five heads turn to stare at me like I farted in church or something.

"Good Lord, Sadie. What's wrong?"

"You look like somebody kicked your puppy."

"Oh my God, did someone kick one of your dogs?"

"Talk about losing it. I'll lose it all over that dog kicker."

"You guys, no. The dogs are fine." I run a training and boarding facility out of my house, and sadly the pups are the only overnight visitors I can claim.

I guess the attempt to fix my face so the emotions tumbling through me aren't written all over it is a massive fail.

The other members of the book club are seated in the charmingly mismatched chairs around the reclaimed oak table, a gorgeous charcuterie board in the center—Molly's creation, no doubt. Molly McAllister, our local flower farmer, has the creativity to make everything she touches, floral or otherwise, look Instagram-worthy.

"No one kicked anybody's dog." I move forward and drop into the chair across from Iris Dixon, our town's recently appointed mayor.

"Then what is it?" Iris frowns. "Because you don't look so good, Sads."

"It's nothing." I try to sound upbeat, but my tone is more feral cat meow than calm and positive. I don't like talking about myself or being in the spotlight. There's a reason I spend more time socializing the dogs I train than talking to creatures who will call me out on my obvious attempts at bullshit.

A poker player, I'm not.

"We should focus on the book." I smile again, ignoring the ache in my cheeks. "It was really inspiring. Good pick, Sloane."

"I'm glad you liked it." The owner of Cover to Cover, and our book club's founder, nods as her gaze drops to my hands. She grimaces ever so slightly. "Do me a favor, and don't rip it up."

I follow her gaze and see that I'm indeed holding the book in a white-knuckled grip. If I had the strength, I'd probably have already pulled the pages apart at the spine.

"We can't concentrate until you spill it." Avah Harris, who made the original puppy-kicking comment, leans forward in her chair. "Sloane has rosé. Do you need a glass?"

Molly tips her glass toward me. "Liquid fortitude helps sometimes. Trust me, I'm an expert."

In addition to living with a cantankerous mother-in-law, Molly is raising her seven-year-old twins as a single parent after a river-rafting accident took her adventure-chasing husband's life two years ago.

To be honest, it's a wonder Molly manages her life as well as she does, with or without liquid fortitude. Despite her big talk,

I've never seen her drink more than half a glass, always vigilant about her responsibilities. I can relate to that.

"I'm not upset." I smooth a palm over the cover of the book then give it a gentle pat for good measure. "My sister called. She's getting married."

"That's good news?" Iris asks, one delicate brow arching. "I don't remember you mentioning Piper having a boyfriend."

"Tonight is the first I heard about it." I try for another smile, but the muscles of my face refuse to cooperate. "They met at the hospital where she got a job after nursing school. Turns out he's also from Skylark." My laugh sounds more like a cat with its tail caught in the door. "Imagine that."

"So you know him?" Sloane asks. "Are there red flags?"

"I *do* know him." I hold my thumb and index finger an inch apart. "Perhaps a teensy yellow flag. My sister's twenty-two, but Brad—Bradley, he goes by his full name now—is my age. Eleven years older. He and I were friends in high school."

"How close of friends?" Taylor Maxwell asks quietly. Taylor, our local librarian, does everything quietly. I might not like attention, but Taylor, with her creamy complexion and soft blue eyes, literally wilts under it.

"We were best friends. Well, I thought so anyway. We were both at CSU for undergrad. He was on a pre-med track, and I was pre-veterinary medicine. Then Mom died, and things changed."

Iris cringes. "Is your sister marrying a guy who's seen your hoo-ha?"

I choke out a real laugh. "No, he never—we weren't...it wasn't like that."

"I remember him," Avah says. She's a couple of years younger than me, and we weren't friends until we both joined Sloane's Cool Girls Book Club. I'm not sure any of us, other than Sloane and Avah, ever identified as cool girls. "He was a dick in high school. You were too nice to notice, or at least to say anything."

When I open my mouth to protest, nothing comes out. She's

not wrong. About him...or me. I take a healthy swig from the plastic wine glass Sloane hands me. "I might have had a small crush on Bradley back in the day."

"Who changes their name *to* Bradley?" Molly throws up her hands. "I'm embarrassed for the guy."

"He's finishing up an orthopedic fellowship. Very prestigious, Piper tells me."

"So when is this...happy occasion taking place?" Taylor asks.

"Fourth of July weekend in Vail."

I close my eyes at the round of gasps that greets this pertinent detail.

"That's like six weeks away," Avah points out. "Is she preggers?"

"No." I shake my head. "At least, not that she's told me. The lodge had a cancellation, and she snagged the date. The other option was waiting a year."

Molly sighs. It's the sound of a woman who, in hindsight, wishes she would have waited instead of falling fast and hard for a man who was a consummate charmer and world-class rafting guide but a less-than-ideal husband. "She's twenty-two. What's the hurry?"

"I don't know," I answer honestly. "I'm happy, just caught off guard. Our mom would be happy she found love." That at least one of us has.

"Love is a many splendored thing," Taylor announces.

The rest of us stare at her.

"It's an old song from a movie of the same name." A blush stains her cheeks. "My grandma used to sing it."

Avah pats her arm. "We'll take your word for it, sweetie."

"Sadie, tell us how we can help." Sloane slides into the chair next to Iris. "I'm sure you'll have tons of planning to do with such short notice."

I swallow back the hurt that clogs my throat. "Piper is still close with a couple of high school friends and the girls from her sorority. I guess the youngsters are doing most of the planning."

"You're thirty-three." Iris looks disgusted on my behalf. "Not exactly an old maid."

I nod my agreement, even though old maid is unfortunately my vibe. I can barely keep up with the turbulent emotions churning through me. I don't like emotions. Compartmentalization is one of my superpowers, and I need to summon every bit of energy before I lose it in front of these women.

We're friends, but the bond still feels tenuous—at least for me. Before Sloane asked me to join the book club, I hadn't made close female friends since my best friend Sally and I met in second grade. She and her wife, Trina, have been it for me until the book club. Sure, I'm friendly with my clients—the ones who are still with me at any rate. But we're not *friends* friends.

I love this group of women. The monthly meetings and occasional nights out in our small town mean the world to me. I don't want to jeopardize that, and I learned a long time ago that being anything but easy and accommodating is a quick way to trouble.

"It would help if we switch topics to the book," I say, not bothering to reach for another smile. I'm not fooling anyone.

"I agree with Sadie." Sloane nods and then holds up our book selection for the month.

According to the book jacket bio, Kristen Quinn is a freelance writer and life coach. I've never met a life coach, but I could probably use one. My life is pretty pathetic. *The Year of Losing It* is Kristen's debut. It documents her path to letting go of the fear she claims had overpowered her since childhood. Also relatable, sadly.

"I found the author's journey inspiring," Molly says.

"I like how she broke the sections down by month, so we could follow her activities as she checked each item off her list," Taylor adds.

Sloane nods. "She really learned important stuff along the way, lessons we can each apply to our lives. She's kind of a role model, you know?"

"Yeah, maybe." Avah pops a piece of cheese into her mouth and chews thoughtfully. "But what did she really learn from a hot air balloon ride or doing a tandem jump out of a plane?"

Iris snorts. "Because it's so easy to jump out of a plane? Maybe she learned to be brave. Or the value of stepping outside her comfort zone."

"Saying yes to something big," Molly murmurs.

"Releasing control," I add, although the thought of jumping out of a plane makes me think about losing bladder control.

"Okay, okay. Don't come at me." Avah holds up a hand. Her fingers are long and slender with a subtle pink polish coloring her nails. Mine can best be described as raggedy-ass. I make a mental note to up my self-care game, but the likelihood of it happening is doubtful.

"I'm not saying a tandem jump isn't cool," Avah continues. "It makes a great bucket list item. But I don't think everything she chose pushed her in a life-altering way. Sometimes she seemed more focused on hyping her basic-bitch nature girl aesthetic, and selling books, of course."

"There's nothing wrong with an author wanting to sell books," Sloane shoots back.

Avah shrugs. "I'm just saying that not every experience has to be a monumental adventure to find meaning in it."

Molly breathes out an overdramatic sigh. "Avah's right. Sometimes getting out of bed in the morning is a monumental accomplishment, but it would make a boring story."

I laugh at the joke before my gaze snags on Sloane. She's swiping a hand across her cheeks, trying to wipe away the tears she can't seem to stop.

"Hey there, girl. What is it?" I climb out of my chair and circle the table to sit in the empty one next to her, grabbing her hand.

"Did I make you cry?" Avah sounds horrified. "I'm sorry. I think getting out of your comfort zone is a good idea. We could all use it. I could use it, and I just don't do it. Yes, I found her tone sanctimonious and—"

"Not helping," Molly says, elbowing Avah.

Iris, who's sitting on Sloane's other side, plucks a napkin from the center of the table and hands it to the bookstore owner.

"What's going on? You don't usually mind divisive book discussions."

"It's not about the book. I didn't want to tell you guys this now. I don't want to make book club about me and my—"

"Oh, my God, you're pregnant!" Molly interrupts.

Sloane laughs as she dabs the napkin at the corners of her eyes. "Hardly. It's been so long since I've had sex that I might be a born-again virgin."

"That's not a thing," I say quietly. I should know.

Taylor leans forward. "Please tell us you're okay."

Sloane wrinkles her nose. "I'll be okay, but I've been getting super tired recently and feeling kind of dizzy. I went to the eye doctor thinking I needed glasses, but it's not that."

Before this moment, I never truly appreciated the phrase "so quiet you could hear a pin drop." No one breathes as we wait for Sloane to say more.

"They ran some tests and...well...I have a little cancer."

"I don't think *little* is an adjective you use to describe cancer," Avah says.

"What kind?" Iris demands.

"Acute lymphocytic leukemia." Sloane's voice is small. "ALL, for short."

I open my mouth to say something—anything—to make this moment better or ease the fear in my friend's voice, but I have no words. Luckily, Iris always has words.

"Leukemia is treatable," she says with the confidence of a top-notch oncologist. "I knew a boy who had leukemia in third grade. He's fine now."

"Yeah, my brother had leukemia as a kid," Sloane tells us. "Rates of recovery are better in younger patients, but I'll be fine. I think."

Molly nods. "Of course, you'll be fine."

"What can we do?" Iris asks, always quick to take charge.

"We can drive you to doctor appointments," Molly offers. "Stock your freezer with meals."

Sloane shakes her head. "They're working on a treatment plan. Hopefully just chemo." She laughs without humor. "I can't believe I'm wishing for chemotherapy. Until the doctors finalize next steps, I want to act like everything is normal."

"But it's not," Iris answers, always pragmatic.

"We can pretend for now," Taylor counters, her tone adamant.

The rest of us go quiet without missing a beat because Taylor never takes a firm tone. It means something.

Sloane offers another smile. "Just saying the words out loud makes them less scary," she tells us, flipping open the book. "I understand what Avah was saying about Kristen's year coming off as inauthentic in some chapters. So I'd like to take this next year, or however long it takes—because we're going to be together in this book club forever—to each check an item off our bucket list."

What if I don't have a bucket list?

"Something from your heart," she continues, looking at me like she can read my mind. Damn that no poker face. "It should be scary, but also have the power to change your life."

"Skydiving has the power to change your life." Iris gives a mock shudder. "Especially if the parachute doesn't open."

Sloane takes a sip of wine. "You know what I mean. I want to do a bucket list club. I need something to take my mind off of..." Her hand is trembling so much, a bit of pink liquid sloshes over the side of the cup, and she places it back on the table. "Off of me."

"We'll do it," Molly answers, glancing from me to Taylor to Iris to Avah.

They each look about as excited as I feel—which is definitely not excited—but I join them in nodding.

"Do we all pick something now or come up with ideas later?" I ask.

Molly shakes her head. "We should go one at a time, so the rest of us can support whoever is working on their bucket list activity."

"They need to be big and meaningful," Iris adds.

"But nothing that takes too long," Avah blurts, then clasps a hand over her mouth. "I hate that I even said those words. I mean, we don't want to lose momentum."

Sloane nods. "I agree."

There's another beat of silence, but not the pin-drop kind. It's heavy and tense, like each of us is well aware of the fears we want to face, but no one is quite ready to volunteer.

Sloane tucks a strand of mahogany-colored hair behind her ear. She has effortlessly beautiful hair—long and shiny, with waves that some women spend ridiculous amounts of money on products to achieve. I barely know how to use a blow dryer. My hair is dishwater blonde and streaky from hours in the sun walking dogs.

Will she lose her hair? Will the chemo get rid of the cancer? This equation has so many unknowns, and she's asked something so small from us.

In solidarity, my hand shoots up like I'm back in the classroom. "I'll do it. I'll go first."

"Thank you," Sloane says, wrapping an arm around my shoulder.

"Way to get in there, Sadie Hart." Avah points at me. "Do you need help coming up with your bucket list item?"

"No." Sloane squeezes me tighter. "We each need to figure out a personal challenge on our own."

"But what if we don't have anything that challenges us?" Iris asks.

"Everyone has something." Sloane levels a look at our meticulous, organized, some might say anal-retentive friend.

Iris lived in Skylark for a few months as a teenager before returning last year for a job in the mayor's office. She and Sloane became friends in high school, and their bond endured. At the start of our book club meetings, Iris seemed even more uncomfortable than me at trying to make small talk, but we're both finding our way.

"I'll think of something when it's my turn," Iris promises.

Sloane pats my shoulder, then pulls her hand away. "I appreciate you going first. Take your time coming up with your—"

"I want to have sex," I say before I lose my nerve.

The ladies take the announcement in stride.

"We've already established there's no such thing as a born-again virgin," Molly reminds me.

"Can you be more specific?" Avah asks. "Do you want to have sex outside or with a stranger or—"

"I'm an actual virgin."

We're back to pin-drop silence, and I feel like I'm going to puke. Avah and Molly gape as if I admitted to having one of those weird obsessions like eating my own fingernails.

"I didn't date in high school." I try to shrug off how ridiculous I feel admitting all of this, only my shoulders bob up and down like they have a mind of their own. "Or college. Then my mom died, and I was raising Piper."

"You weren't conjoined," Avah points out. "And you're not ugly."

"Crushing it with that compliment." Molly pats Avah's arm. "Absolutely crushing it."

"You know what I mean," Avah mutters.

"It's perfect for our bucket list club," Sloane says, and even though I'd like to crawl under the table until my cheeks stop burning like they're on fire, which might take a while, something in her tone makes me turn to face her.

Sloane is smiling with tears in her eyes, but not the sad kind from before. These seem grateful. "This is exactly the kind of life-changing decision I hoped you all would find a way to make. Kristen Quinn would be so proud."

Avah lets out a not-so-delicate snort. "She's probably sad she didn't recount her cherry-popping for an essay she could make money off."

"She's not about the money," Sloane insists.

"Girl..." Avah's blue eyes roll to the ceiling. "Have you looked at her Instagram? She's living life like a Kardashian."

"We are still in the 'you need to shut your mouth' part of the discussion," Molly says and grimaces at Sloane, but Avah's not exactly wrong. She's been sending screenshots of Kristen Quinn's posts and stories.

Sloane waves off their concerns. "We're talking about Sadie. This means something to her."

"I want to do it before my sister's wedding. If I don't give myself a timeframe...who knows how long it will take me. I've already got cobwebs in my vajayjay at the ripe old age of thirty-three."

"How can we help?" Taylor asks.

Sloane claps her hands. "Let's set you up on a dating app."

"You need to try The Club," Iris suggests. "That's the one for casual sex. Unless you want insta-love and committed sex, in which case—"

"No dating app. I can figure this out," I tell them. "I just needed the motivation, and now I've got it."

Hopefully, by next month I'll no longer be a virgin. What a strange and wonderful and terrifying concept. There was a line in *The Year of Losing It* about opening your mind to possibilities so the universe can bring you what you need. I sure as hell hope that's the case because it's been a very long dry spell and I need a man... stat. This could be the first step to a new and improved version of Sadie. One that's way overdue.

"Yay for Kristen Quinn and *The Year of Losing It*," Taylor says.

"Literally," Avah adds and gently smacks Molly on the arm. "I will not be silenced."

"Next month, I'm bringing duct tape," Molly answers, winking at me.

2

SADIE

I MUST BE DREAMING. Why else would Captain America—or the actor who plays him on screen—be kissing his way along my bare shoulder?

They're soft kisses, a featherlight whisper against my skin. As dreams go, I'll take this over the usual scenario of showing up for my high school prom wearing only a bra and panties.

High-waisted granny panties, no less. White. Always plain, boring white, just like real life.

I shiver as dream Cap nibbles the sensitive spot at the crook of my neck, and then...ew...why does his breath smell like ham?

"Stop, Max. Down. Blech."

Sputtering, I scramble to sit and shove away my ten-year-old rescue mutt. All thoughts of hottie Chris Evans vanish as I wipe away the residual dog drool coating my chin.

"Sweet Maxie, I set the alarm for a reason."

Max wags his bushy tail, jumps off the bed and then back up again, wildly excited to start another day.

I give his scruffy ears a scratch. "Okay, okay. Gotta drain the main vein? I get it, buddy."

I flip off the covers, pick up my phone, and shove my feet into the fuzzy slippers beside the bed. Grabbing a flannel shirt from the hook on the closet door, I follow Max downstairs.

There are three dogs boarding with me at the moment and a couple more arriving for daycare this morning. I let Max out into the fenced backyard before opening the other crates. One of the perks of being canine master of the house is first dibs on the bush you pick to hydrate each morning.

First out of the boarders is Princess, a five-month old corgi who is energetic, curious and spoiled rotten by her high-strung owner. She bounds into the yard and immediately starts trying to herd Max, who is infinitely patient with her. Next up is Lilly, a three-year-old goldendoodle. She blinks her long eyelashes as I release her from her kennel, while Stoop, the elderly dachshund in the fake wood crate that also serves as an end table, waits patiently.

"Did anyone else have sweet dreams?" I ask the dogs as they greet me before trotting to the patio door. Mornings mean serious potty business around here.

Neither dog answers, not that I expect them to. I might spend more of my life with four-legged creatures than two, but I understand they can't talk back.

It doesn't stop me from continuing my one-sided conversation. I pour a glass of water, hit the brew button on the coffee maker I filled last night, and stroll into the backyard.

"Your mommy's coming home today," I tell Lilly, who's sniffing one of the hardy shrubs I planted along the fence line.

I've given up on a golf-course-worthy lawn. Operating a dog boarding operation out of my house for the past ten years has proven that no amount of water and love can prevail over a steady onslaught of canine acid.

My yard is tidy-ish with a landscape plan that includes swaths of mulch, large boulders, and grasses native to Colorado. Even without the dog traffic, the Rocky Mountain foothills aren't a hospitable growing climate for anything other than the most rugged plants and flowers. I only bother with flowers on the front porch, and they have to be drought tolerant.

I love my hometown of Skylark, Colorado, but choose to leave the business of bountiful baskets of blooms to the cute storefronts downtown. My clients are more concerned with sniffing and digging holes than admiring my non-existent gardening prowess.

After gulping down a few swigs of water, I button up the flannel. The end of May in Colorado means cool early mornings before the bright sun warms to another glorious day.

My phone buzzes, and I smile at the text from my sister.

> Piper: How's my Maxie this morning?

> Me: picture of Max rolling on his back in a pile of who knows what.

> Me: Missing you as always.

> Piper: 🖼 I found the perfect ring bearer pillow for him.

> Piper: A screenshot of a puffy silk saddle

> Me: He'll love it.

"You'll love it, right, Max?"

The dog gives me a dubious look.

"Yeah, humiliating," I agree, although I'll never say that to my sister. Piper is thrilled to have our beloved dog participate in her upcoming nuptials, and I won't put a damper on her excitement.

There's nothing I won't do for my half-sister. My mom and I were a dynamic duo for the first ten years of my life, and I thought that was all I needed. Then came Piper, the result of an unexpected pregnancy from a short and disastrous attempt at dating by our perpetually single mom.

I'd been horrified at the thought of a baby sister, but from the moment Mom placed the wriggling bundle into my arms, it was instant love and devotion. Piper became the piece of my heart I hadn't known was missing. She's also the reason I chose to forgo the unicorn of scholarships—a full-ride to a private university in California—when the time came for me to go to college.

Instead, I took out loans and worked evenings to put myself through the pre-vet program at the state university an hour away from Skylark so I could stay close to Mom and Piper.

I gave up even more, everything really, when a drunk driver careening down the wrong side of the highway on a snowy night stole Mom from us.

I'd been one semester away from graduating and had already been accepted to the veterinary school at a top-rated program in Texas. But my life dreams—and the sorrow of losing my mother—didn't seem to compare to Piper's overwhelming grief. I moved into Mom's house, which a meager life insurance policy had blessedly paid off, and became guardian to my younger sister.

For weeks, I worried about how I'd pay the bills and keep my twelve-year-old sister from disappearing into her despair. Then a middle-aged neighbor knocked on the door and asked if I'd do her the massive favor of dog-sitting while she tried to reignite the spark in her marriage with an erotic weekend getaway. A cringey TMI tidbit, but I agreed. The woman's goofy black lab galloped into the house, whacked everything off the coffee table with his wild tail, and made Piper smile for the first time since our mother's accident.

The dog was a new lease—or leash, as it went—on life for us. *Sadie Hart's House of Dog* was born.

At the time, I hadn't planned to add a permanent dog to our family of two. I was plenty busy growing the business through word of mouth and daily pack walks through the neighborhoods of our bustling small town. As often happens with meant-to-be connections, Max found us. He was a three-month-old ball of fluff abandoned on the playground and scooped up by my sorrowful sister, who needed him as much as he needed her.

Even though Piper transitioned through her grief and her

sunny personality returned, Max's devotion never wavered. He might be my dog at this point, but his heart belongs to Piper. Just like mine.

In a few weeks, Piper will be starting a new chapter with my childhood crush. Not on purpose, of course. And thinking too much about how my sister and the guy I pined after for a humiliating number of years came to be a couple makes my heart ache for what I might never have. But Max and I will show up for the wedding weekend in the mountains with our best foot—and paw—forward.

Even if I wind up grinding my molars to tiny nubs trying to keep a carefree smile on my face while ignoring the pitying looks and gentle snubs from my sister's cliquey friends and Bradley Carlson's snobbish family.

Even if my date for the weekend wakes himself up at night with the potency of his own dog farts.

Because that's the kind of loyal I am.

"No, no, no!" I jab my fist toward the bluebird sky in protest. All three dogs freeze. "Sorry, guys. Not you. No, me."

I pace through the yard, watching where I'm going so I don't step in any random piles of poo. "Sadie Hart isn't loyal like a dog," I tell my rapt audience. "I don't sit or stay. No fleas. I sure can't reach around to lick my private bits."

A choked laugh reverberates from the other side of the privacy fence, and my heart plummets to my toes right along with my self-respect.

What in the world is my newish next-door neighbor, the mysterious specter of a man who moved in a few weeks ago, doing in his backyard?

The guy never leaves the house. And based on the number of boxes deposited on his porch by the UPS drivers each day, I suspect he's an agoraphobe with a compulsive shopping disorder.

It isn't like I've been spying, but that giant brown truck

pulling to a squeaky-braked stop at the curb multiple times a day sets my posse of dogs into a frenzy. Every single time.

Yet I haven't met the man or even caught sight of his face. On occasion, I've seen him pull out in a massive SUV with blacked-out windows, but no one in our cul-de-sac seems to know much about him.

The close-knit community of Skylark, Colorado doesn't take kindly to suspicious behavior, and being antisocial tops that list.

Of all the times for the new guy to be outside.

"It's not polite to eavesdrop," I shout, pretending my face isn't flaming with embarrassment.

"Your voice probably carried to the other side of the street," he calls back. "Out of curiosity, what would happen if you could reach those bits?"

I gasp. "Rude."

Lilly barks as if to let me know she's got my back.

The answering chuckle from the other side of the fence is deep and a bit gravelly. Definitely not the reason for the unexpected goosebumps that prick my skin.

I glance up to see the top of a thick mop of sandy brown hair —impressive since the fence is six feet tall—moving closer.

Oh, hell, no. I'm not meeting my deranged hoarder neighbor under these circumstances.

"Let's go," I say to the dogs and make a dash for my back door.

Stoop is slow on the uptake, blind in one eye, and I trip over his stubby back end as he stops directly in my path. My slipper catches on the edge of a weathered Adirondack chair, and my knees and palms hit the concrete patio.

Go-time for the dogs, who circle like this is the best game they've ever played. I can't help but welcome their exuberance, even if it means when growly neighbor guy peers over the fence, I'll look like the weirdo dog lady people in town have labeled me for the past decade.

Except, when I manage to stand and turn, the mysterious

neighbor has vanished. My eccentricity isn't enough to keep a potential international super spy, hoarder, or shopaholic interested.

I'm not shocked, although the disappointment that lances my belly is a bit of a surprise. Go figure. I'm suddenly invested in seeing the face that rumbling laugh belongs to, even if he's laughing *at* me.

3

IAN

I REMEMBER my Super Bowl win like it was yesterday. The energy. The crowd. The adrenaline. Existing in the coveted flow state of elite athletes. The flow meant I was ready.

My gift as a quarterback is—was—the ability to become one with the game. All those hours of practice and conditioning, beating my body and mind into submission until nothing could pierce my confidence. Not to go all Jerry Maguire on you, but I'm the entire package. The Quan.

Any given Sunday, I made miracles happen.

I managed that feat with a screaming stadium of fans and millions more watching at home, so surely I can fake the whole confident dad thing for one twelve-year-old kid.

Why won't my damn palms stop sweating?

I've been pacing the living room of my new house for the past hour. Pausing in front of the distressed white shelves I set up on either side of the room's gas fireplace, I adjust—what did the catalog call it—the love knot.

The clay sculpture looks more like a pile of dog crap to me. But the trendy design catalog I ordered almost everything from to fill the two-story space assured me it's farmhouse perfection.

I want my daughter to consider this house her home. Maybe this piece of— this love knot will prove I'm serious. Trustworthy. Responsible. Worthy of her love.

I hope Riva approves. And that Monika, my ex and Riva's mother, agrees.

Hell, earlier this morning, I was half-tempted to ask my canine-chatty neighbor if she approved. For the past four weeks, I've listened to her talk to the dogs that amble around her backyard without her once noticing I'm out there.

The dogs sense my presence often enough, but haven't given me away. They seem to realize her monologues make me feel like I'm not alone.

My neighbor has plenty of conversations with humans, too. These mainly occur in her driveway when people drop off or pick up their precious Fidos and Fifis.

At first, based on the snippets of gut spilling I heard through my open kitchen window, I thought she was a professional therapist. Considering the verbal diarrhea the woman next door elicits from her customers, maybe dog trainers are the new hairstylists.

This solitude is my own doing.

I'm waiting for Riva to arrive so we can start our lives together in this new Pleasantville-esque town. A happy life—just the kind my daughter deserves.

One I'm determined to give her.

The doorbell rings, and I startle, wiping damp hands on my athletic shorts. This is it. Go time.

But it's not Monika and Riva on the other side of the door.

"Hi, I'm Sadie."

I recognize her, of course. She comes and goes multiple times daily, loading dogs in and out of her ancient Land Cruiser. Still, her face up close is a surprise. A beautiful, beguiling surprise.

I bet she's close to my age—thirty-five a month ago—or maybe a few years younger, with creamy skin and freckles dotting the bridge of her nose. Her brown eyes are wide-set with flecks of gold around the edges, and her mouth is soft with a lower lip fuller than the upper.

An incredibly kissable mouth, I'm shocked to discover.

She usually wears shapeless clothes: faded jeans with a flannel over a loose T-shirt. Utilitarian, basic, no-nonsense. This afternoon it's pushing eighty degrees, so she's in cut-offs and a gray tank top that skims her oddly delectable curves and has a hole near the bottom hem.

Her raggedy-ass wardrobe fascinates me. My girlfriends are models, actresses, or influencers—women who preen and gallivant and take pride in their fashion sense. I could give a rat's ass about fashion, and living next to a woman who doesn't care either validates my decision to move to this nondescript little town.

I picked it sight unseen based on a Buzzfeed ranking of the happiest towns in America. Skylark, Colorado topped the list. It was a risk, but I want to raise my daughter in a place where people are normal. I want to *feel* normal.

"Hello?" A hand waves in front of my face. "I don't mean to interrupt anything, like finishing the build-out of your freaky basement dungeon. I thought I'd officially introduce myself. I'm your next-door neighbor."

I blink. "I know who you are. The dog lady. What's this about a dungeon in my basement?"

It's her turn to blink—like she didn't realize she said that part out loud.

"Oh, well...never mind." She takes a step back, and I half expect her to turn tail and run as her face goes slack, like she's seeing me for the first time.

Her gaze travels up and down my body. I might have retired from a career as a professional athlete, but I still work out. Not to sound like an egotistical jackhole, but I'm not hard on the eyes.

Except Sadie squints and swallows, like taking in all six-foot-four inches of me might make her sick to her stomach. Okay, that's a first from a woman. Or anyone.

Huh.

"Tell me more about this dungeon," I suggest with a wink. "Are there handcuffs?" Flirting always works for me.

Or it has until now.

She visibly shudders. *Shudders*. And crosses her arms over her chest. I'm trying hard not to notice her chest, but it's damn near perfect.

"It's just that no one in the neighborhood has met you," she explains, craning her neck to look over my shoulder. "Your shades are always drawn and you drive an SUV with blacked-out windows and have loads of boxes delivered. Big ones. Remember the scene in *Twilight* when Bella calls Edward out on being a vampire?"

Is the cute dog lady on something? "Who the hell are Edward and Bella?"

She grimaces then waves away my question like dandelion fluff. "It doesn't matter. To each his own. Anyway—"

"I'm furnishing a house. I'm having *furniture* delivered. Not paraphernalia for a dungeon. I don't even own handcuffs."

"You must not listen to true crime podcasts." She shrugs. "Lots of creepers keep rooms like that in the basement. Not lots I guess, but you know what I mean."

Unfortunately, I do.

I rub a hand along the back of my neck. "People around here think I'm a creeper? I've been trying to keep a low profile."

A no profile until Riva arrives, because I don't want the fact that she has a famous father to affect her getting settled.

Sadie studies me for a long moment, as if trying to assess whether I'm telling the truth, and I wait for recognition to dawn.

Unless this woman lives under a rock—which I can tell you she doesn't since her house is next door—she's seen what my agent calls my enviably chiseled jawline on TV at some point. I have commercial endorsements for products ranging from car insurance to burgers to high-end fashion lines.

She draws in a deep breath. Here we go.

I'm ready for her to fawn, but instead she says, "There are online quizzes you can take to determine whether your neighbors might be serial killers based on their observed habits."

My chiseled jaw goes slack because it's clear she's done some research. Research that doesn't involve my career stats.

"What's my score?" I ask, genuinely curious despite the peculiarity of this exchange.

"You don't want to know," she says simply. "Anyway, nice to meet you, mystery guy. I'll spread the word that the neighborhood won't be featured on *Dateline* any time soon."

She glances past my shoulder again. "I had a dog escape into your yard. Is it okay to go through your side gate to grab her? I wanted to ask first before heading in. Trespassing and whatnot."

"You all but accuse me of being a deranged murderer, and you're concerned about trespassing?" I cough out a laugh and then pin her with a severe glare, the kind that used to make upstart reporters and unprepared defensive coordinators quake in their shoes.

Dog lady nods, seemingly unfazed. But I catch a hint of color rising to her cheeks and like the thought I put it there.

"It's Princess's first time overnight with me. She slipped under the fence when my back was turned. Wiggly little thing. I can't lose a pup during her first stay, you know? Her owner is already nervous about being away from her."

"Wow, you talk fast." I'm focused on her mouth so I don't miss anything and find I like how her lips turned up at the corners when she said wiggly. A little more than I should.

A sleek black Mercedes pulls to a stop at the curb. It has to be Monika and Riva. "Sure, go get your lost dog. The gate is unlocked." I step onto the front porch. "I won't even try to kidnap you while you're on my property."

"Appreciate that," she says with a bright smile but still no recognition.

Maybe I lucked out by moving next door to the one person who exclusively watches the Puppy Bowl on Super Bowl Sunday.

I want a regular life. Sadie, the dog lady, isn't what I had in mind when I imagine my perfect neighbor, but she's quickly converting me.

She hops off the side of the porch as the back door to the Mercedes slams shut.

"Hey, there," I call with a wave that neither my ex nor my daughter return.

"You weren't joking about going low-profile," Monika says as the driver unloads several duffle bags from the trunk.

"Is there a pool?" Riva asks as she surveys the modest neighborhood like she's never seen a house less than five thousand square feet. Maybe that's true, which is one more way I've failed her up until now. I try to see Elmwood Circle through the eyes of a kid who's lived most of her life in posh Beverly Hills.

Monika and I only dated for a few months at the start of my NFL career. I was on cloud nine with the money and fame from my hefty rookie contract, and she was a fledgling starlet intent on getting her name in the headlines any way she could. Our spark flamed hot and fast, burning out quickly, but not before Monika's surprise pregnancy. Much to the shock of both our agents, we agreed we wanted the baby and have been somewhat effectively co-parenting ever since.

In truth, Monika does the heavy lifting. I got traded from LA to Atlanta after one season and two concussions. I stayed healthy and focused long enough to achieve a Super Bowl ring and four respectable—if disappointing in the end—playoff runs.

I did my best—or told myself as much—to see Riva on bye weeks or in the off-season. Mostly, I sent elaborate gifts and FaceTimed while Monika took our daughter to various shoots and sets as her career took off. Easy enough, she claimed, when Riva was younger, but once she started school, things changed.

Monika hit it big with an ongoing role in a superhero franchise, while I was downed by a dirty sack during a Monday night game that knocked me unconscious for twenty minutes. I came to in a smelly locker room at a stadium far from home. I'm not saying my life flashed before my eyes. But the gravity of what I was risking did.

To my agent's chagrin, and the speculation of various sports channel pundits, I announced my retirement at the end of my team's dismal finish last season.

"No pool, but there's a big maple tree in back that's perfect for a tire swing." I smile and try to portray a confidence I don't feel.

"Riva is allergic to rubber," Monika tells me with a sniff.

"And peanut butter," the girl adds.

I'm familiar with the nut allergy, but is there such a thing as a rubber allergy? I grab bags while the driver pretends to ignore this first-world-problems conversation. "We can find a non-rubber swing."

"I'd rather have a pool." Riva kicks the toe of her sparkly sneaker against the cobblestone path leading to the front of the house. "Or go with Mom to Hawaii. Everyone there has a pool or lives near the ocean."

Monika is filming on location in Maui for the next six weeks, which is why Riva is with me for the summer. And beyond, since the plan is for her to live here full-time when the school year resumes. I want a do-over on being a dad, full stop.

"You and your dad are going to have a great time together," Monika says, wrinkling her nose like one of the dog lady's pups has deposited a turd at her feet. "So much fun to be had in... Pleasantville." Oscar-worthy performance, it's not.

"Skylark," I correct.

"Sure," she agrees.

In the beat of silence, while the three of us contemplate the irony of the town I chose to move to based solely on an online quiz, I hear the side gate to the yard squeak open.

"A dog," Riva practically squeals. "Daddy got me a dog."

Uh...first of all, my heart flips at the word daddy, which she hasn't called me for far too long. Then it plummets because 1. I didn't get her a dog, 2. Monika made me promise no pets, and 3. Sadie, the dog lady, is staring at my ex the way I want her to look at me.

Complete astonishment and awe.

Monika Graham is a bona fide A-lister.

"We agreed," Monika reminds me through clenched teeth as Riva hurtles toward Sadie and the wriggly pup trying to escape her grasp.

"I didn't." I take a step forward. "Riva, that's not—"

"Hello." Sadie tears her gaze from my ex and holds up a hand like she and Riva are playing a game of Red Light, Green Light. My daughter digs in her heels and stops mid-stride. Impressive. "Do you like dogs?"

Her voice is calm and commanding in a weirdly appealing way. I've heard the tone before. It's how she talks to the dogs she trains in her backyard. However, she doesn't sound so self-assured when she's conversing with herself or voice texting—badly, based on the insults she hurls at auto-correct.

"That's my dog." Riva holds out her hands. "Give it to me."

I shoot Monika a look, although I have zero right to judge our daughter's atrocious manners. I've offered little to the equation besides DNA, gifts chosen by a professional shopper, and a hefty monthly child support payment.

"This is Princess," Sadie says, ignoring Riva's rudeness. "And she already has an owner who loves her very much."

"She's in my yard," Riva counters.

Sadie's confused gaze flicks to me. She lifts a brow and mouths the word *basement*.

Despite how in over my head I am, my lips twitch. "She didn't escape from the dungeon," I assure Sadie, moving forward with the bags. "This is my daughter, Riva. She's living with me."

"Even though Hawaii is way cooler than Colorado," Riva clarifies, then glances over her shoulder. "I want that puppy, Dad."

She sounds like that bratty girl from the old *Willy Wonka* movie. I can't remember her name, but it's not a comparison I like making.

"We agreed no pets." Monika's voice is calm, and she bestows Sadie with a megawatt smile. "Although that little ball of fluff is a cutie."

Monika was bitten twice as a girl, so has always been terrified of dogs, but her people don't think that's a good optic for social media.

"Rivs, give me a kiss and hug goodbye."

"I want Princess. I'll name her Sophie."

"She's got a name." Sadie displays more patience than me. "I need to bring her back to my house. Loved you in the last *Revstar* movie, Ms. Graham."

"Thank you," Monika says, adjusting her sunglasses. "Riva, a hug."

"Dad, you can't let her take my dog."

"Who needs a dungeon," Sadie asks no one in particular, "when you can have fun family times on the front lawn?"

Does she realize she's speaking out loud? The mix of authenticity and snark fascinates me.

Riva watches Sadie hurry across the driveway that separates the two houses, the dog cradled in her arms like a baby.

"Say goodbye to your mom, and I'll give you a house tour."

"No pool and no puppy." Riva rounds on Monika and me. If the girl has a superpower, it's shooting fire from her crystal blue eyes—the same color as mine. That fire is clearly meant to turn her parents to ashes. "I hate this place."

She stomps toward the house, banging through the front door like it did her wrong.

Except nope. I'm the one who hurt her, and it has nothing to do with the dog. "That went well."

"She's nervous about staying with you," Monika explains.

"We'll figure it out."

My ex nods but doesn't bother to pretend she believes me. I don't blame her.

"I'll call tonight after I check into the hotel." She gives my arm an awkward pat. "How are the headaches?"

"Better." Mostly.

She nods. "I hope you're happy here, Ian."

There are plenty of things I regret in life, but those few months of dating Monika and the daughter we have as a result will never fall into that category.

"Riva and I will find a way to be happy. How can we not in a town the internet assured me is so damn happy?"

She cracks a smile. A real one, not the Hollywood version she's perfected over the years. "I'm not sure why, but I believe you."

Makes one of us, I think, as I watch her climb into the backseat of the Mercedes to be driven away.

4

SADIE

"How could Ian Barlowe move to town and I didn't hear about it? Have you seen him in his underwear?"

I nearly trip over a rock on the trail in the foothills behind my neighborhood, and Max immediately moves to my side. He's enjoying the off-leash hike with the other dogs in my care today, my best friend Sally, and her terrier mix, Aspen. Max has never been much for adventure—we have that in common—so tends to stick close.

"Are you joking? Not that I'd peep, Sal, but he keeps the blinds drawn."

Although, since his daughter arrived two days ago, I've noticed the shades open from early morning to sunset.

Sally Mortensen, my bestie since second grade and owner of The Roasted Sky, the most popular coffee shop in Skylark, turns to face me, hands on hips.

"Google Ian Barlowe boxers." She draws in a few belabored pants. "Also, get me out on the trail more often. It's embarrassing to suck wind this badly."

The thought of my blue-eyed, golden maple-haired, drop-dead gorgeous neighbor wearing nothing but boxers makes my breath catch for an entirely different reason. Captain America has nothing on Ian, in my dreams or real life.

"I'm not an internet fangirl." I sound like a matronly aunt scandalized by the idea of a half-naked man. "I'm not sure why you are, either. What does your wife think?"

Sally laughs then rolls her eyes. "Trina's one-night stand pass is Scarlett Johansson."

Trina is a high-powered marketing whiz who worked in Manhattan for years but opted to go remote after falling in love with my best friend when they were set up on a blind date.

"Don't get me started on how many times we've watched the *Avengers* movies," Sally continues. "Even the lame ones. I doubt she'd have a problem with me internet ogling Ian's fine ass."

"Is he your pass?" And why do I feel a sudden stab of possessiveness?

The dogs congregate around us, wondering why we've stopped. All but Aspen, who never stops in her mission to flush out wildlife or discover decaying animal bones.

"Zendaya is my pass." Sally grins. "Big dick energy doesn't do it for me anymore." She jabs a finger at me. "But he could do it for you, Sads. I still don't agree with the whole bucket list V-card punching, but if you're going to have a first time with someone..."

I come close to swallowing my tongue at the thought of sex with Ian Barlowe. Boxers are one thing. The Playmaker in the buff would definitely be more than I can handle.

"Don't think so," I manage between wheezes.

"I thought you wanted a story to tell the book club. No one could top Ian Barlowe as an adventure. Even if you didn't recognize him, he's a bona fide big deal."

I don't follow football, not even Sally's beloved Denver Grizzlies. I might be the only Colorado native who doesn't subscribe to the belief that sunsets are orange to pay homage to our NFL franchise.

"Of course I'm not going to share details." Cue the matronly aunt tone again. I need to lock that shit down. It's embarrassing. Almost as embarrassing as my loose lips making my virginity an acceptable topic of conversation. Why didn't I pick something easy like skydiving or swimming with sharks?

"Not that I know either of them, but it's hard to imagine Ian and Monika Graham as a couple," I tell my friend, hoping to distract her. And to distract myself from thinking about meeting my bucket list deadline. "She's tinier than she looks in the movies. Doesn't like dogs."

Sally frowns. "She said that? Weird. I saw a post of her at the launch party for a book about a dog who kept watch over its owner for weeks after they got lost in the wilderness. I think she signed on to star in the movie version. Something like that. But she seemed to like dogs."

"No. I could feel her fear across the front yard. The daughter was all about Princess, but not Monika."

I point to the clouds gathering on the edge of a distant mountain. "Speaking of Princess, I should let her out, and we need to get off the trail before the rain hits."

"Praise the Lord for afternoon storms," Sally mutters. "At least your neighbor isn't a deranged serial killer. I heard he and the kid showed up for breakfast at The Diner this morning. Maybe one of these days, he'll drop by to grab a coffee, and I can snap a picture for Insta."

"You can't do that. He clearly moved here for a life out of the public eye. We need to respect his privacy."

It makes no sense to feel protective of Ian Barlowe. He's the last man on earth who needs my help with anything. Plus, we have nothing in common. But now that I know he was feathering the nest for his daughter's arrival, I feel kind of... Well, I have all sorts of emotions I wouldn't expect about my new neighbor.

The protective kind are easier to manage than the fluttering in my belly ones.

"Mmmmkay." Sally doesn't sound convinced. "Talk to me after you see him in his boxers."

"I will *not* be searching that." Totally Googling him later. My cheeks heat at the thought, and I turn to head down the trail before Sally notices.

This is my second hike of the day, which is typical. Often, I break up my daily dog clients based on personalities. Princess needs a few months before she'll be ready for a trail hike, and I hope to have her as a client for that long.

Her owner, Penelope, is high-strung, so it's not a given. However, the pup is back with me for a second day of training after being too exhausted yesterday to leave her usual trail of post-dinner destruction. Princess needs mental and physical stimulation, and I'm good at providing both.

She's anxious around animals other than Max, who tends to be a dog whisperer in his own right. I took the two of them for a leash walk around the neighborhood before doing a half-hour of obedience training in the backyard and then settling her in a crate to rest.

I noticed Riva Barlowe watching from an upstairs window, her furrowed brow clearly communicating she's still upset that her dad is holding fast to the no-pets rule.

Good for Ian. I know from experience that a united front is essential. At least to the extent you can compare puppy parenting to handling human children. The most challenging dogs to train are the ones who have unclear boundaries set by different members of their pack.

And, yes, I understand that raising a child and a dog are not the same. Better than most since it was trial-by-fire becoming Piper's guardian after Mom died.

"Have you told your sister you don't have a date for the wedding?" Sally asks as we approach the trailhead.

I stop and call the dogs, leashing them up one at a time.

"There's still time." I don't meet Sally's gaze since I already know how she's looking at me. Frieda, the standard poodle who comes to doggy daycare every Friday, lifts her head as I clip the leash to her paisley collar, soulful brown eyes reproachful. Et tu, Frieda?

"For what? Are you going to hire a boyfriend for the weekend? This is your life, not a sappy movie where everything can be neatly tied together in a flannel bow."

"Don't knock flannel. It's an underrated fabric."

"Sadie, I'm serious. You deserve better," Sally says then calls Aspen. She's always the last dog to relent to being put back on her harness—more wolf than canine, that one.

"I don't want Piper to stress. She was so relieved when I told her I've been dating someone and plan to bring him to the wedding."

"Piper is an adult now, not the broken-hearted little girl you returned home to rescue."

"We rescued each other," I clarify.

"You gave up your life for her. The career you dreamed of and the guy you'd had a crush on since sophomore year of high school."

"Bradley and I were never more than friends."

"You kissed him."

"Once." I shake my head. "One drunk kiss after finals doesn't count. It didn't mean anything. I doubt he even remembers, and Piper doesn't know. She can never find out either. Let it go, Sal. I have."

Her lips press into a thin line. I can lie to myself and fool my sister, but Sally knows. My crush on Brad Carlson—Bradley—is a secret I vowed to take to the grave after Piper revealed the identity of her mystery boyfriend, now fiancé.

It felt like a punch to the gut hearing how surprised she'd been to run into Bradley in the hospital cafeteria during her first week on the job in Kansas City last fall. They'd bonded over long hours, job stress, and their mutual homesickness for the mountains.

I have no right to care, no dibs on him. His family only lived in Skylark a few years, and we became friends after being assigned as chemistry lab partners.

His parents moved to Arizona once we left for college. After I dropped out of school to take care of Piper, Bradley reached out several times, but I never responded.

My heart felt too broken, and I was reeling from all the things I had to do to keep our heads above water.

My crush was just another layer of skin to shed as I became the new version of myself—the one who only cared about raising my half-sister.

"She's happy," I say as Aspen barrels toward us from deep within a copse of scrub oak bushes, proudly displaying her latest find, which looks relatively fresh. "Just like this four-legged bone collector."

Sally makes a retching noise. "How does she always find animal parts? Gross. It still has fur."

Aspen trots closer, tail wagging. "Drop it," I command, and she deposits her prize at my feet. I pick up the section of deer femur and reach around to place it in the plastic bucket carabinered to the outside of my backpack. It's where I stow bags of poo plus other flotsam and jetsam from the trail until the end of the hike. And why Sally walks upwind of me.

"You deserve more than carrying around garbage that makes the people or dogs in your life happy," my friend reminds me.

"It makes *me* happy to see Piper happy." Not a lie but also not the whole truth.

We've made it to the trailhead, close enough to my house that I walked over.

"A piece of your blueberry sour cream cake would make me happy." I smile. "Save me a day-old slice?"

She rolls her eyes. "How about I make it tomorrow's special pastry and pull aside a fresh piece for you?"

"You don't have to—"

"It's coffee cake, Sads. A low bar as expectations go. Stop accepting less. Take something for yourself. It's time." She leans closer. "Also time for you to be honest with Piper."

The dogs watch with rapt fascination and then glance at me like they're expecting a sublime retort from their fearless leader.

"Sure," I agree with a shrug. I can feel the letdown from friend and canines alike, and hate to admit they're all right. I'm a disappointment even to myself, but is it too late to become someone else?

With a smile so brittle it might cause my cheeks to crack, I wave and start walking toward home.

5

SADIE

"What's so wrong with caring about my sister's happiness?" I ask the pack as they lead me down the street. The walk home is a breeze since they're all worn out.

No one answers, so I continue, "I might meet Mr. Right tomorrow. There's still time. It could be love at first sight."

Max yawns.

"Could I hire a date? There are services for that, right? Not for the...you know what part but—"

Trigger, the shaggy sheepdog, woofs, startling me out of my thoughts. I'm in front of my house and Ian is standing in his driveway, washing his giant black SUV. And watching me.

Please tell me he didn't hear my out-loud ramblings. Again.

"Big crew," he says with a smile and wave of the hand holding the soapy sponge. After weeks of being a complete recluse, he's now an average suburban single dad taking care of household chores.

Molly Burton and Abbie Jokerst peer out of Molly's front window across the street. The two empty nesters and best friends probably hope he'll take off his shirt.

Not the worst thing that could happen.

"It's going to rain." I point to the sky, which is quickly filling with clouds headed our direction from the west. How does my ability to make casual conversation vanish so suddenly in this man's presence?

Guys with giant muscles aren't my type. Bradley and I wore the same size jeans back in high school. I make a mental note never to ask my sister if her waist size matches his.

Ian's smile dims. "I'll pull it into the garage. Thanks for the tip."

"We might get hail," I blurt like an armchair meteorologist. "When a storm blows in so quickly from the west, that can happen. It's a thing on the Front Range." I clasp a hand over my mouth to keep from blabbering any more.

Ian slowly places the sponge into the bucket of soapy water like he's worried that quick movements might agitate me further. "Appreciate the warning and weather insight."

"Sure," I mumble. Would anyone at my sister's wedding even believe I could get a date, other than if I hired one?

The dogs lose interest in him when I tug on the leashes to communicate we aren't moving closer for a greeting, and turn toward my house.

"Is that a deer leg in your bucket?"

"Yep," I call over my shoulder, pretending it's completely normal. "For my collection."

Okay, now I've crossed a boundary into totally weird.

Maybe I subconsciously want Ian Barlowe to go back to hiding out. Despite my usual indifference to broad-shouldered men, the things he does to my lady parts are no joke.

I hear him laugh like he finds me amusing. It makes my stomach zip and twirl in a lustful little dance. Oh, no. Are those my ovaries clenching? Sweet baby Jesus, say it isn't so. I can't be lusting after a man so out of reach we're barely breathing the same air.

Eyes on the prize, Sadie. I need a wedding date and a willing vict—partner for my first time between the sheets. Ian Barlowe isn't a candidate for either.

I toss the poop bags in the trash can next to the garage but leave the backpack on the front porch to deal with the bone later. Once inside, I release the dogs and press myself against the door, willing my knees not to tremble.

Ian will be swooped up by some thirsty single mom or cute twenty-something in town. Maybe he already has a girlfriend— probably a Monika Graham lookalike.

I'm the eccentric dog lady next door.

Speaking of eccentricity, I check my watch. Penelope texted that she'd pick up Princess at three for the dog's weekly appointment at the groomer. But when I turn to greet the pup in her crate, it's empty, the door shut and locked like it's been that way all along.

I've seen a lot in my decade as a dog trainer, but an animal that can teleport is new even for me.

A giant boom sounds from outside, and Trigger gives a little whimper of protest. I need to put him in his thunder shirt before the storm starts. But first, I need to find the disappearing dog.

My heart races as I open the crate like that will make her reappear. Only this isn't some two-bit magic trick.

"Princess?" I call, and two of the dogs amble toward me. Neither of them is the missing animal.

Then I notice the curtains ripple and realize the patio door is open.

I quickly crate the other dogs except Max, who's already snoring away on his dog bed in the kitchen. After a quick scan of the yard and a rushed search of the house, I step out back as another crack of thunder reverberates. My heart pounds just as loudly.

Calling the dog on repeat, I scan the yard and then glance toward the space under the fence where she crawled through the first time. I secured the gap with netting, which is holding fast. But still...

I hurry through the gate at the side yard just as Penelope's car stops at the curb.

No, no, no.

Where is that puppy?

Ian's garage door is open, and he steps out, his brows furrowed. "Everything okay?"

"Princess is gone. I don't know what happened, but..." I hitch my chin toward the woman with the high ponytail and pink velour tracksuit moving toward us. "I'm in big trouble."

"I'll check my yard," he offers without missing a beat.

"Where's my sweetie baby?" Penelope calls in her trilling voice. "I want to get her to the groomer before the rain starts."

Based on the scent of rain and the wind picking up, the storm is nearly upon us.

"Hey, Penelope." I clench my hands into fists as I move toward her. "A strange thing happened today."

"Was that Ian Barlowe?" she asks in a stage whisper, nodding toward the open gate he's just walked through. "I heard he's Skylark's newest resident but had no idea he lives next door to you."

"Yep." I offer a strained smile. "I can introduce you."

"Yes, please, mama," she says with a wink, then shakes her head. "But not today. I want to look my best to meet him, so I need to grab Princess and take off before he returns. First impressions are important."

And second and third. I inwardly cringe, imagining what my hot-commodity neighbor thinks of me.

"About Princess..."

Penelope's gaze sharpens. "What about her? I'm sorry I haven't been following up on the obedience training homework but—"

"She's gone."

"Gone where?"

I lick my dry lips. "I'm not sure yet."

Penelope's gaze flicks over my shoulder for a second, and I turn, hoping to see Ian holding the dog. Instead, those strong arms are empty. He offers an apologetic shake of his head.

Crapola. "I'm going to find her, Penelope," I promise.

Penelope makes a sound somewhere between a shriek and a sob as she lunges for me. "You lost my baby."

I stumble back into a wall of...well, Ian. Hard and warm, his calloused hands grip my upper arms. It's like being held steady by a mountain. I catch the faint whiff of laundry detergent and male spice, and resist the urge to turn my head so I can breathe it in. Do not sniff the man, I tell myself.

"This isn't Sadie's fault," he explains to my infuriated client.

It's not? It feels like my fault.

His tone is calm and commanding, and for a moment, Penelope blinks up at him with her mouth forming a perfect "O".

"Sadie lost my precious pup." She glares at me. "Did you put out an Amber Alert?"

"That's for missing children," Ian clarifies.

"She's my *baby*," Penelope cries, tears welling in her kohl-rimmed eyes. "We need to find her."

She points a finger at me. "And there better not be one hair on her perfect head harmed. I trusted you. You, Sadie Hart, are the worst. I'm going to make sure everyone in town knows they can't rely on you with their dogs."

A raindrop lands on my heated cheek, a harbinger of what's coming. We're going to be soaked in minutes.

Ian doesn't release me.

"I'll find her," I shout like Penelope can't hear me over the imminent storm.

Or maybe it's the throbbing in my head. Ten years, and I've never had a mishap with an animal. Scratches, accidents, even a random bite a few times. But I've never lost an animal in my care.

"I'm going to post on my socials and call the humane society," Penelope yells back.

"We'll find your little dog," Ian promises.

Penelope draws a breath and nods like she believes him.

I do, too.

I want to, anyway. His hands around my arms give me comfort. His body is a wall of certainty, relaying a confidence I don't feel. Is this what it would feel like to not be alone? Is this what my sister has with Bradley?

Is it what I could have had if things had gone a different way?

There's a strange three-second lull in the swirling wind, and in that preternatural silence, I hear the most remarkable sound.

Princess's plaintive bark.

I look up to see Riva quickly backing away from her upstairs window, the puppy cradled in her arms.

Ian mutters a curse and then takes a step away from me. I shouldn't miss his touch, but I do, even as I realize what this means. His daughter stole the dog.

"My baby." Penelope lets out a relieved breath and takes a step toward his house.

"Oh, right. Sorry." I place a hand on Penelope's arm to halt her movement. "I forgot I asked Ian's daughter to watch her while I hiked with the other dogs. The barometric pressure is doing funny things to my brain."

I'm not going to give Monika Graham any competition in the acting department. Still, I manage to not sound as angry and confused as I feel.

Ian growls behind me, his feelings on the matter crystal clear.

"She was never lost?" Penelope demands, her tone uncertain. She wants to believe me. I *want* her to believe me.

"I'll get your dog," Ian says, the gravity in his voice making it seem like he's heading out on a covert ops mission instead of into his house. He levels Penelope with a steely stare. "This isn't Sadie's fault."

My breath hitches when his ice-blue gaze meets mine, and then he turns and stalks across the front lawn.

"I'm so sorry I worried you." I squeeze Penelope's hand. "I would never let anything happen to your baby."

She's still frowning as she glances up at the sky. The storm remains contained other than the wind and a few sporadic raindrops. "I'm getting wet, and Princess will miss her appointment at the groomer."

"I'm sorry." I don't bother to ask if she's going to reconsider trashing me around town since I didn't, in fact, lose her dog. That question can wait. But it doesn't stop panic from clawing at my gut.

My business relies on my reputation. As much as I want to believe many long-time clients will remain loyal, I've lost more than a few to a new national-chain training center that opened on the other side of town. Dogapalooza, if you can believe that name.

Penelope flicks a raindrop off her forehead. "I guess it's okay since Ian Barlowe's daughter is the one who has her. Although if I'd known, I would have curled my hair before meeting him. But if she likes Princess, that might give me an in with her dad, right?"

"Sure," I agree. "And you look great, Pen."

As attractive as someone can be in a fuzzy tracksuit the color of Pepto Bismol.

"You look like you need a shower." She sniffs.

Of course I do. If only a shower could fix my life.

As soon as Ian reappears on the front porch, Penelope hurries forward, cooing at Princess and thanking my neighbor for saving the day.

The rain starts in earnest as she rushes past me toward her car. "I'll be in touch," she calls, and there's a promise of retribution in her tone that adds to my headache, barometric pressure be damned.

I press my lips together and hold up a hand before Ian can take a step off his porch.

"It's fine," I lie. "Totally fine." Thunder booms again like it's offering a retort, but I turn and head to my house.

Stick a fork in me today. I'm officially done.

6

IAN

"Riva, open the door."

I pound on it again then pull my hand away when the wood quivers like it's going to give way under the force of my fist. The last thing I need is my daughter's nightly FaceTime call with her mom to feature a splintered bedroom door.

Growing up with a dad who used force to prove a point and keep his wife and two kids in line, I promised myself long before I became a father that I'd be different. I *am* different. But how do I manage a kid with a stubborn streak even wider and longer than mine?

My former teammates would get a kick out of this. I earned my nickname, The Playmaker, because I'm always prepared. My backup plans have backup plans.

But being a dad doesn't come with an instruction manual. Despite what the half-dozen parenting guides I've read in the past few months preach, kids aren't exactly by the book. Riva has been in her room for hours, although she did at least take the tray of dinner I left in front of the door. No one is going hungry on my watch.

"I'm not leaving until you come out," I tell my daughter when she still doesn't answer. I wonder if she's even listening.

Since her arrival, she's barely taken off her noise-canceling headphones, and I'm not proud to admit I mostly stopped trying to convince her. I don't know how to connect with her. Before we've truly started our life as a father-daughter duo, I'm already a failure. And I don't like to fail.

I turn and lower myself to the carpeted floor, leaning back against the door and gazing up to the rubbed-bronze light fixture above me. "Please open the door."

Unexpectedly, that murmured entreaty does the trick, and I have to catch myself before I pitch backward into her thin legs.

"It's your fault," she says like that's a given. Of course it is.

I turn and stare but don't stand yet. Maybe looking down on the father who has so clearly disappointed her on some soul-deep level will make her more willing to talk.

The women I've dated would be cackling in sadistic pleasure to know that all I want is for my kid to talk about her feelings.

I hate talking about feelings.

"What part of you breaking and entering into our neighbor's house and stealing a dog is my fault?"

"Take a hint, *Ian*."

"You may call me *Dad*."

Her wide-set eyes narrow. "A *good* dad would realize his daughter is desperate for a pet. You and Mom move me away from my friends and a house with a pool to a place where I know no one and there's no pool."

"We can join a pool."

She snorts. "I've wanted a dog my whole life. Now I have to live next to a woman with *all* the dogs."

"Dog sitting is her job. They aren't *all* hers. The one you stole is not hers, not that it would be more excusable if you'd taken *her* dog. Maybe I didn't appreciate your lifelong obsession with pet

16

ownership, but I didn't purposely choose this house based on our neighbor's ability to torture you with her dog-lady lifestyle."

She crosses her arms over her chest. For the first time, I notice her nails are chewed down to nubs.

My brother bit his nails when we were kids, and that compulsion led to other, more self-destructive behaviors when Felix hit his teen years.

I don't want that for Riva.

How did I *not* know the hardest thing about being a parent is that you can't control so much of it? I built a career on control and moved here because I figured I could control our lives in a small town in a way living in Los Angeles would never allow. And at the moment, I got nothing.

"Just get me a dog, and I won't mess up your life anymore."

"Your mom and I agreed..." I shake my head as the meaning of her statement sinks in. "Back up a sec. Riva, you aren't messing up anything. I'm happy you're here."

She rolls her eyes so hard I almost crack a smile. "Mom says you're trying too hard to really mean it."

Ah, hell. Thanks, Monika. So helpful.

"She's wrong. I wish I'd been a bigger part of your life before now, but I really do want to make up for lost time."

"You know what would make me feel better?" she asks with so much fake sweetness it makes my teeth ache.

"Apologizing to Sadie Hart and thanking her for covering for you instead of calling the cops?"

Her face goes pale. "I didn't mean to steal the dog for good. I just wanted to borrow it while she was gone."

I straighten and run a hand through my hair. "Did you engage in petty crime in LA?"

"People in LA lock their doors."

As if that's the point.

"No more, Riva."

"It's boring here," she complains, jutting out a hip in defiance. "I don't have friends and—"

"Why won't you sign up for one of the summer camps we looked at online? There's a community center with—"

"I don't want to do stupid pottery or play volleyball with a bunch of losers."

"How are you so sure they're losers?" I ask, genuinely curious.

"Because...duh...they're playing volleyball instead of lying by the pool."

Are all twelve-year-olds so cynical? I think about asking, but in this case, ignorance might be bliss.

"I played sports as a kid, and I wasn't a loser."

"Says you."

Fair point.

"We can deal with your boredom later. Right now, it's time to face the music next door."

Riva tilts her head. "The dog lady plays music?"

"Figure of speech. Stop trying to distract me."

"What if she yells?" Riva looks uncharacteristically worried.

"I don't think..." How do I know how Sadie will react? I've never seen anything like the look of terror in her caramel-colored eyes when she thought she'd lost her client's dog. I blame myself as much as I do Riva—nearly as much anyway.

I've been working on my next career move, a task that so far involves researching the careers of other retired sports stars and leaving her alone in her room, which I thought she wanted. But she's a kid, and I'm the adult, and I screwed this up.

"I don't know what she'll say, but I'll be at your side for whatever happens. Owning up and taking responsibility for your screw-ups is important, Riva."

"I don't think you're supposed to say screw in front of me."

"Sorry," I say, then nod. "See how easy that was?"

"Sure, but I didn't steal your dog."

She lifts her hand to her mouth, chewing on the cuticle before quickly lowering it back to her side. For the first time since she arrived in Colorado, Riva seems like an actual twelve-year-old girl, uncertain of the changes in her life and floundering about how to handle them. Not unlike her father.

"Yes, but you stole my heart, and that's even more serious."

She breathes out what might pass as a laugh. "Oh my, gosh. What a dad thing to say."

"That's the best compliment I've gotten in a long time." I hold out my hand. "Let's go, kid."

She doesn't take it but bumps into me on her way past. It almost feels like a hug.

I follow her downstairs and through the house I worked so hard to put together. Unfortunately, this perfect catalog-furnished house doesn't make a difference the way I need it to.

The air is still humid as we step outside, although the sun is out and the driveway and road are dry. Maybe if it hadn't been raining so hard earlier, Sadie would have stuck around after Princess's owner claimed her dog and stomped back to her car. Maybe I made a mistake in laying so low before Riva arrived. Now people probably assume I'm an egotistical former athlete who thinks he's too good to mingle with the locals.

I just didn't want my name to influence anything. From comments Monika has made over the years, Riva isn't a fan of dealing with her mom's adoring public. I wanted the first time people met me to be as the regular dad I'm trying to be. Now I might have to lean into my fame. I'll autograph some footballs or maybe guest coach for a local pee-wee team to meet some of the parents with kids.

There's a lot more to the parenting thing than I realized. Saying screw in front of my kid might be the least of the ways I'm going to mangle it.

"If I do a good apology, can I get a dog?" Riva asks as we head up the steps to Sadie's front porch.

"I admire your tenacity, but you gotta lay off, Rivs."

"How do you feel about girls crying?"

Is that a joke? "I support people—women or men—being free to express any emotion."

"Mom's last boyfriend couldn't stand to see a woman cry, so every time she wanted something from him, she turned on the waterworks."

Monika used the same tactic on me back in the day. I hate that she'd set that example for our daughter, although maybe I deserve it. I sure hope I can convince Riva there are better ways to deal with our problems.

She squares her shoulders and then knocks on the door, the sound greeted by a chorus of barking dogs. A moment later, the cacophony dies down, and Sadie opens the door.

She's wearing baggy sweatpants and a yellow tank top, a bright pink bra strap peeking out from one edge. I should not be reacting to a glimpse of her bra, but my lower half doesn't get the message.

"Hello," she says quietly, looking between us with a decent amount of wariness.

After a moment, her gaze holds on Riva. "I appreciate you knocking this time instead of letting yourself in."

My daughter's chin tips up. For a moment, I worry that this apology is going to go horribly wrong. Sadie Hart doesn't seem like the type of woman to want an autographed football. She didn't even recognize me when we first met, but I'll find some way to—

"I'm so *profusely* sorry I borrowed a dog that didn't belong to me." Riva clutches her chest like her heart is pounding with the pain of the apology. "And for entering your very beautiful and understated home without permission."

She could have left out the understated part. It sounds like another word for plain, and I see Sadie's eyes flash. She knows it, too.

"I have no excuse other than the fact that I'm a child who's been forced away from the only home I've ever known..."

50

Also not exactly true since Monika has moved several times over the years.

"Then shipped off to a father I barely know. The loneliness inside my soul knows no bounds. And although it was very, very, *very* wrong, I hoped that the sweet dog might offer a bit of solace." She sighs deeply. "Since I have no friends and my father is consumed with his own life."

How does she know so many fifty-cent words? I clear my throat. "That's not exactly an accurate portrayal of your life," I tell my daughter, but her attention is riveted on Sadie.

"You seem like such a nice, understanding lady, and I appreciate that you didn't call the cops the way a certain person threatened."

"I never threatened," I mutter.

Sadie stares at Riva wide-eyed, like she's unsure whether to hug the girl or applaud her performance.

A laugh sounds from inside the house. "I like that kid," a female voice calls. "She reminds me of me, other than the part about committing a felony in elementary school."

Riva's eyes go wide, and her shoulders slump.

"Come in here, sweetheart," the same voice calls. "I want to take a look at you."

Riva glances at me and I shrug, because after being thrown under the bus with her poor pitiful me routine, I'm not inclined to jump in and rescue her.

Sadie still hasn't responded, so I'm unsure how my daughter's overenthusiastic apology landed. I'm also slightly unsure whether I'm supposed to follow Riva as she enters the house, or remain on the porch.

"Come on," Sadie says after a moment, and I'm weirdly relieved but almost equally terrified.

The house reminds me of Sadie—casual and welcoming. Like it's been put together with love not a platinum Amex and expedited shipping. She leads me into a cozy family room with well-worn furniture and bookcases filled with colorful paperbacks. It's painted pale yellow with white trim, but framed prints with brightly colored nature scenes adorn the walls. At first glance, the house is similar to mine, but it feels like a home without even trying.

"This is my friend Sally and her wife, Trina."

I nod and wave to the two women sitting on the couch, a dog that looks more like a dust mop than an animal lounging between them.

Max, who I've now met on several occasions, trots over and shoves his snout in my crotch. I'm embarrassed to say I'm not fast enough to deflect, a fact that doesn't go unnoticed by Sadie's friend Sally.

"Your reflexes aren't quite as sharp as they used to be, huh, Playmaker."

I swallow a choked laugh. "Guess I'm not used to defending against avid fans of the four-legged variety."

"Max, leave it." The dog reluctantly turns away, and Sadie's cheeks bloom with color. "I'm sorry. If it makes you feel better, he only goes for the comfort crotch with people he likes."

Weirdly, it does. "If it makes you feel better, my daughter doesn't have a history of B&E and she's more than learned her lesson."

Sally and Trina both grin at Riva. "We've been telling Sadie for years she needs to lock her doors," Sally says.

Trina holds up a finger. "Skylark isn't the town it used to be." She points that finger toward Riva. "But an unlocked door isn't an open invitation."

"I understand," my daughter says with a sigh.

"What are you going to do to make it up to our sweet Sadie?"

Riva blinks. "I said sorry."

"Not good enough," Sally offers conversationally.

"I accept your apology, Riva," Sadie interrupts quickly.

"What do you want me to do to make it up to you?" Riva asks, surprising me with the genuineness in her tone.

I wonder if I should interrupt or offer to donate to Sadie's favorite charity to make amends. But this moment is about Riva handling her own problems, even at the tender age of twelve going on twenty-five. I don't know much about parenting, but I know this is the right thing to do.

Still, I'm squirming right along with her as we wait for Sadie Hart's next move.

7

IAN

"How about you give me a few weeks of volunteering?" Sadie asks like it's no big deal either way. Could she truly be willing to let Riva off that easy after the terror I saw written all over her pretty face earlier.

"What kind of volunteering?" It's funny my kid thinks she has any choice in the matter. Whatever Sadie wants, she'll do it.

"Well, scooping poop for one. It's summer, so a lot of my clients go on vacation. That means I have more dogs boarding, especially on weekends. I could use help walking, training, and generally keeping them entertained." She scrunches up her nose and sighs. "That's assuming Penelope keeps her word and doesn't spread it around town that I lost her dog."

"She can't say that," Riva counters. "You didn't lose the dog. I took her, and I really am sorry. Promise."

My daughter's voice trembles, but she doesn't try to hide it. This apology is real and so different from the one so patronizingly offered on the front porch. Sally meets my gaze behind Riva's back, winks, and then gives me a quick thumbs-up.

How is it that Sadie Hart has managed to reveal Riva's soft underbelly without yelling or lecturing? Instead, she's offered my kid a chance to do exactly what will make her happiest in the world while also potentially learning how much work dogs can be.

My daughter looks like an animal about to flip on her back to be loved up just the right way. Sadie has managed to connect with her at a soul-deep level while I'm completely clueless, and I'm not convinced Monika is any more insightful than me.

Why didn't I think about volunteering with animals to bond with my kid? Because I have no idea what I'm doing. Now I owe my dog-lady neighbor even more than she realizes.

Whether or not Sadie understands the impact she's making, her friends do. Trina scoops up the dust-mop dog lounging beside her and offers it to my child. "This is Tempest. She arrived this afternoon and happens to like doing her business with an audience. Would you take her out in the backyard?"

You would have thought the woman offered Riva front-row tickets to a Taylor Swift concert. Her eyes light up with a brightness I've never witnessed.

"Yeah, of course. I love watching dogs go potty."

I watch in disbelief as Riva practically skips out of the room toward the back of the house with Tempest in her arms and Max automatically trailing behind. I rub a hand along the back of my neck as I stare after her, feeling the gazes of the three women on me.

"Thank you, Sadie. You've been way kinder than my kid deserves, and if there's anything I can do—"

"There is." Sally points toward me with what can only be described as a diabolical smile at the same time Sadie shakes her head.

Sally ignores her. "In fact, Playmaker, I think you might be the perfect person to help with a situation we were just discussing."

Her wife's pale green eyes go wide as she offers a vigorous nod, which isn't any more comforting than the finger-pointing.

"Oh, no." Sadie steps in front of me as fast as any lineman I've ever played with. "I do *not* need Ian's help with what we discussed, so..."

The scent of the citrusy perfume—or maybe it's lotion—she's wearing hits me as she shakes her head. The ends of her long dark blonde locks are damp and I'm momentarily lost in a vision of Sadie Hart in the shower.

The visceral physical reaction I have to this woman makes no sense, but is absolutely undeniable.

Right now, a beguiling, wholesome, and sexy-as-hell dog lady is voluntarily trying to protect me from something, and I'll do any favor she wants if it means more time with her.

Which is a mistake because I don't do wholesome.

Yes, I decorated my home thanks to a farmhouse-decor-inspired shopping binge, determined to make a life in a place that could be the setting for every cheesy Christmas movie ever filmed. But at my core, I'm not the person I want to convince my daughter I am. I'm not a guy who dates nice women who might have expectations of me beyond the bedroom.

Sadie hasn't given me any indication she's interested in me that way, but either way, she's not *my* type. Despite what my body is intent on convincing the modicum of good sense I possess.

"What's the favor?" I step closer to Sadie. I want her to feel the heat of my body, which runs at the temperature of an overworked furnace. The little hairs on the back of her arm stand on end, and it makes me weirdly happy.

She might not be a football fan, but at least she's not immune to me. I don't know why that matters, yet it sets my mind at ease.

"On second thought, it doesn't matter the favor. I'll do it."

Sadie spins on her heel and stares at me like I've lost my mind. She's not even aware of her power, which makes it even more formidable.

Thanks to the scooped collar of her tank top, I witness the flush that starts on her chest and travels all the way up the smooth skin of her neck to her cheeks. I wonder if the favor might involve making that flush cover her entire body.

Hell, yes, my dick twitches.

Nope, my brain commands. Dangerous territory.

"I don't want a favor from you." Sadie shakes her head. "Riva helping with the dogs is more than enough."

"She needs a date for her sister's wedding Fourth of July weekend," Sally explains.

Sadie's eyes briefly drift closed, like she's in physical pain, before she turns to face her friends again.

"Why don't you have a date?" I ask quietly.

"It's complicated," she says over her shoulder, "but I'm handling it."

"Now Ian Barlowe can handle it," Sally insists, "and you'll have way more fun in the process."

Sadie shakes her hands like they're filled with pins and needles or she's nervous as hell. "You don't know him. How do you know he's fun?"

"I'm fun," I say to no one in particular, unsure why I feel the need to convince Sadie or involve myself in something she's admitted is complicated.

Complicated and me don't mix. At all.

Trina holds up both hands, one in Sadie's direction and one in front of Sally's face, when the two women look like they're about to start arguing again. "Sadie's little sister is marrying the man who was Sadie's secret crush when she and Sally were in high school. A crush that unfortunately intensified in college. But nothing ever happened between the two of them."

"Not true. They kissed." Sally looks like she wants to launch off the sofa to make her point.

"Who kissed who?" Riva asks as she returns to the room, cradling Tempest like a baby.

"We are *not* having this conversation." Sadie looks horrified, which makes me want to smile. Everything about her makes me want to smile.

"I'm not a baby." Riva plants her own kiss on the dog's fuzzy forehead. "I know grown-ups kiss. It gives me the ick, but still..."

I'm not sure what the ick is, but I'm pretty sure I have it at the thought of Sadie's sister marrying the guy she might still be hung up on.

"Well, Bradley Carlson will definitely give you the ick," Sally says. "I wish Piper would wise up, but there's something about that dou—" She clears her throat. "About that doofus the Hart sisters find appealing. It's never made sense to me."

"Maybe because you like girls," Riva suggests.

"Even if I liked boys, that dude would give me the ick," Sally tells her.

I feel completely out of my element, which is a novel experience given the structure and influence I'm used to wielding. In particular, I do *not* want to discuss girls, boys, or kissing with my daughter. However...

"You need a date?" I place a hand on Sadie's shoulder like we're old friends and ignore the flash of electricity that skitters along my arm. "I happen to look great in a tux. I can be your date."

My daughter nods, and I appreciate the unexpected show of solidarity. "My dad would be a great date for a wedding. Mom says he's a terrible boyfriend because he can't do commitment, but he's fun at a party."

Is there any manner in which my daughter's mother hasn't disparaged me? Not that I don't deserve it, but come on.

"Like I said, it's complicated." Sadie ducks out of my hold, and I let her go. I may be commitment-phobic, but I'm not a jackhole.

Sally grabs her wife's hand and kisses Trina's knuckles. "I'll take it from here, hon. Sadie not only told her sister she's bringing a date to the wedding, but that she has a boyfriend. So we need you to be her boyfriend for that weekend."

"We are no longer friends," Sadie says to Sally without emotion. "I don't even know you."

"Dad *isn't* a good boyfriend," Riva says, and she's not wrong.

Sally pats the space on the couch between her and Trina. "Come here, little one, and take a load off. This is not a real boyfriend-girlfriend arrangement. Have you ever seen your father play football?"

Now it's my cheeks that feel hot. Riva hasn't been to one of my games since she was a toddler, and I doubt she remembers. It's also unlikely Monika tunes into football during the season. She dated a couple of athletes after me, but quickly moved on to high-profile businessmen and A-list actors. Football was my world, but it kept me from being a real part of my daughter's life.

"I watch sometimes." Riva mumbles the words, focused on stroking the dog's lopsided ears.

My heart seems to skip a beat even though I'm probably reading more into this moment than it deserves. But I want to believe it means something. Maybe she cares about me more than she lets on. Maybe there's a way for us to rebuild our relationship here in this little town.

Sally gives her an approving smile. "Well, one of the plays that made The Playmaker famous is the flea flicker."

"Like how dogs have fleas?" Riva grimaces. "Ewww."

"It's a trick play," Sally explains. "Your dad takes the snap and pretends to hand it off to a running back like a standard rushing play." She leans forward and whispers, "Then the magic happens."

"It wasn't magic," I mutter, feeling the back of my neck warm.

Sally shoots me a quelling glance that clearly says 'dude, I got this.'

"The running back pitches it to your dad again," she tells Riva. "The defense is fooled into thinking it's a run, so there are receivers open down field. Your dad uses the arm that made him famous to throw a deep pass and the crowd goes wild. It's a high-risk, high-reward play that produces spectacular results when executed correctly. That's what this weekend would be."

"This is not football, and he's not going to flea flick me," Sadie argues.

"I could flea flick the *shit* out of you," I mutter.

"Dad, language. And all the ick."

"I don't want to be flea flicked." Sadie looks horrified. Damn if even that pruny face she's making isn't adorable.

"Do it for Piper," Sally says, and the weighted silence that follows affirms those words are some sort of mic drop.

Sadie shakes her head. "We don't need a trick play. It will be easier if my imaginary boyfriend and I break up right before the wedding. She'll understand."

It's a good thing Sadie has a career as a dog trainer, because she would never be hired anywhere for her acting ability.

"She won't and you know it," Sally counters.

"The wedding is being held at a fancy-schmancy resort in Vail, so it's not like anyone around here needs to know the truth," Trina says.

"Did you and your sister grow up in Skylark?" I ask Sadie.

"Yes, but that doesn't matter."

"If she has friends from here going to the wedding, it matters," Riva says.

"My thoughts exactly, my girl." I offer her a slow grin that she returns almost shyly.

It's a strange way to bond with my daughter, but I'll take it.

"You can't be serious about this." Sadie takes several steps away, as if done with all of us, and then turns. "We can't lie about being in a relationship in front of your daughter."

Riva shrugs. "It can be part of my punishment."

"Volunteering isn't punishment," Sadie argues.

"Neither is dating you," I point out.

Sally and Trina applaud.

"I think it's funny." Riva makes kissy lips at Tempest. "Do you think Sadie and my dad in loooove is funny, Tempy?"

"At least consider it," Trina implores Sadie.

"For Piper," Sally adds with a knowing smile.

This little sister must be something special. Maybe the two of them weren't close to their parents. I can relate, although I make a mental note to text Felix when we're back at the house.

Sadie seems to want to argue as her gaze settles on me, but she slowly nods. "Fine," she whispers. "I guess I'll do it."

Spoken with about as much enthusiasm as a dental patient agreeing to a root canal.

Trina squeals with delight, earning an eye roll from Sadie. She looks irritated as hell. And still adorable. I need to get a grip.

She waves a hand at the group in general. "You all need to leave now so I can go to bed."

"It's seven-thirty," Riva says with a giggle.

"This is going to be awesome, Sads." Sally high-fives her wife over my daughter's head. "Brad-*ley* is going to shit a brick when The Playmaker shows up. Poop a brick," she amends as Riva elbows her.

I can't believe how comfortable my girl is with this quirky trio of women, and how grateful I am to see her smiling so easily. At the same time, a twinge of jealousy tugs at my heart. Why can't I have this kind of connection with Riva when I've changed almost everything about my life in order to facilitate it? Shit. I'm the problem.

"This isn't about him," Sadie answers, and it takes me a moment to realize she didn't just read my mind. "I'm *only* agreeing so I don't stress out Piper any more than she already is."

Falling on the sword of fake dating me for her sister? So much for my irresistible charm. Immune to me—another thing she and my daughter have in common.

I can tell her friends are trying to tamp down their glee. They aren't the only ones. I haven't done much right in my life lately, but I'm going to rock this arrangement. Sadie deserves a hell of a fake boyfriend, and I plan to deliver.

"I totally ship the two of you," Sally says as she stands, not too subtly pumping one fist in the air.

"Leave now," Sadie answers.

Sally envelops her in a tight hug before leaving, and even though Sadie tries to act irritated, I see her sink into the embrace.

Before moving to Skylark, I didn't give much thought to having friends. I had teammates, and that seemed like the same thing. Now that my football career is over, it's become glaringly obvious it isn't.

The two women head for the door like they're determined to beat my daughter and me out. Sally turns at the last minute and nods her head in my direction. "I'm glad you agreed to this, Ian."

The use of my given name rather than Playmaker tells me that whatever she's about to say is serious.

"I hope you're as good a fake boyfriend as you claim to be. Because if you hurt my friend, the best offensive line in the league won't be enough to protect you."

Sadie groans, but I nod. "Got it."

"Nobody is getting hurt because none of this is real." Sadie shoos her friends out the door.

"Let's go, Riva."

"Can we stay longer?" She crouches down next to Max, the canine mop still in her arms. "Your house is boring compared to this one. A dog would help." She flashes a smile so sweet it makes my teeth ache.

"You know the answer to that." I try to sound patient. "Your mom—"

"Isn't here," she points out. "I could—"

Sadie holds up a hand. "Oh, right. That's another stipulation of you making amends by volunteering with me. You're going to be around a lot of different dogs, and you'll definitely bond with some of them. No borrowing." She uses air quotes for the last word. "And no begging your dad. Your parents have set rules, and you need to follow them."

The no-dog policy isn't my rule. Monika tells people she's deathly allergic, but I'm one of the few people who knows that's not true. She simply doesn't like animals, which her agent told her feels harsh in a world of celebrities who at least give lip service to being dedicated to their pets.

I've seen both sides. I had some teammates loyal to their furry companions and others just as happy to let the animals be raised by an assistant or housekeeper or random family member until they needed a dog for a photo op.

"But I really want—" Riva begins.

"It's a non-negotiable part of the deal," Sadie interrupts. "Take it or leave it."

"Take it," my daughter agrees, and I want to throw my arms around the woman smiling at her.

I'd like an excuse to get close to Sadie for a number of reasons, not the least of which is how good she is with my daughter. And she smells like a fucking dream come true. Like oranges and lemon and the secret to happiness all mixed into one heavenly scent.

She raises her gaze to me and that blush colors her cheeks again. "Now that they're gone and nobody is around to pressure you, you can admit—"

My turn to hold up a hand. "It's all good. I'm happy to help. We can talk about the parameters and expectations once you decide on them. I'm game for anything." Even without trying, my voice drops on the last word, sounding gravelly to my ears.

Sadie pulls her bottom lip between her teeth, and I nearly groan. "Okay, thank you. Just so you know, I don't expect much."

Why do I have the urge to change that?

"What time do you want me here in the morning?" Riva asks, unaware of the strange tension that's crowding the air between Sadie and me. It's probably for the best, at least for the moment.

"How about eight? Four dogs are coming for daycare

tomorrow, and one six-month-old puppy will also be training. I want to introduce you to the owners as they drop off."

I wait for my daughter to complain that eight is too early for summer break, but she nods. "See you then." She glances at me. "Can we make brownies tonight?"

"Sure." I try to keep my jaw from hitting the floor. She wants to hang out with me. I haven't turned on the oven since I moved in, but I did buy a box of brownie mix at the grocery store before Riva arrived because she likes chocolate.

At least I did something right, although not nearly as much as Sadie Hart. Still, I'm grateful for any opportunity to spend time with Riva, even though her favor is fickle.

"Bye, Tempest." Riva kisses the dog again, then sets her on the sofa and heads for the front door. "See you tomorrow, Sadie."

When the screen slams shut, I turn to my neighbor. "Thanks again for being cool about Princess," I tell her, trying to sound casual. Could she possibly understand how much I mean it? A simple thank you is inadequate to communicate everything I need to.

"You're welcome." She glances out the screen door instead of making eye contact. Riva is already halfway across the driveway. "You're doing a good job, Ian."

That isn't true, but I appreciate her confidence in a man who has more confidence than sense and is relying on a woman I barely know to bolster my courage.

Whether she believes it or not, I owe Sadie Hart big time. The biggest. And I'm damn sure going to be the best fake dater the world—and more specifically the town of Skylark—has ever seen.

8

SADIE

After avoiding talking to Ian for a couple of days, I begin to wonder if I imagined his enthusiasm for being my date to Piper's wedding weekend.

Sure, I acted cool about his daughter entering my house and stealing one of my clients' dogs. That's what I'm known for—handling any situation without fuss or fanfare. The unofficial town doormat. Suddenly the one man who wants to treat me well is famous and smoking hot. Talk about a potential complication. As much as it's fun and flattering to think of walking into the wedding on Ian's arm, he doesn't owe me. I could throat punch Sally and Trina for suggesting the ridiculous arrangement.

Well, not Trina. I can't assault a pregnant woman. Sally is fair game, though. Besides, will anyone believe me showing up with somebody like The Playmaker is anything but fake? Can I even pull it off?

Oh yeah, I've done my homework. Including a ridiculous amount of hours the past couple of nights watching interviews and highlights from Ian's college and NFL careers.

Realizing what a big deal he is makes my insecurities blossom like allergies during hay fever season. Several clients have already asked about my neighbor, especially when I introduce his daughter as my summer assistant.

Apparently, the impression around town is that my life is so dull, not even a twelve-year-old would want to be involved. Gives a girl the warm fuzzies.

But Riva seems happy to hang with me and is doing a fantastic job so far, especially for a kid her age with no prior experience working with animals. And I like having someone to talk to other than the dogs, even if the girl refuses to say much about her dad and my level of curiosity is embarrassing.

"Barkley, heel," she tells the two-year-old doodle mix I put her in charge of as we walk the perimeter of Skylark's biweekly farmers market. The dog slows his stride to match hers, and she gives him a shoulder pat as a reward, just like I taught her.

The bright sunshine and warm temperatures make it a perfect afternoon for the farmers market, and the Skylark community is out in force. People around here love any excuse to gather, so we host more festivals and events than could be featured in a dozen Hallmark Channel movies.

This propensity to celebrate any holiday no matter how quirky or obscure with a town-sponsored activity is a serious bone of contention with our interim mayor. Iris has big ideas for how to improve Skylark's services and infrastructure, but has to contend with the fact that most of her budget is earmarked for, as she calls it, "fluff and nonsense."

Several people greet me, and I wave but don't start any conversations, because most of them will more than likely involve Ian. The fact that Riva is the product of two megawatt stars—her mother even more famous than her dad—seems to be a sore spot for the girl. Piper and I got a lot of attention after Mom died, and we both just wanted to blend in. The situation with Riva isn't the same, but I still want to protect her.

. . .

I NOTICE Riva pause as a group of kids who look to be about her age walk out from the end of one of the open-air aisles.

"Have you met anyone in the neighborhood? Your dad's right about the community center being a hub of summer activity." She's confided that as much as he wants her to get involved in organized sports, it's the last thing she'll agree to.

"No." She eyes the group but subtly ducks behind me. "There's no actual point to making friends." She looks at the ground as she speaks. "I probably won't be here when school starts in the fall."

This is news to me, and oddly disappointing. "Where will you be? Do you want to go back to LA with your mom?"

"Not really. But even if I did, she's got three movies in the pipeline back-to-back. She'll be on set or doing press junkets for at least a few years, so...they'll probably send me to boarding school."

My stomach drops at how nonchalant she sounds. "I don't think your dad is planning on boarding school, sweetheart. He bought a house here."

"My mom has bought and sold four houses around LA since I started kindergarten. Houses don't mean anything, and Dad doesn't like commitment. I'm sure he'll get sick of me."

I want to tell her that isn't going to happen, but my own experience was similar. Not the boarding school part, but after I begged her incessantly, my mom sent me to stay with my dad for a month the summer I turned nine.

I'd had minimal contact with him since they never married and the relationship didn't last through her pregnancy. He lived in what I then believed to be a magical state called Minnesota. I was so excited to finally tell my friends I had a dad in my life. Only, my timing was off that summer. He'd just started dating a woman with kids a few years younger than me and decided nine was the perfect age for a built-in babysitter. After two weeks of indentured servitude, I called my mom and pleaded with her to bring me home.

Other than a random birthday card with a wrinkled twenty on the years he remembered, I haven't been in contact with dear old dad since. Not even after Mom died.

"See, you don't think he's going to keep me around," Riva laments when I take too long to respond. "Why should I try to make friends or give him a chance?"

"Because he's trying," I answer. "I think he's doing the best he can. He offered to be my fake date for *your* benefit. I'm not the kind of woman your dad would date unless he was forced into it."

She looks like she's trying to hold back a laugh, which is better than the scowl from minutes before, even at my expense. "He doesn't have good taste in women."

While not exactly a compliment, I take it as one. I'm not hideous in the looks department, more classic girl-next-door-cute than striking supermodel, which has never bothered me. I've also never tried to be anyone other than me, and I have no intention of starting now.

"His girlfriends are pretty," I say, more to myself than her.

"Pretty awful," she answers, and I laugh.

There's a crowd gathering in front of the produce stand at the far end of the market. Odd, because this early in the season, the Colorado harvest is slim pickings. Most of what's good to buy now is handmade soaps, breads, and various jarred foods.

"It's my dad." Riva sounds horrified. "I knew this would happen. Look at how everyone wants his autograph. It's so weird and cringey."

"We don't see a lot of famous people in Skylark. That's more the Aspen vibe. The novelty will wear off once people get to know him."

"It *never* wears off," Riva insists. "It's only gotten worse with Mom. At least there aren't paparazzi here. They follow her everywhere."

"Your dad is different." I'm out of my element, knowing almost nothing about famous people, but I try to sound convincing. "He's retired and out of the public eye. Do you want to say hi? There are a few kids in the mix you could meet."

"No way. Being the kid of someone famous is the worst," Riva mutters, and I do *not* roll my eyes at the absurdity of the statement. Because she believes it. "How am I supposed to act when strangers act like they're friends with my parents?"

I get that. I know loads of people around town, but the level of attention Ian draws makes my stomach clench with nerves. Invisible is my preferred mode of operation.

He agreed to the fake dating thing for Piper's wedding, but we haven't discussed parameters or how heavy we need to sell the two of us together in the weeks leading up to the big event.

Like I said, I've been avoiding him. Seems prudent to continue that path for now.

I start to change direction, then hear my name called.

"We should ignore him," Riva says as Ian calls to her as well.

I choke out a laugh. "We can't ignore your dad. Time to put on your Skylark happy face. You do realize he moved you to a town consistently ranked one of the top ten happiest in America?"

She looks up at me with a funny expression but nods. Skylark happy is what Sally termed the moments I forced a public smile in the months after Mom died and I came home to care for Piper.

Even though I'd been listed as her guardian in our mother's will, it was evident from the looks we received—a mix of sympathy and gentle reproach—that most people thought I was too young to raise my sister on my own. Which was true, but didn't stop me from being committed. Sally was my biggest cheerleader. She was also the person who insisted I fix my face when the grief became too obvious. It's a skill that applies in a variety of situations, and I take my own advice when the crowd in front of him parts like the Red Sea as we approach.

Speculative gazes land on me, which is annoying. Why wouldn't he know me by name? We're neighbors, and his kid is at my side.

"Hey ladies," he says, and although he's smiling, his voice is tight. Looks like I'm not the only one doing Skylark happy. "What kind of vegetable should we have with dinner?"

The idea of weighing in on Ian Barlowe's side dish decision knocks me for an unexpected loop. There's a peculiar intimacy to the question, like my opinion matters in some meaningful way.

"Potatoes," I blurt before anyone—Ian especially—notices my shock.

One of the women flanking him leans closer, her breast grazing his arm, and jealousy I have no right to feel grips my chest.

"I have an amazing recipe for roasted potatoes with olive oil and fresh rosemary. I'd be *so* happy to share it." She holds up her phone. "Just give me your number and—"

"I'm good." Ian's blue eyes meet mine over the woman's phone. The spark of mischief in his gaze gives me pause. "I think my girl can handle the potatoes."

My girl? Is he talking about Riva?

"He means you," she says under her breath.

I blink and notice his smile widen.

"I mean you," he confirms, crooking his finger. The fabric of his navy blue T-shirt stretches tight across his broad shoulders and molds to his chest and flat abs, no doubt covering at least a six-pack, if not more. Ian Barlowe challenges my perception of the term dad bod, and I move like there's an invisible string drawing me to him.

"I'll bag up a few," the man behind the vegetable stand says.

"Appreciate it." Ian reaches out and pulls me forward the last couple of steps.

I hold three leashes, and the dogs attached to them don't understand what's happening. Miles, the cocker spaniel new to walking on a leash, gets tangled between my legs and nearly takes me down.

Nearly, because Ian tugs me even closer. He loops a heavy arm around my shoulders then drops a kiss on my temple.

A kiss.

I'm standing on the ground but my body is floating several inches above the earth.

Let's be honest. Did I briefly entertain the possibility of killing two birds—the wedding and my V-card—with The Playmaker?

Yes, ma'am, I most assuredly did. And the idea felt almost too good to be true. Now I know it is. If a chaste brush of his lips makes my panties feel like they're about to spontaneously combust, anything more might literally kill me.

Ian crouches down to pet the dogs, then surveys the people staring at us. He waves to Riva, who looks relieved to be left alone to blend into the crowd. And now I'm jealous of her. Being the center of attention is giving me hives.

"Nice day for a pack walk." He glances up, his blue eyes pinning me in place with their intensity. "I'll be around this afternoon. Mind if I stop by around pick up time? I'd love to meet some of the dogs Riva keeps telling me about."

Before I can respond, Phil Mazza elbows his way through the throng. "Hey, Sadie, I've been meaning to call you about getting Trixie back in for some daycare and training."

His gaze shifts to Ian. "So, Playmaker, I'm sure you know this already, but Sadie here has quite a way with dogs."

"Animals of all kinds," Ian says with a chuckle, his breath warm on the shell of my ear. It sends a shiver through me.

"I thought Trixie was happier at Dogapalooza," I say to Phil. He was one of the first clients to ditch me for the fancy facility that offers puppuccinos and extra belly rubs—all for an additional cost of course. They did a splashy ad campaign before the grand opening, offering monthly membership packages and a live video feed of the dogs.

I couldn't help but take it personally when several longtime clients ghosted me in favor of a facility that branded itself the Ritz of doggy daycare.

I'm completely devoted to the well-being of the animals in my care, but it isn't swanky with all the bells and whistles. No indoor splash park or a groomer on site, but I use behavioral methods that are scientifically proven to bring out a dog's best. Unfortunately, that doesn't tap into the need certain pet owners seem to have to give their furry friends the five-star treatment.

However, the potential opportunity to get close to a famous retired quarterback because he might be close to me is apparently a bigger draw than a pup cup.

"I guess you would know that since Sadie is your *girlfriend*." Phil clears his throat at the gasps his declaration elicits from the crowd. His squinty brown eyes focus on Ian, who is holding onto me like I'm a football, and he's two strides from the end zone.

Riva is grinning wildly.

"I mean I *assume* she's your girlfriend," Phil continues. My mortification amplifies at the same rate as his booming voice. "Because you're acting like her boyfriend."

I'm a deer caught in headlights, and Max—always so attuned to my nerves—lets out a low whine as Phil's gaze catches mine. Here it is. The moment when Skylark locals bust a gut laughing at the idea of little old me dating Ian Barlowe.

"I like to keep my personal life private," Ian says without releasing me. "Sadie and I have that in common."

Riva has drifted closer, and he places the hand not holding me on her shoulder. "This is my daughter, Riva. She just arrived in Skylark and we couldn't be happier to call this our new home."

Skylark happy. That's the three of us.

"I'm sure you understand I also need to protect my private life for my daughter's sake. She's my priority." The sincerity in his voice makes my heart melt like ice cream left out in the hot summer sun.

Phil nods. "Sure, sure. We're all about discretion in Skylark. It's a tight-knit community of regular folks. Not like some of those snooty mountain towns that cater to celebrities."

"Here are your potatoes." The farm stand owner hands Ian a

canvas bag that he loops over one shoulder. He then releases me long enough to pull a wallet from the back pocket of his cargo shorts. It is completely unfair that he can simultaneously look casual and so damn gorgeous.

The older man shakes his head and rubs two fingers over his handlebar mustache. "Oh, no, Playmaker. You standing here has driven more business to me than I normally see in a month of farmers markets. Potatoes are on the house."

"I appreciate that," Ian says. "You can bet I'll buy my produce from you all summer."

The man beams like Ian Barlowe is the vegetable pied piper.

"That was fun," Ian says as the remaining looky-loos walk away. He bends down to scratch Max behind the ears, which happens to be the old boy's sweet spot and...good lord...are my ovaries clenching?

After putting my life on the back burner to raise my little sister, I didn't think I'd ever have a maternal urge of my own. Clearly, my body isn't on the same page where Ian Barlowe is concerned.

"Dad, will you hold Barkley's leash so I can get a cupcake before we leave?" Riva asks, pointing to The Sugar Shack booth at the other end of the aisle. It's the best bakery in town.

"The salted caramel is my favorite," I tell her. "But everything they make is delicious."

Ian takes the leash and offers his daughter a twenty. "How about a couple salted caramels and a vanilla for me?"

She grins. "Vanilla is boring."

"I'm in my boring dad era," he answers with a wink.

There is *nothing* boring about Ian.

When it's just the two of us, I take a purposeful step away from him. "I wonder how long it will take for the whole town to be buzzing with assumptions about us." Preemptive mortification invades my gut.

Ian gives me a funny look. "I thought that was the point. I'm selling us."

Right. Selling us.

"I figured you'd come to your senses and back out. It's not too late."

"I'm in this." He glances around at the people—women mostly—still glancing in our direction. "You're doing me a favor, too, and not just because Riva is speaking to me now in more than monosyllables. I want my life to be normal here without the attention of..."

He makes a face and rubs the back of his neck.

"Thirsty women drooling all over you while the local dude brigade competes to strike up a bromance?"

"Um, yes." He nods vigorously. "I know people mean well, but it's not what I want for Riva. Dating you will give people time to get used to me. You're my safe space, Sadie."

I'm not sure why I like the idea so much, but I do. Like maybe I have more to offer than most people—including myself—give me credit for. Ian also seems more relaxed without his adoring fans hovering.

"Okay, then," I concede. My voice sounds weirdly breathy, and I clear my throat before continuing. "We'll be each other's safe space."

His ice-blue eyes darken to the color of the sky at twilight, the pastel flecks at the edges mesmerizing me. And when he licks his lips and leans slightly closer...hold me.

The idea of being partners with Ian is intoxicating and almost irresistible. It's as if decades after being the last picked for any team activity in PE class, the cool kid is finally choosing me. Like I mean something.

I don't want to think about how much I like it. Or what's going to happen when this arrangement comes to its inevitable end.

9

IAN

FOR A GUY who's gone to great lengths to avoid serious relationships, I'm blown away at how much I like being in a fake one with Sadie. So much so that I want more. More than she's willing to give, anyway.

That's right. The one woman who makes me consider lowering a few of my rock-solid defenses so she can come closer, is a woman who doesn't seem to want to be near me at all. Well, other than for the purpose of putting our fake dating life on display for her sister's friends in town before the wedding weekend anyway.

Which makes me an idiot, and I can't even stop myself. That's right. A man known for his discipline and composure is being undone by a woman who doesn't want me. Not like I want her.

It was adorable how flummoxed she got at the farmers market when I called her my girl. But it's annoying as shit the way her demure blush makes my heart race. And let's not even get into what that sweet smile and her habit of biting down on her bottom lip does to the rest of my body.

Or the fact that I want a chance to have my way with her full mouth. I want to see those lips wrapped around my—

Nope. Not going there again. I'm already taking multiple showers a day so I can jerk off in an attempt to keep my dick under control.

Spoiler alert: it's not working.

I tell myself I have a legit reason to spend time with my sexy neighbor. Something more than showcasing the chemistry I'm not faking. Riva likes her. And whether she realizes it or not, I'm learning a crap ton about relating to a preteen girl from Sadie.

I also respect the hell out of her for the dedication she shows to her job. She's so good with my daughter and the dogs who adore her, it blows my mind that she's not married with kids of her own.

The comparison between being a dog and human mom might offend some people, but it takes a lot of patience to do what she does plus deal with the owners, who are a pretty high maintenance bunch. She's always getting last-minute phone calls or urgent texts with requests to drop everything and pick up a dog who isn't on her schedule so that the owners can go live their best lives. Since we've been hanging out, she hasn't taken a day off or even had an hour to herself that I can tell.

I'm used to worrying about only myself—and now my daughter. It's a real eye-opener to watch someone do so much for people and expect nothing in return.

I've started channeling my inner Sadie when I'm dealing with Riva and the responsibility of single fatherhood. Having Sadie in our lives to run interference when I misstep in the parenting department—which happens plenty—eases a lot of the pressure.

I tag along with them more than I should because I also miss my daughter when she's helping take the dogs on a hike or doing errands during the day. It's not like I can get a do-over on all that time I missed when she was younger, so I'm soaking in every moment I can now.

Instead of being their shadow, I should be figuring out what I'm going to do next with my life. I had a few lucrative broadcast offers when I first announced my retirement, but that means traveling during the NFL season, and I'm not doing that to my kid. She needs me to be steady and stable, so I have to find something that will keep me in one place.

Now I understand why so many ex-athletes end up owning car dealerships. I'm hardly qualified for anything that would take more skill or training.

But I want whatever I do next to mean something. Problem is, the only thing that's ever meant anything to me is football.

"Sally and Trina are here," Riva calls as she pounds down the stairs. "I'll see you later."

"Use your good manners," I tell her as I intercept her at the front door.

As soon as the words are out of my mouth, I regret them. I sound like a tool. Or an octogenarian grandma who sucks on those disgusting butterscotch candies all day. Maybe Riva won't notice.

"Really?" She pulls to a stop and cocks her head as she shoots me a glare. "Do you think my manners are bad?"

Another misstep.

"Your manners are perfect. Sorry, Rivs. It just seemed like something a parent would say," I admit. "That sh—crap is new to me, so I'm still working on my technique. There's no doubt in my mind you'll be polite and a pleasure to be around."

A pleasure? Sheesh.

"I mean you'll be awesome. Sadie's friends are going to have an awesome time with you. Because you're awesome. Amazeballs. The best. I'm going to shut my pie hole now."

To my surprise, her shoulders soften and she smiles. "Hey, Ian. Don't strain yourself trying too hard."

"Call me Dad. And are you teasing me? Because I think that means you like me. Admit it, kid. You like me."

Riva rolls her eyes but giggles. "You're being weird, *Dad*."

She's right, but at the moment my heart is expanding in my chest. Who knew I'd like the role of the weird, cringey dad so much? Not me, but I do.

"Have a good time tonight."

"You, too, on your big date." She waggles her eyebrows. "Remember there are no gross paparazzi in Skylark, so if you kiss her, it's not going to end up all over the internet."

She starts to open the door, but I put a hand on her shoulder. "I'm not planning to kiss her..." No matter how much I want to. "And if we do kiss, it's for show. You understand that, right?"

"Yeah."

"You also understand a kid shouldn't have to see photos on the internet of either of her parents kissing people."

"It's not a big deal," she answers but keeps her gaze on the doorknob.

We are both aware that it is, indeed, a big deal, although it took me until now to realize it. I've been naive to think of my daughter as a little kid who isn't affected by her parents' public personas. Twelve-year-olds are way more worldly than I remember being. It's become abundantly clear my daughter has been exposed to a lot more than I would have wanted. And I have no right to pass judgment on Monika since I haven't played the role I should have in raising her before she came to Colorado.

"Well, since you put all those dumb parental controls on my tablet, I can't search anything interesting." She makes a face. "Not that seeing pictures of Mom and her boyfriend canoodling on the beach is interesting."

"Canoodling moms are the worst," I agree with a grimace, prompting both another eye roll and smile. "For the record, I might order a 'dum dum dad' bumper sticker and slap it on the back of my car."

She laughs out loud.

I smile broadly, feeling the satisfaction of that moniker all the way down to my toes. Dumb parents are boring and normal, which is just what I want for my girl. It's what my brother and I would have killed for growing up, but never got.

A dad who regularly made booze-fueled scenes and got carted

off for drunk and disorderly in a town where everyone knew our business didn't feel normal. Trying to run interference so he wouldn't take his frustrations with life out on our mom was never boring. In the worst way possible.

My daughter might be worldly and wise in her own way, but she doesn't know the constant anxiety of my turbulent youth. And she never will.

"I love that for you, Ia—Dad. Bring Sadie flowers or something. She likes daisies."

"Daisies. Got it. Thanks." I wave to Sally and Trina, waiting at the curb in their white Jeep. They're taking Riva to dinner and a movie because Sally thinks Sadie and I should be seen in town on a date, just the two of us.

I expected my daughter to protest. I might not be her favorite person, but she doesn't seem to be in any hurry to make friends her age, and still won't talk to anyone in the neighborhood other than Sadie and her clients. Yet she's thrilled to be hanging out with Sally and Trina, and happy for me to have a night out with Sadie.

She's not the only one. Although, I shouldn't admit that even to myself. This is fake. Sure, I like Sadie, but not because she's sweet and beautiful and smells like summertime. I like her because she's helping smooth the waters with my daughter, and that's not enough of a reason to make this anything more than a good show for the Skylark public.

It also turns out I'm a man who wants a sure thing, which doesn't speak highly of my confidence or courage when it comes to relationships or things that matter in general. I was fearless on the field, but that was about what I could do, not who I am as a human.

If I could be the kind of man a woman like Sadie Hart deserves, I'd do it in a second. A heartbeat.

But I can't. Because football is all I'm good at, just like my dad always told me.

10

SADIE

WHEN THE DOORBELL rings at six on the dot, I toss the wet washcloth I've had pressed to the back of my neck onto a side table and wipe my damp hands on the soft cotton of the flowy floral skirt I've chosen for tonight's date. Is thirty-three too early for a stress-induced hot flash? Because nerves have my insides sizzling like an egg in a frying pan.

Sally texted an hour ago to let me know they'd picked up Riva, as if I wasn't peeking through the curtains.

I'm showered and shaved—not that this night is going to require silky smooth skin. How many times can I remind myself of that before my body gets the memo?

I check my reflection in the mirror one last time, convinced a scarlet V will appear on my forehead given how much I'm overthinking all of this.

Max slowly pads to the door, curious but calm. I could learn something about self-possession from the old boy. The two boarders staying the night are already crated. It's a slow week for me thanks to Dogapalooza announcing a big summer special—book two nights of boarding and get a third free.

Certain clients—the ones who appreciate my bond with their

furbabies—will stick with me no matter what financial incentive is thrown their way because they understand the level of care I give their dogs. The pack is my priority. Still, the slow migration of clients to Dogapalooza has been chipping away at my margins more than I care to admit, and I'm not in a position to discount prices.

But that's a worry for another time. Most of the time, in fact. Just not tonight.

Max nudges my leg, and I take a deep breath, plaster on a smile and open the door.

Then cough and sputter as I swallow my own spit at the sight of Ian wearing an olive-colored polo that sets off his tanned face and makes his azure blue eyes pop. Faded jeans sit low on his hips and leather flip-flops give the outfit just the right amount of Colorado casual cool.

His hair stands slightly higher than usual, like he might have used product after showering. Ian doesn't strike me as a product guy, but it's working for him. I also like that he made an effort for tonight more than is healthy.

As I bend forward in a futile attempt to stop choking like I'm about to hork up a chicken bone, he thumps me hard between the shoulder blades.

Out of the corner of my eye, I see that he's holding a small bouquet of daisies—my favorite flower because they'd been my mother's favorite.

Suddenly, the understanding that this night is all for show disappears. I want it to be real, and that's a terrifying realization. It makes me vulnerable. I haven't done vulnerability for over a decade, and have no intention of starting now.

I should stand up, step back, and slam the door in his face, then call my sister and admit the whole farce before I well and truly fall for Ian Barlowe.

Too late, my ovaries chorus, doing jazz hands as they shimmy with excitement.

I straighten and wipe a hand across my mouth to stem the drool I feel oozing down my chin. An outstanding way to start the evening, if I do say so myself.

Sure, sure.

It's not like I live on an Amazonian island. I'm familiar with hot guys. There are plenty of them in Colorado. Not one can hold a candle to Ian as far as I'm concerned.

"Do you want water or a cough drop or something?" My cheeks flush as he searches my gaze like he's worried I might need the Heimlich. My back tingles when his giant palm presses against it, the fact that I can register any feeling other than humiliation at the moment a testament to the potency of his touch.

"I'm fine," I insist. "You didn't have to—"

"Are you okay, Sadie?" Marla Pierce shouts from across the street. My longtime neighbor has lived on Elmwood Circle since the dawn of time and prides herself on keeping tabs on anything that involves one of the street's residents.

"Fine, Marla," I call back. "Nothing to see here."

Ian's lips twitch as he removes the hand on my back to wave. Max gives me a supportive headbutt.

"What a gentleman to bring you flowers. Daisies were your mom's favorite."

"Yep. Have a good night, Marla." I grab Ian's arm and yank him into the house, muttering, "That woman needs a hobby," as I close the door. "This isn't the most auspicious start to the night."

He grins. "I expected it. And I'm kind of into the whole small-town busybody vibe. It beats paparazzi hiding in the bushes. Bet money she's already blowing up her grandma group chat with the news that we're on a legit date."

The words hit me like an ice bucket challenge.

This. Is. Fake.

Ian brought me flowers because he's selling our lie, and I have to both play along and remember it's not real.

He holds up the cheery bouquet. "Would you like to put these in water? Riva told me you like daisies," he adds gently.

Right. The flowers. Thankfully he doesn't mention Marla's comment about my mom. "Yes." I pluck them from his grasp. "Thank you. Flowers are a nice touch. Way to sell it."

His thick brows draw together, but he nods, and I hurry toward the kitchen, blinking away the tears that sting the back of my eyes. My mother *adored* daisies, and even after all these years, sometimes the emptiness of not having her here threatens to overwhelm me.

"I'm still not convinced this whole public dating scenario is necessary," I tell him as I return and open the front door. It's still sunny, and the light has that coveted golden-hour quality. The landscape appears softer, like everything is luxuriating in the lazy transition to summer.

The hiss of a sprinkler travels down the block and kids' laughter rings out from a nearby backyard. And while the world spins merrily on, I'm about to publicly deceive an entire community because I'm too much of a chicken to have a hard conversation with my sister.

I shove tortoise-shell sunglasses onto my nose, grateful for a brief reprieve from Ian's too-knowing gaze. It's ridiculous. The guy doesn't know me, so why does it feel like he can read me like the plot of some old-school romance? The kind where the virginal heroine is breathless and bewitched as she waits for the devilish duke to ravish her.

Heat pools low in my belly when he places that massive paw on my lower back, guiding me down the porch steps like I might take a tumble without him. As if he knows I'm distracted, thinking about being ravished. By him.

"This doesn't have to be a big deal," Ian assures me. "I need to eat. You need to eat. We're eating together—the kind of food served at a barn dance."

"Barbecue."

"Love it." He smiles. "We're having barbecue and dancing. A date. If people infer there's something-something going on between us, that sells this arrangement even more. That's what we want, right?"

Right. And I'm not a virginal Victorian heroine. Virgin, yes. Heroine, no. Regular people don't think in terms of ravishing, they think in terms of a little something-something. No strings attached...just checking off my bucket list item. I need to think like that.

"There's also a good chance no one is going to care." It's a lie. Everyone will care. The bigger question is whether anyone will buy it.

"Yoo-hoo," Mrs. Morris shouts from her porch. "It's so good to see you getting out, Sadie. With a ma-a-an," she adds, drawing the word into at least three syllables.

"Thanks, Mrs. Morris," I call with a wave.

"When was the last time you went out with a ma-a-an?" Ian asks. "Why does everybody seem so shocked that you're dating?"

"Those are two very different questions, but equally loaded," I answer. "They're mostly shocked by the thought of me dating you. Plus, I typically keep my private life private from our nosy neighbors."

It's a less humiliating answer than *I can barely remember the last time I went on a date.*

He opens the door of his SUV. "But let's discuss this Bradley guy your sister is marrying."

I trip over nothing and come close to smacking my forehead into the door's corner, but Ian's warm hands steady me. He's kind enough to ignore my reaction as I straighten.

"I take it you're still hung up on him?"

So much for ignoring my reaction. I smile as I hoist myself into the weirdly elevated vehicle.

"I'm not hung up on him, and I'm happy for my sister. What

kind of tires are these? Do you do a lot of off-roading? Why are they so tall?"

His mouth quirks, and he leans in, his breath fanning my cheek. "I do everything big, Sadie."

I huff out a laugh. "Bigger isn't always better."

He stares at me for a long moment. "But sometimes it is."

Add a British accent, and Ian Barlowe would have the part of the rakish duke locked up.

No whimpering, I silently command myself as he shuts the door and walks around to the driver's side.

"So are you sure this little favor you're doing for me isn't cramping your style?" I ask as he pulls out of the driveway. We both need a bit of grounding in the reality of our situation. At least I do. "I don't want to be on the bad side of whoever you're dating now."

That hint of a smile disappears. "I'm not dating at the moment. You don't have to worry about making anyone jealous."

Of course, I won't make anyone jealous. That's never been a possibility.

I turn and look out the passenger-side window. That's a harsh reminder, even delivered in his deceptively gentle tone. Who knows what people from Ian's real life will think if they see pictures of me with him? Probably that he lost a bet.

We drive in awkward silence for several minutes until he breaks it, asking, "So is this dance popular?"

I nod. "People around here love any excuse to congregate. We have a festival or art show or obscure event almost every weekend. As far as summer, the barn dances draw a decent crowd. Not quite as big as when the rodeo comes to town next month, or the Apple Festival and Brewfest in September. Not to mention the Christmas Extravaganza. I could keep going."

He chuckles low in his throat. "Extravaganza. That's a good word."

I adjust the seatbelt, cursing the fact that I've worn a thin T-shirt and a bra that isn't padded. One harmless chuckle from The Playmaker and my nipples are standing at attention.

Down, girls. I'm unsure how to ignore my body's repeated reaction to Ian, but I'm determined to stay in control no matter what.

"Extravaganzas are kind of our thing in Skylark. We have a rep to protect."

"Do you attend every one?"

"Mostly," I tell him. "A lot of my business comes from word of mouth, so I like to be out and about with the dogs. And the socialization is good when I'm training."

He turns onto the two-lane highway that leads toward downtown.

"I mean when you're not working. Do you go with friends or boyfriends? What does Sadie Hart do for fun in her off time?"

I swallow, because I need a minute to formulate a response. Should I make up stuff to sound less boring? This is all fake, anyway, so what's to stop me from being a different person with him?

Then reality sinks in. It's not easy to keep secrets in a small town, and we're already dealing with a whopper trying to sell this relationship thing. Mrs. Morris is the tip of the reactionary iceberg as far as my dating life is concerned, and it's ridiculous to think someone won't mention my story. Might as well head it off at the pass.

"My mom died when I was in college." I keep my eyes forward, unwilling to witness his reaction to that TMI bomb. "Piper was twelve, and she took it hard. I came home to raise her."

"I imagine you both took it hard," he interjects softly.

"Yes, well." I start to shrug, realize my shoulders are already hovering near my ears, and force them back down. "Of course it was hard for both of us, but I had the fact that I needed to find some way to support us to distract me.

"And I needed to be available for Piper. Mom cleaned houses

and office buildings around town and did whatever else she could to make ends meet. She was gone a lot, especially after Piper was born, so I didn't want to be. She had nightmares about me getting in a car wreck or having an accident or leaving her. She needed to feel safe. So, long story short, I threw myself into building the dog business and caring for her.

"When she left, the routine kind of stuck. I have friends like Sally and Trina and my book club, but people know me as the dog lady. My social life is nearly non-existent."

I take a breath and add, "I haven't been to one of the barn dances since high school."

"Did you go with *Bradley*?"

Ian says my soon-to-be brother-in-law's name with all the enthusiasm he might show a wet fart.

"With his friend group. We were always in a group, and that's fine. My life probably seems pathetic." I feel compelled to add that so he doesn't think I'm unaware of how mind-numbingly dull I am.

He drums a hand on the steering wheel. God, he has big hands. Hands that look like they could cup...well, a football for one thing. My ass for another.

"It doesn't sound pathetic," he answers. "I grew up in a postage-stamp town outside of Tulsa. My parents worked hard but never made much money. Football was a way out of the small town I desperately wanted to escape. It was the way out for me and my brother, and I was as singularly focused as you, although my motivation wasn't quite so altruistic. Still, it was me and Felix against the world, and I knew if I made it out, I could pave the way for him, too."

"Your brother plays football?" I ask.

He flashes a quick grin. "You really don't follow sports."

I shrug. "Piper played soccer, so I follow women's soccer. Megan Rapinoe is my favorite."

"She's cool," he agrees.

I feel my mouth drop open. "You know Megan Rapinoe?"

His grin widens. "We've met at some ESPN events. Have you Googled me at this point?"

"Maybe."

"What did you think of the underwear ads?"

"Didn't pay much attention, to be honest."

"I don't believe that for a second, Sadie. I think you're a secret fan of me in my skivvies." His voice pours over me like warm honey, and I don't want to think about all the ways he could make me sticky sweet.

I remind myself that all of this comes easy to Ian. Men like him can flirt and dole out sexual innuendos like dime-store bubble gum.

It doesn't mean anything. I don't mean anything. Which is how I want it.

It's why I'm in this predicament with a V card I can't shake. I don't know how to do a fling or a one-night stand.

Except Ian will be my fake boyfriend for the next few weeks until my sister's wedding. And if I'm going to toss my virginity down the field, I might as well throw it to a man with giant hands who knows how to use them. The thought has me squirming in my seat, but I manage a smile.

"Maybe I'll take a second look." I try to sound flippant, like I'm not a big fat failure at flirting. "And, at some point, maybe I'll compare the glossy ads to the real thing to see if bigger really is better."

11

IAN

I GRIP the steering wheel and try not to swerve off the road as we approach the property nestled into the foothills west of town where the weekly barn dance is held.

Did I underestimate Sadie Hart? Because you can about knock me over with a feather—or at least crack my suddenly rock-hard dick in half with a feather-light touch—at her bigger is better comment. Not to mention how she looked at me from beneath those long lashes of hers, a rosy tint coloring her cheeks and making me wonder if her whole body will flush pink when she breaks apart in my arms.

"I'm on a dating hiatus," I respond.

You're on a complete hiatus, I tell my dick, which twitches in response and ignores my warning. "A fake relationship is the only kind I'm interested in at the moment."

The last woman I dated posted pictures of me grabbing her thong bikini-covered—or not so covered—ass on social media. Monika took great pleasure in revealing that Riva had been shown those photos of her dad at school.

And the woman before that shared a photo of my naked ass with her family chat.

That's not to say that I blame anybody but myself for the current tension in my relationship with my daughter, but staying away from dating seems like a good start for getting things back on track. Being with Sadie isn't real dating. And Riva approves because it gets her close to the dogs.

All the more reason why I can't screw this up by complicating things with sex.

I remember a time when sex seemed simple. I took advantage of all that simplicity. But just like the aches and pains that plague me every time I get out of bed in the morning, the older I get, the less things stay simple.

It's incredible to me that Sadie believes my lie without any hesitation. What's more inconceivable is that I want to accept her explanation that dating isn't a big deal. It's obvious Sadie Hart is not a casual sex type of woman. She has white-picket fence and commitment written all over her adorable face.

"Be careful, darling," I say, letting the slightest tinge of my Oklahoma accent lengthen the vowels. "I might just take you up on your generous offer. I don't think that's what the neighborhood welcome wagon had in mind when they promised the people of Skylark are sure to make me feel right at home."

Sadie Hart would feel right at home underneath me. Somehow I know that deep in my soul, and it's a bad, bad idea.

She sucks in a breath, and I try not to notice that she needs a bra with more padding. One that hides the fact she's as affected by me as I am by her.

But it's hard.

No, not hard.

It's difficult. I have to stop thinking about the word hard and start thinking about my third-grade English teacher. Or calculus. Or something other than the way Sadie smells like sunshine and how appealing the freckles that dot her neck and arms are to me. How I want to touch every birthmark on her body with my hands and tongue.

We pull into the parking lot in front of the barn. It's more than half full, and the doors are wide open with a small crowd congregating. I park and then hit the button to kill the vehicle's engine.

"This place does look like a popular spot. You haven't been here since high school?"

"Almost fifteen years," she confirms, her hands balling into tight fists. "Some things about a small town never change."

The words sound hollow. Like she wants to change, but the past won't let her. I get that. Football did that to me, even with everything it did for me.

Some guys cry when they retire, unable to imagine their lives without the competition, camaraderie, fans, and fame. Some guys continue to live off stories of their glory days and remain steeped in the halcyon memories of their youth.

Not me. My brother might follow that path when it's his time to hang up the shoulder pads, but I didn't hesitate after the day when my life flashed before my eyes in that locker room.

For me, walking away was about Riva. I had an inkling I didn't have much time left before the relationship with my daughter would be beyond repair, and I'm hell-bent on fixing it. Sadie Hart is part of that whether she realizes it or not, and I'm a man who pays my debts.

"Let's get some supper and dust off our dancing shoes."

I climb out of the truck, but Sadie doesn't move.

"I'm guessing you aren't waiting for me to do the gentlemanly bit of opening your door," I tell her after opening her door.

"No one is going to believe this," she murmurs, her gaze focused straight ahead.

"People will believe what we show them, sweetheart."

"Everyone thinks I'm still pining after Bradley even though he's marrying my sister." She glances at me, sparks flaring in her brown eyes. "I'm not, by the way."

"Of course you're not." I drape one arm over the top of the

door like I could stand here all night talking about her dipshit high school crush. I'm already convinced the guy must be a complete tool. Why else would he have let Sadie go? If she's half as loyal and protective of the people in her life as she is to her menagerie of mutts, those people are damn fortunate.

The lengths she's willing to go to, taking on things that fall well outside her comfort zone, to ease her sister's worries also speaks volumes. I'd do the same for Felix in a heartbeat.

"Not to toot my own horn." I give her a slow wink. "But I might be just the type of man your close-knit community will believe could help you leave ole' Brad in your rearview mirror."

"Toot-toot," she whispers, and hell if those ridiculous syllables don't sound sexy.

What in the world is wrong with me?

I don't have time to puzzle it out because Sadie gets out of the truck and reaches on tiptoe to kiss my cheek. "Thank you for being a nice guy."

"I'm not nice." My voice sounds like I've just swallowed a giant frog, but I'm speaking to Sadie's back as she's maneuvering through lines of cars toward the barn's entrance.

I slam the door and catch up, taking her hand as we move closer. A shiver runs through her, and I want to pull her into my arms and give the crowd, which has turned to watch our approach, something to talk about.

She slows, but I keep us moving forward.

"Oh, my God, you're here," a woman calls as she rushes to greet us. For a moment I assume she's talking to me even though I've never laid eyes on her.

She has glossy blonde hair, supermodel cheekbones, deep blue eyes, and innate confidence that screams *I was a popular girl with rich parents who gifted me with a BMW for my sweet sixteenth birthday.* Okay, I can't tell all that from a first glance, but I'd bet it's close.

I'm used to being approached by strangers, but she completely ignores me and hugs Sadie tightly. "It's so good to see you out in the world, Sads."

Sadie laughs and returns the embrace with one arm. I notice she does not loosen her grip on my hand, and I like it more than I should.

She draws back from her friend and lets out another nervous laugh. "Come on, Avah. It's not like I'm a hermit." She glances nervously in my direction like I'm going to judge her for any supposed anti-social tendencies.

I'm the guy who didn't leave his new house for two weeks. No judgment here.

Her friend makes a show of looking on either side of Sadie before her gaze snags on our joined hands. "You're not carrying a leash," she points out. "And you've upgraded your companion from four-legged to two."

"Debatable whether it's an upgrade," I offer.

As if only realizing we're still holding hands, Sadie pulls hers away.

"Avah, this is Ian, my..." She pauses as if unsure what label to place on me.

"Her boyfriend," I supply.

Sadie looks like she wants to roll her eyes. "Ian, this is my friend, Avah."

"We're in a book club together." Avah offers a hand. "One where we actually read books, which was a surprise initially. I thought the books were an excuse to drink wine and gossip. But I like it. Nice to meet you, Ian. I know who you are. Everyone knows who you are."

I arch a brow. "Not everyone."

Avah quickly grasps my meaning and grabs Sadie by the shoulders. "Tell me you recognized Ian Barlowe."

My fake girlfriend's eye roll can't contain itself any longer. "I knew. I do now, anyway," she amends.

Avah gives Sadie another hug. "You're the best. So how long have you two…"

"It's new," Sadie says. "Can we talk later? I'm starving."

"Me too," I agree and shift closer to Sadie so my meaning is clear.

The woman's eyes widen. "Call me later," she tells Sadie, already backing away. Then she gives me another look. "Or tomorrow."

"Tomorrow will work," I confirm and nudge Sadie toward the barn.

"You don't need to lay it on so thick with my actual friends," she complains. "They aren't the ones we need to convince."

"Avah believes it. Are you familiar with the concept of manifestation, Sadie?" I ask as we walk into the barn.

Strings of fairy lights hang from the rafters, adding a rustic charm to the scene. Hay bales are arranged along the sides, and in the center, there's a large open area for dancing. Round tables with checkered tablecloths are scattered around, each adorned with centerpieces featuring mason jars filled with wildflowers. In one corner, a band is warming up on a small stage, the space filled with the twang of country music.

More eyes turn to us. These are speculative and curious. "You have to believe to receive," I tell her. "You have to feel the feeling and speak things into existence."

We're heading to the section of the barn dedicated to the barbecue buffet. Long tables contain a spread of smoked meats, cornbread, coleslaw, baked beans, and an assortment of sauces. She stops so quickly I almost run her over.

Her arms cross over that perfect, perky chest. "Are you telling me you believe in woo-woo shit?"

I shrug. "It's backed in science and sports psychology. Hell yeah, I believe it. I believe in my mind's power and ability to manifest the life I desire. I believe in visualizing an outcome to make it happen."

I let a little bit of my desire for her show in my eyes. Not the entire level of my need, because it's embarrassing and would probably freak her out. It freaks me the hell out. "You need to see us together in your mind." I will her to truly listen and feel even a portion of what I do. "You need to visualize what you want to show up in your life. Can you see it, Sadie?"

Her pupils dilate, and she drags that bottom lip between her teeth again. If there's any doubt whether the two of us have chemistry, no one in this barn will be able to deny it after this.

She gives a small nod.

"Good girl." I've never been much for good girls, but Sadie Hart might convert me. "What are you thinking about?"

I want her to tell me. I want her to say it. My body wants her to say it. She opens her mouth, but there's a clattering of metal against metal that breaks the connection between us. She blinks and the veil falls over her eyes again.

"I'm thinking about barbecue." She smiles, but it's as fake as our supposed relationship. "With a side of cornbread."

I laugh. She has zero poker face, but the fact that she keeps trying is cute. "Then let's eat."

I don't push the issue of our mutual attraction, because I've proven my point. Now I need to figure out how I'm going to manage to spend the next month pretending to be her boyfriend and keep myself from falling for her. Damn, it's going to be hard—and not in the good way.

12

SADIE

By the time the band starts their first set, my emotions are pulled as taut as the fiddle strings, and I try to manage the vibrant sensitivity shimmering inside me without snapping under the pressure.

Ian and I took our food to one of the picnic tables. It wasn't long before everyone I knew in town—and some people I didn't—found an excuse to plop themselves down and visit for a while.

Most wanted to talk to Ian, and those who sought me out did so to ask for dog training advice or explain why they'd stopped patronizing my business in favor of Dogapalooza.

"So, Ian Barlowe, huh?" Iris slides onto the picnic bench beside me.

Ian has been whisked away to the cornhole boards set up near the edge of the gravel driveway surrounding the barn. Based on the way the guy who recruited him is cheering and backslapping his buddies, Ian's athletic ability also extends to yard games. It doesn't surprise me. I'm sure his prowess is evident in any physical activity a person could undertake.

I need to stop thinking about one in particular if I'm going to have any chance of convincing myself to make a move on my fake boyfriend. Anticipation is not my friend.

I glance around then mock slap Iris's hand as she tries to steal one of my remaining chips. "Is everyone talking about me?"

She wrinkles her nose and snatches the chip. "Would it help if I lie and say no?"

"They'll get used to it," I answer. "You think everyone will calm down, right?"

She studies me for a long moment. "Will *you*?"

I'm not going to admit that by the time I'm used to it, if that's even possible, our arrangement will be over

I had planned to tell my friends the truth, of course. The book club members are the people closest to me, after Sally and Trina. However, watching Iris watch me, I realize I don't want to deal with the inevitable looks of pity if I admit this is all fake. What's one more lie in the grand scheme of things?

"I hope not," I tell her. "I sort of like the idea that people might realize there's more to me than they thought." That much is true.

"You're going to make quite the splash at your sister's wedding," she muses. "He's going to the wedding with you, right? Talk about getting over your high school crush in a *big* way. Huge." Her grin is contagious, and I return it, feeling just a bit self-satisfied.

Iris isn't a native of Skylark, or even Colorado, but knows enough about my history with Bradley and coming home to raise Piper. "That part is awesome."

"What about checking off your bucket list item?" Her smile turns sly. "I imagine that part is awesome, too. You know I'm up next for the challenge. I have a whole spreadsheet of ideas. Is it time to whip it out?"

"Not even close." I shake my head. "This relationship is new. Also, a spreadsheet? Seriously, Iris? The bucket list challenge is about choosing something that feels right, not a spreadsheet making the decision for you."

"No doubt Ian Barlowe would feel exactly right, so what's the hold-up? Is it your lack of nice underwear?" she asks, her voice dropping to a whisper. "I'll take you shopping. If you want to try stuff on, let's drive to Denver. Maybe hit one of those fancy lingerie stores in Cherry Creek. Otherwise, order something online." She wiggles her delicate eyebrows. "Expedited shipping, if you know what I mean."

The mayor is a woman who gets things done. She's organized and meticulous in her planning, to the point that her spreadsheets have spreadsheets. Having her sharp focus on me is overwhelming, but in a different way than Ian's attention feels. No less intimidating, although I need all the help I can get. I'm learning to accept help—sort of—and I definitely appreciate the offer.

"I don't even know if we're going to get there." What a ridiculous statement. Who wouldn't want to *get there* with a guy like Ian? I'm halfway there just looking at him. Could he ever want me the same way?

Iris nods and grabs my hand. "He's big," she says like she's imparting great wisdom. "I'm guessing he's big everywhere, but it will only hurt for a few seconds."

Yikes. Leave it to all-business Iris to get right to the meat of the matter, so to speak. "I hadn't thought about that," I confess. So much for bigger is better.

"We have to assume he knows what he's doing." Iris sounds serious. She could be prepping for a town council meeting, not parsing my lack of a sex life. "I'm guessing he's had a lot of experience. A *lot*."

I yank my hand from hers. "You aren't making me feel more confident."

She looks contrite, as if she hadn't realized what she was doing. "It's not a big deal, Sadie."

"Stop using the word *big*," I snap. "I don't want to think about having sex with Ian Barlowe."

Iris's face freezes, her gaze trained directly behind me. Oh, no.

"How about dancing?" Ian asks in that low, grumbly voice. I hear the amusement in his tone.

"This is *not* chill," I tell Iris. "Not at all."

She pops up from the table. "Hello, Ian. Welcome to Skylark. I'm Iris Dixon, the town's mayor. Interim mayor until I'm officially elected this fall. We're happy to have you as a new resident of our lovely community. If you need anything as you settle in, give me..."

She shakes her head and flips her shiny chestnut-colored hair over one shoulder. "I'm sure Sadie can handle anything you need."

I don't turn around but feel Ian smile behind me.

"She definitely can," he confirms.

Iris swallows hard before glancing at me again.

"I hate you," I mouth.

"Love you, too," she answers, then turns on her heel and strides away.

"I never took the mayor for a coward," I call after her.

"Would you care to dance?" Ian asks as I blurt, "I didn't mean for you to hear that."

He sits down and places his hand on the worn picnic table in front of me, palm facing up. My gaze stubbornly focuses on a little splotch of barbecue sauce next to his thumb.

"Let's talk while we dance," he suggests.

As much as every survival instinct I have tells me to bolt, I place my hand in his and force myself to look at him.

"We could also *not* talk." I immediately regret the unintentional innuendo of those words. If only I could swallow my tongue at the moment. "I didn't mean that to sound suggestive. I meant we can dance, enjoy the music, and pretend the past five minutes never happened."

He smiles as he stands and pulls me to my feet to lead me to the crowded dance floor. My palms are sweaty, and my mouth is filled with sandpaper.

Nerves flit around my stomach as we assume the position. Oh, gah. The thought of Ian and *positions* makes my knees go weak. Iris's comments about his size only add to my trepidation as his giant hand grips my hip.

Luckily, I know just the thing to make anxiety less awkward. Verbal diarrhea. That's the ticket.

"If memory serves, the band starts with the classics," I tell him like a cub reporter with my first scoop. "Mostly country—Patsy Cline is a favorite with the older crowd around here. Then they move into the line dancing era with early nineties covers. Once it's just the partiers left, they start the rowdy stuff. Closing time is upon us when they play 'Friends In Low Places.'" Bradley and his buddies loved belting out the Garth Brooks classic back in high school.

"It wouldn't be the first time I ended a night with Garth," Ian says close to my ear. Cue the shivers.

"I certainly won't be here long enough to sing along." I don't mean the words to sound prudish, but to my ears, they do.

"Where are you going to be?"

The question is casual, but my mind is completely muddled from his thumb drawing teasing circles over the small of my back, so I answer without thinking.

"At home in bed." I feel the shock ripple through his body even though he doesn't react. "Alone," I nearly shout. This night cannot get worse.

He continues to guide me around the dance floor effortlessly, like I'm not making a complete fool of myself because I can't seem to shut my damn pie hole. "Have you thought about doing *Dancing With the Stars*?" The words tumble from my mouth in fast progression like I'm possessed or mainlining caramel macchiatos.

"Nope," he answers and pulls me closer. "I also don't expect to have sex with you tonight. In case you're worried."

Worried, no.

Disappointed, a thousand times yes.

Humiliated beyond belief. Absolutely.

Where's a spontaneous earthquake, tornado, or other distracting natural disaster when a girl needs one?

Plastering on a smile, I put a little distance between our bodies. He doesn't resist because he might be big and strong and totally alpha, but he's a gentleman. I should appreciate that and kind of hate the part of myself that wants to be thrown over his shoulder and hauled off—or God forbid spanked—like we're in caveman times. Who am I right now?

"Ian, I need to apologize." The words sound stilted, and I try to get a hold of myself. "I shouldn't have been talking about us with Iris or anyone. Not about sex or even hinting at it. I appreciate what you're doing, but this is fake. You agreed for your daughter's sake. You're a good dad. A good guy. You're also not the type of guy who wants to have sex with someone like me. So we can just—"

He stops so abruptly that the older couple nearest us, two-stepping their way across the floor, runs into his back.

I understand how that feels. Slamming into a solid, sexy brick wall. "Sorry about that, Mr. and Mrs. Moore."

The man is my dentist, and his wife has worked the front desk of his office since I had my first cavity back in second grade.

"Good to see you out and not covered in dog hair," Mrs. Moore says, her hand resting on Ian's shoulder for balance. I don't think I imagine her eyes going a little glassy. I understand that reaction.

Ian still hasn't moved, and other than a grumbled, "Sorry," he doesn't acknowledge the roadblock we're causing.

"Are we done dancing?" I glance around confused, because the song has another verse and the bridge still to come. "Listen, if I offended—"

The noise that comes from my throat can only be described as a yelp. He doesn't throw me over his shoulder, but the force with which Ian takes my arm to lead me toward the barn's front entrance might set a land-speed record.

I jog to keep up, my skirt flapping in the cool evening breeze. The sun has dropped below the mountains to our west. I adore this time of evening in Colorado. While our much-hyped three hundred days of sun are lovely, sometimes a girl wants a few shadows to hide what she doesn't want other people to see.

I expect him to drag me to the parking lot so he can race home and end this painfully awkward night sooner rather than later. Instead, he leads me around the side of the barn.

"There's nothing and no one over here," I point out in case he's lost his way. Maybe all my ramblings scrambled *his* brain along with mine.

"I know," he answers. He doesn't quite sound annoyed, but he sounds *something*.

Before I can puzzle out the emotion, he spins me, pressing my back against the rough barn siding.

Ian bends his knees until we're at eye level. "I said I don't *expect* sex."

I'm still struggling to name that tone, but if I had to guess, I'd say frustration. God, please don't let him cancel our deal. I'll find somebody else for the bucket list V-card challenge. But I not only don't want to go to Piper's wedding alone, I want to go with Ian.

"I never said I don't *want* to have sex with you, Sadie."

I'm so lost in my own thoughts, my own wants, that it takes me longer than it should to catch the meaning of his words. I blink and focus on his eyes, which have turned the vivid blue of a flame's scorching center.

He leans in closer, and I think he's about to kiss me for real. My tongue darts out and wets my parched lips. He groans softly, then tilts his head and presses his mouth to the underside of my jaw.

"Sadie. You need to know..."

He drags my earlobe between his teeth, and I practically melt into a puddle of desire. Praise the Lord for the barn at my back.

"I definitely..."

He looks at me again, kissing first one corner of my mouth, then the other.

"Want..."

His tongue traces the seam of my lips.

"To have sex with you."

"Oh." It's the only response I can manage—just the barest puff of air.

Ian takes advantage of my open mouth to kiss me full-on. A deep, heady kiss. A kiss like I've only imagined receiving.

"Can you feel how much?" he asks against my mouth as he tilts his hips forward.

He's rock hard between us. Granted, I don't have much to compare it to, but I think Iris might have underestimated big when it comes to describing Ian Barlowe.

It's a good thing he claims my mouth again before I can answer, because I'm pretty sure I don't have words that would do justice to what I'm feeling.

He's wrapped an arm around my back, ensuring the rough barn wood isn't biting into my skin. As if I could register anything but the feeling of being kissed by Ian. His lips are soft but demanding, and every part of my body is thrumming with need. The rest of the world fades away and it's like being smack in the middle of a perfect moment, but still longing for more. Because his mouth on mine isn't nearly enough.

His other hand cups my cheek, then trails down my neck and collarbone until he covers my breast with his palm. Forget that thought about wishing I'd worn a bra with more padding.

Need spears through me as he circles my taut nipple. I want to beg him to take me right here. I didn't even know I had it in me to *beg*, and we're both still fully dressed.

What in the world could this man do to me naked?

A throat clears behind us. Ian stills and draws back ever so slightly to offer a hint of a smile. "No expectations, sweetheart," he whispers. "Just a whole hell of a lot of want."

I assume whoever caught us has walked by, but no such luck. Even worse, I recognize the voice calling, "Is that you, Sadie?"

I feel Ian's reluctance when I push him away, but he steps to one side, not turning around to face the woman staring at us, her coral-tinted lips pursed in a scowl.

"Imagine being caught canoodling at the barn dance as an adult." Amanda Sinton giggles. "I suppose you're making up for lost time. You most certainly never made out with anyone back in high school." She clucks her tongue. "Or college, from the stories Bradley used to tell."

I automatically raise a hand to my chest, hating that her verbal arrow has pierced right where she aimed it.

"Nice to see you, Amanda," I lie. "Piper told me you're coming to the wedding."

"Of course I'll be there. I'm happy for Bradley and your sister. Are you going to introduce me to *your new friend*?" She puts special emphasis on the words as Ian turns to face her.

"Amanda, this is Ian Barlowe."

"Her boyfriend," Ian clarifies, just as he has with every person we've met tonight. You've got to appreciate the man's commitment to the game. But he doesn't smile at Amanda. In fact, he looks annoyed—potentially both at the interruption and her digs at me. Maybe that's wishful thinking on my part, but somehow I have the feeling Ian has my back. The idea gives me enough confidence to offer him a shy smile.

"This is Amanda Sinton. She works at the elementary school."

She takes a step closer and holds out a manicured hand, her fingers long and elegant, the French tips on her nails perfect half moons. "*Principal* Sinton," she tells him. "I understand your daughter is joining our school community this fall."

Ian nods. "Sixth grade," he says.

"We're excited to have her and you as part of our Skylark Wolves family," she says, tilting her chin skyward. It gives us a perfect view of her creamy skin and the subtle cleavage exposed by her V-neck sundress. She lets out a howl, dainty as noises go.

"Okay, then." Ian glances at me then back to Amanda, who stands there like she's not done with us—with me, more likely. "Nice to meet you, Principal Sinton. Sadie and I should be heading home now."

"It's a close-knit community at the school," she elaborates, "and we look out for our children and parents. We pride ourselves on being pillars of the Skylark community. Feel free to reach out if you need help meeting the *right* people."

Quicker than I've seen anyone move in a long time, she pulls a business card from her cross-body purse and presses it into Ian's hand, giving that hand a squeeze. "My cell number is on the card. Please call *any* time."

Is Amanda trying to steal my fake boyfriend right in front of me?

"Thank you," Ian says, no emotion in his tone. "Riva is a good student, and I already feel *very* welcome in town."

"You're new. You'll find your way," she tells him with a wink. "Good to see you, Sadie. If not before, we'll visit at the wedding."

She turns to walk away, then glances over her shoulder. "My secretary sent sponsorship applications for the school's summer fun run. We're raising money for new playground equipment—such a worthy cause. Dogapalooza has already signed on as a gold sponsor. Ian, you'll get more information from PTO about signing Riva up. I'm sure she'll want to participate. Sadie, I understand that times are tight for certain small businesses in town, so whatever you can contribute would be greatly appreciated."

"You bet," I answer with a smile that might crack if I have to hold it much longer. She disappears around the side of the barn, and I slump back against the wood, head lowered, chin resting on my chest. "Amanda Sinton is a Colorado native who missed her calling as a southern belle," I tell Ian.

"You were friends in high school?" He leans against the barn next to me and crosses his thick arms over his chest.

"She dated Bradley, and he and I were friends. Because of that, I was included in his group. I stupidly thought that meant they were my friends, too."

Ian laughs softly. "If it makes you feel any better, I think you dodged a frenemy bullet with Principal Sinton. She's extra extra, as Riva would say."

I blow out a breath. "Why did it have to be her who caught us?" I wonder out loud. "She's going to tell everyone."

Ian nudges me with his elbow. "Isn't that a good thing? If nothing else, what your former non-friend witnessed should seal the deal as far as people believing what's between us is real."

Ouch. That stings, even though it shouldn't. I can tell myself all I want about losing my V-card to Ian being the right thing, but the truth is, my heart was just as engaged as my body when we were kissing.

That won't work.

At all.

"I'd like to go home." I push off the barn and head for the parking lot.

The sky is inky now and stars twinkle above us like the fairy lights strung across the barn's interior, making the night feel both intimate and expansive. A bonfire glows at the edge of the property with couples swaying to the music drifting out. It's like something out of a romantic movie, only the chill that tinges the evening air seems to be coming from inside me.

I wrap my arms around me to ward off the cold. Ian doesn't

take my hand again, and we're silent as he drives away from the barn.

"Thank you for tonight," I tell him, unbuckling my seat belt before he's even pulled to a stop in my driveway. As if I can't make it the short distance between his property and mine on my own.

"I'll walk you to the door." He puts the truck in park.

"Not necessary. You still need to pick up Riva from Sally and Trina. I can make it on my own." Story of my life, in fact.

"Are we okay, Sadie?" It sounds like he cares about my answer.

"All good." I chuck him on the arm like nothing happened between us. Like I hadn't been on the way to my first big O with another person right there on the side of a barn in plain sight of half the town. That's embarrassing to admit, even to myself.

"I'll see you later, Sadie." Before he can say anything else, I hop out of the car and walk to my house without looking back.

Max is waiting by the front door, tail wagging and a half-destroyed stuffed toy in his mouth as an offering. Good old Max. My most stable relationship.

I head for the freezer, because this night is begging for a bowl of Rocky Road. Ice cream and dog kisses. A girl could do worse.

13

IAN

I'VE SPENT the better part of the past two days castigating myself for letting my dick get the better of my common sense. I haven't acted with the reckless abandon I displayed, pressing Sadie against the side of a barn Saturday night, for a long time.

More specifically, since my rookie year in the NFL and the decision to forego a condom with Monika *just that once* because she wanted to really feel me inside her and she was on the pill.

Spoiler alert: she was *not* on the pill.

I don't regret the outcome. Riva is the best thing that ever happened to me. Even my twenty-two-year-old idiot self recognized it. But the comparison confirms how impulsively I acted with Sadie.

And it's not cool.

I don't care about the principal's not-so-subtle innuendos, or what anybody in this town thinks about me, but they should think a lot better of Sadie than most of them seem to. If I mess this up, and she decides she doesn't want my daughter as her summer helper...

Well, I know who Riva will blame. And she'll have every right.

Let me be clear: my body has waged an all-out war against my brain and the willpower I'm trying to muster. For a guy who spent most of his career leading with his body and not his brain, it's a hell of a battle.

I dream about Sadie. I think about her every waking minute. I walk past the window that faces her house so often, I'm wearing grooves in the hardwood floor. Still, I haven't done so much as wave at her this week because I'm a damn coward. It's been easier to give her the cold shoulder while I try to lock down my emotions.

No doubt, the unofficial neighborhood watch is keeping track of both of our comings and goings. Hers involves dogs and my daughter, while mine includes early morning runs to work off pent-up frustration, mostly of the sexual variety.

We're touring the local country club this afternoon, and Riva invited Sadie to come along. Thankfully, it doesn't sound exclusive or snooty like the country club I belonged to in Atlanta. Joining might give Riva an opportunity to make friends. Plus, until I figure out the next move in my career, I need a hobby—something other than obsessing over my fake girlfriend and how good she felt in my arms.

Golf should do the trick.

At least it'll give me an excuse to hold something between my legs that won't derail my future or tarnish my daughter's opinion of me any further.

I walk out of the house when I see Sadie's garage door open.

"This is Beast," Riva announces as she moves toward me, glancing down at the bundle in her arms.

I try to hide my visceral reaction to whatever it is she's holding. The creature certainly doesn't look like a Beast.

"Are you sure it's a dog?"

Wrong reply based on the exasperated sigh that comes from my daughter.

"He's a Yorkie Apso." Sadie exits her garage and hits the code to shut the door. At my blank look, she explains, "A mix of a

Yorkshire Terrier and a Lhasa Apso." Her nose wrinkles. "We're unsure if there are other breeds in the mix."

"Perhaps a half-plucked chicken?" I'm only half joking.

"Dad, that's so rude." Riva snuggles the dog closer. The animal is trembling like he's facing a firing squad. "Beast has a skin condition, and you're making fun of him. That's as bad as body shaming."

"Whoa, now. No shaming intended, but you gotta admit that is one ugly mutt."

"He has alopecia, which causes patches of hair loss," Sadie explains in a patient voice like she's talking to a three-year-old. "The vet has him on a treatment plan."

"How's that going for him?"

I notice she hasn't made eye contact with me. Believe me, I'm watching.

Sadie sighs. "Slow. His owner passed away a few months ago, and now the woman's son has him. He's a pilot, so he travels for work and has an active social life. He isn't around a lot, and—"

"He wants to date Sadie for real," Riva announces with a grin. "It was *so* obvious when he dropped off Beast this morning."

"Daniel does *not* want to date me." A blush colors Sadie's cheeks.

Add this Daniel dude to the list of men I want to stab—along with Sadie's soon-to-be brother-in-law.

"Beast's condition has gotten worse because he isn't giving the dog the medicine or daily oatmeal baths that keep it under control."

I'm feeling stabbier by the moment. "Why doesn't he take the mutt to the pound?"

"The pound?" Sadie and Riva chorus, giving me twin looks of...I hope the right word is horror, but it could be disgust.

"Dad, just because an animal or a person isn't social-media beautiful doesn't mean they're less worthy of love."

Okay, that got serious fast. "I'm not implying Beast isn't

worthy of love." I try to figure out what I *am* saying, because this feels like way more than commenting on a butt-ugly dog. "If his new owner can't take care of him, he should be rehomed with a family who can meet his needs."

Riva is about to give me another lecture when Sadie touches her shoulder. "Your dad might be right, sweetie. I'm going to help Daniel take care of Beast, but if he can't do what he needs to, we'll find a better home for him."

"We could adopt—" my daughter begins, but Sadie cuts her off with a sound somewhere between a whistle and a grunt.

"What's the rule about asking your dad for a dog?"

Instead of the side-eye or sass she likes to bestow on me, Riva nods and cuddles Beast, the canine chicken, closer to her chest. "I hope Daniel figures it out," she says softly.

This is getting more complicated by the second, and complex is not my favorite thing. But I owe my sweet and sexy dog lady for keeping my daughter happy this summer in a way I can't manage on my own. I'm also frustrated as hell that she makes me feel things I haven't in years.

Now I'm wondering if she's the smartest person I know. After all, she realized that not begging to adopt every animal in need had to be part of the agreement with Riva. For my sanity at least.

If I had plans to adopt a dog, which I do not, it would be something more respectable. Maybe a German Shepherd or a barrel-chested yellow lab. Man's best friend. *Not* a chicken dog.

"Me, too." I reach out to pat Beast's head, and he growls low in his throat. Less chicken, more Rottweiler.

"He hasn't been well socialized." Sadie grimaces. "I have him for the next week while Daniel's out of town. We have a lot to work on." She wraps an arm around Riva's shoulder, and my daughter leans into her. "Luckily, my amazing assistant has the magic touch."

"I can't wait to see what the two of you accomplish," I say. Trust me, I'm drawing on every ounce of acting ability I've displayed in commercials hawking insurance, fast-food and laundry detergent to keep a straight face. "Why don't you take him back to the house now, Rivs? We're due at the country club in a few minutes."

Riva smiles at me, but it's not as sweet as the one she bestowed on Sadie moments earlier. "Beast's going with us."

I choke out a laugh. "I don't think so. We're touring a country club, not a dog rescue."

"It's all good." Sadie's smile borders on sheepish. "The club's membership director is a client of mine. One who hasn't deserted me for Dogapalooza. I called her when Riva invited me and asked if we could bring Beast. He needs to get used to people and learn to walk on his own."

"He can't walk? I thought that was intuitive for dogs."

"His former owner carried him everywhere," Sadie tells me like it's just one more tiny hurdle to jump, "and he has some sensory issues."

"Sensory issues," I mutter. How is this my life?

"He can sit in the back with me." Riva walks past me toward the SUV still parked in my garage.

"Is this necessary?" I ask Sadie, crowding her a little. Wanting to crowd her a lot.

"Oh, I'm sorry." She frowns but doesn't look the least bit contrite. "I would have asked, but it's pretty clear you're avoiding me, so I didn't want to bother you." Still not making eye contact, she moves to walk by me as well. "The invite is a nice touch, public and all that. The country club should be busy this time of day. Maybe you can feel me up in the tennis bubble."

I'd love to snap off a witty comeback, but just that sarcastic reference to her breasts causes my breath to lodge in my chest.

How did I think this arrangement would be easy? When have I ever done anything easy when it comes to a relationship with a woman—even a fake one? I'm committed, and although it's clear she's pissed at being ghosted for the past couple of days, Sadie isn't calling things off either.

I need to find a way back to neutral ground. Maybe if I flew to Vegas and lost myself in gambling, brown liquor, and the thighs of a random hookup...

I slap a palm against my forehead. What the hell am I thinking? Vegas isn't an option. I'm a single dad and an upstanding citizen of the happiest town on earth. A man who's given up being wild and reckless.

I'm The Playmaker, I tell myself as I jiggle the keys in my pocket and follow Sadie and my daughter to the car. I'm used to victory, and this is a game I'm damn sure going to win.

Riva gives me the rundown on her morning as we drive, surreptitiously slipping in another request for a cell phone. She's been asking for one since she got to Colorado. Unlike the dog rule, there's no agreement stopping her.

It sounds like Sadie is busy this week with multiple dogs attending day school and extended boarding stays for clients on vacation. I want to ask her about Amanda's comments that threw subtle shade at her business and get more info on the other boarding facility in town. But I don't want to put her on the spot, and it's hard to define the actual parameters of our relationship. Is talking about whether or not her business is failing too personal?

It seems ridiculous after I practically polished her tonsils with my tongue Saturday night. But I know sex. I understand physical attraction. *Those* are easy and simple. If we hadn't been interrupted, I would have gladly dropped to my knees, lifted her skirt and pressed my face to her sweet center without a single regret.

What I don't know is how to approach the other topic without hurting her feelings or overstepping my bounds. Or let's face it, invite questions about my own life that I'm too chicken-shit to answer.

Maybe I have more in common with Beast than I realize.

"Are you a member of the Mountain View Country Club?"

"Me?" Sadie rolls her eyes. "No. Mountain View isn't the kind of place for people like me."

A glance in the rearview mirror confirms that Riva has put on her headphones. At some point I'm going to have to cave on the iPhone, but for now the MP3 player is getting the job done. I hear the tinny sound of Lainey Wilson's drawl, so I know my daughter isn't paying attention to this conversation.

"What does that mean?" I reach my hand across the console, intending to place it on her denim-clad leg, but she shifts away.

"No one's watching," she tells me. "You don't have to make this look real."

I want to argue, but press my lips together and nod. Boundaries are healthy, even if they're bullshit.

Up ahead, a dark wood sign with gold lettering announces the entrance to the Mountain View Country Club, renewing the topic that invited my reaction to begin with. "People like you?"

"My mom worked here. Five nights a week, she cleaned locker rooms. At the very end of the summer, when they were about to drain the pool for the season, they'd let the families of staff come for an afternoon. That's when I got to swim in the rarefied water of Mountain View. In high school, Bradley and Amanda belonged. He sometimes invited me, but it felt weird."

Irritation pumps through my veins because I hate that Sadie feels like I'm the type of tool who'd hang out with a major tool like Bradley. I turn onto the road leading to the clubhouse. It's lined with tall maple trees, their verdant leaves shimmering in the bright afternoon sunlight.

"I want to be somewhere you'd be comfortable, too. Is there a community pool I could take Riva to? A public golf course? I'm mainly joining for the golf."

She meets my gaze, and her eyes aren't exactly sad, just resigned. "You should join Mountain View. You'll fit in here."

I've slowed nearly to a stop, and the car behind us honks.

"What does that mean?"

Riva's bopping along with her tunes as she pets Beast, unaware of the tension that's crept into the vehicle. Tension I don't want anywhere near my daughter or the woman sitting next to me.

My teeth clench when she doesn't answer, and I hit the gas again. "I'm not going to apologize for having money, Sadie. I worked hard for my success. And I've got the scars, aching joints, and too many concussions to prove it."

I've never been the kind of guy who flashes his lifestyle. I don't carry gym bags with designer monograms or flex my collection of blinged-out watches. But I have them. Some part of me—mainly the kid with the angry dad and the sad mom, who listened to countless fights about paying the bills—needs proof that I made it.

Sadie touches my arm. I'm tense all over but relax as her soft fingers wrap around my wrist. She might think I'm a rich prick, but my body doesn't care. It wants to snuggle into her like a kitten...a very hard kitten.

"My issues with the country club..." She pauses, drawing in a deep breath. "My issues with a lot of things are my own. I don't want to put them on you. There's nothing wrong with Mountain View. By and large, the people who belong here are lovely. Trina and Sally are members. They're part of a weekly golf league that they'll no doubt try to convince you to join. I don't judge them for being members."

She draws back her hand, and when I glance over, she smiles. "I'm not judging you either. The wedding and our arrangement are bringing up feelings I hadn't expected."

"Tell me about it," I murmur. "By the way, I'm sorry if I crossed the line Saturday night."

She looks over her shoulder toward the back seat then back at me, her eyes sparking with the same need I feel whenever we're together. "We crossed it together, and I liked it."

She liked it. Hot damn.

Relief courses through me along with another healthy dose of desire. It's somewhat embarrassing how much I wanted—possibly even needed—to hear those words.

"So what happens now?" I ask as I throw the truck into park. There's a valet stand under the portico at the front entrance, but I want to finish this conversation.

"I'm your plus one for the country club tour," she says, tightening her ponytail.

"I liked seeing your hair down on Saturday night." I reach out and trail my finger over a wisp that's pulled free from the rubber band. "You have beautiful hair, Sadie. *You* are beautiful."

Her nostrils flare, and she leans forward slightly. I can't kiss her with Riva in the back seat, but damn I want to.

Then a terrible, horrible, no good, very bad scent hits me like a sledgehammer.

"Hey guys, Beast farted," Riva calls from the back.

Sadie wrinkles her nose. "He's a little gassy."

"That smell better come out of the interior of my car," I shout as I roll down the windows and drive toward the valet stand. "I am *not* dealing with that dog's putrid odor."

"At least he didn't get car sick this time," Sadie says.

My mouth falls open. "That was a possibility?"

"I have a towel wrapped in the blanket to clean it up," Riva assures me.

"The two of you were going to let that dog puke in my car? Oh, hell no. Let's go," I tell them, opening the door.

When I hear their answering laughter, tinkling together like the melody of my favorite song, I know I'll put up with a lot more than dog vomit to keep both my daughter and Sadie Hart happy.

14

SADIE

"At no point did I have 'sipping lavender lemonade while gazing out over the country club golf course' on my summer bingo card." I take another drink of the sweet and tangy beverage as Ian chuckles.

"If it makes you feel any better, I didn't have 'holding a dog that looks like a chicken' on mine."

I return his smile, sinking back against the cushion of the Adirondack chair on the country club's patio.

It's just the two of us at this point. Halfway through the tour, Riva spotted the daughter of one of my clients, and Kaya invited her to join a group of girls at the pool. Riva wore her swimsuit under her T-shirt and cut off shorts, so she went along, much to Ian's shock and my delight.

After the girls dashed away together, it took a few minutes to talk him down from the worried-dad ledge. His overprotectiveness when it came to his little girl heading off into the wilds of the country club pool deck without him was more than a little adorable.

When we finished with Heather Martin, the club's membership director, she suggested we grab a drink and then take

Beast to check out one of the nature trails that border Mountain View's championship golf course. Although I offered to make myself scarce so he could meet the moms of Riva's potential new girl squad, he and Heather rolled their eyes in unison.

"What do they put in this?" he asks, holding the clear glass to study it. "It's ridiculously good."

"It's sweetened with honey. My mom used to make the same recipe during the summer. We'd sit out back with sweet toddler Piper and dunk our feet in the baby pool while she splashed. Mom told me it was just like being at the country club."

He doesn't laugh at my mother's attempt to romanticize our circumstances, but I feel his gaze hold on me. "Was it?"

I roll my lips together as I think about how to answer. "Better," I say finally, "because the three of us were together."

He nods. "My mom worked a lot, too. My brother and I got into all kinds of trouble when she was gone. Our version of a country club was the local swimming hole."

"Have you ever taken Riva to your hometown for a visit?"

He gives me an odd look. "No. She'd hate it."

"Why?"

"I hated it." His voice is solemn, like he's admitting something he doesn't want to say out loud. "Plus, they both moved after they divorced. Felix got Dad a boat in the Keys when he got his first big contract. I bought Mom a condo in Ft. Lauderdale with my money. Took Rivs to Disney World after my first Super Bowl win. We spent a few days with her grandma on that trip, and I fly my mom up when I have Riva for holidays. My dad is in his own world, and that's best for all of us."

"Are you close to your parents?"

He drains the last of his lemonade and places the empty glass between us. "I wouldn't say that, but I do my duty." He gestures at me. "You do more than yours by your sister."

"I love her." I offer those three words like they explain everything.

"I hope she appreciates how much."

My stomach tightens, and I press a hand to it. Piper wouldn't want me to pretend to have a boyfriend to make things easier for her at the wedding, but making things easier is my love language with my sister.

Okay, that's a cop-out. I've used Piper as an excuse for not living my life to the fullest and playing small for too long. Being with Ian—even though it's not real—makes me understand how much I want that to change.

Turns out, change is scary as hell.

I set my glass next to his on the teak table between us and stand. "Let's take Beast for that walk. I need to snap a pic of him with the golf course as a background. Daniel loves to golf and won't believe he spent the afternoon at the club."

He makes a strange growling sound low in his throat but hands the dog to me.

Beast is more relaxed than usual and almost seems curious about the world around us instead of frightened. I like that for him. I also like the idea of it for me, even though it's absurd to compare myself to a dog.

"Do you want to date this Daniel guy?" Even though Ian asks the question casually, there's a thread of something in his tone that makes goosebumps erupt along my skin.

"We're friends, and he's a flirt. That's all Riva saw."

I walk down the patio's wide stone steps toward the nature path a few feet away.

His long legs easily match my stride. "Why didn't you ask him to go with you to the wedding?"

"He's a client and a friend. It would have been weird and not served the purpose."

"I serve the purpose?"

I bend down to place Beast on the ground without answering. When I straighten, Ian is so close my ass brushes the front of his cargo shorts. The touch is casual, inadvertent...and electric.

He makes me feel things I've cut myself off from the whole of my adult life. It's easy for him—the physical part. He's so in control of his body. Trusting what he's doing comes without effort for him.

I trust his experience, but sadly, not myself. It's frustrating, intoxicating, and confusing as hell.

"Remember it was Sally and Trina who put you up to this. Not me."

I keep my gaze on Beast. He's staring at the trail like he's never seen dirt under his dainty paws.

"Are you saying our arrangement isn't working for you?" He sounds amused, not irritated. He leans in and drops a featherlight kiss on the skin at the base of my neck, his lips grazing the collar of my thin tank top. "Because earlier you told me you liked what happened the other night."

Keep it together, Sadie.

"I'm hoping you liked it enough for more."

I laugh, and where did that husky note come from? "I imagine women fall at the feet of The Playmaker like dominoes. You can get more any time you want it."

"You don't fall," he points out.

"I'm no one." As my words reverberate in the air around us, I realize how much I believe them.

"You're someone to Riva." His breath is warm against my skin, and I want to lean into him. To beg for more. To be the type of woman confident enough to beg. "And to me."

Because of how I help the relationship with his daughter, I remind myself and step away.

The pathetic pity party that starts every time I think about the terms of our arrangement needs to end. I have a good life and great friends. Even if people around town make jokes about me being covered in dog hair and needing to get a life, my mom would be proud that I took care of my sister.

Would she be proud of me outside my role as Piper's guardian?

Hard to say. I've never let myself consider becoming more than that.

Losing my virginity is supposed to be the first step in reclaiming my power. Now it feels convoluted in my head and heart thanks to this fake relationship. Beast trots forward a few feet and continues along the path as we follow.

"If we have sex," I announce, rounding on him, "I understand it doesn't mean anything."

Oh, dang. Listen to the verbal diarrhea spewing once again. It's almost as bad as Max's first Halloween, when he pilfered a bag of chocolate, and it came torpedoing out his back end the next day. Is there no limit to the ways I'll embarrass myself in front of Ian?

"Are you trying to convince me or you?" He's so close that I'm captured in his magnetic orbit.

His gaze is intense as he watches me, and I bite my lower lip. His step falters, which makes me feel strangely powerful. Like I know what I'm doing and can handle whatever comes next, when, in fact, I have no idea what comes next.

Beast moves to the edge of the path and stops. He hates walking on grass.

I can tell Ian realizes this moment is a big one, and not just for the two of us. He focuses his attention on the dog. All that gentle consideration from such a big guy for a dog that weighs less than most cats melts my heart. Everything about him affects me at this point.

"You've got this, buddy," I tell the dog, half expecting Ian to repeat his question of who exactly I'm trying to convince, but he remains silent and watchful.

After a long moment. Beast places a tentative paw on the grass, lifting and lowering it twice before stepping down with his full weight. A moment later, he has all four paws on the grass and lifts a leg like he hasn't been using pee pads his whole life.

"Good go potty," I praise. "Well done, Beast. Good boy."

Ian chuckles and takes my hand, linking our fingers like it's the most natural thing in the world. "You have a way with animals. He looks like a normal dog. Sort of."

Beast finishes his business and then ventures off to explore. I'm not worried about him running off. Beast is about as adventurous as me.

"It's all I know," I answer, although I don't expect him to understand what I mean.

"You know how to make people feel comfortable," he tells me. As we follow Beast off the path and through the trees, he tugs on my hand and spins me around. "You also know how to kiss."

He presses his mouth to mine, and it's easy to lose myself in the feel of him once again. Before Ian, I'm not sure any of the few guys I've kissed would compliment my skill, so maybe things could be different with him.

Maybe *I* can be different.

He draws back to look into my eyes. "It can mean nothing if that's what you want. Either way, we'll keep it simple and stay friends after this ends."

I don't react to the reminder that our arrangement is temporary. I *need* to be reminded.

"You understand I can't commit to anything serious in my personal life other than Riva?" he continues.

I want him to stop talking and keep the excuses vague—the kind I can ignore in my secret daydreams—but I'm the one who started this conversation. I need to see it through.

"I understand." I offer a placating smile. Sadie Hart, master placater. "Your daughter is your priority. I respect that. And let's face it, in the real world of dating, we aren't exactly each other's type."

He blinks. "Is Daniel the pilot your type?"

"I suppose he could be," I say, which is true, although Daniel the pilot doesn't come close to making my body tingle like Ian the Playmaker. "But this is about you and me. It's smart for us to define what this is and isn't before we move forward."

When his mouth is on mine, it's too easy to forget. He doesn't answer with words, but claims my lips again. The spell is broken minutes later when Beast lets out a string of high-pitched barks. Ian and I break apart as two women power walk in our direction.

We're far enough off the path that they might have walked on by if it wasn't for the dog. Instead, their attention is drawn to us.

Because my luck is shit, one of them is Amanda Sinton. The other is Casey Chambers, one of the teachers at the elementary school, and my sister's best friend and maid of honor.

Casey waves. "Hey, Sadie," she calls. "I haven't gotten your RSVP for the bridesmaids' spa day in Vail before the rehearsal dinner. Piper says there's no way you'll miss it."

I hold up a hand in a stiff wave. "Yep, I'll be there."

They look like they're veering off the path toward us, but Ian tugs on my hand. "We should find Riva," he tells me.

"Need to get going, ladies," I call as he scoops up the dog, and I follow him without hesitation.

We don't speak until we're lounging poolside, watching as Riva splashes in the water with her new friends. The moms throwing us curious glances aren't familiar, but Ian has been holding my hand since the first woman lowered her sunglasses to get a better look at him. He's also cradling Beast like a canine football as the dog drools on his forearm.

"Why did you pull me away from Amanda and Casey?" I ask when I can't hold my serene smile any longer. "Casey is Piper's maid of honor. I need to make an effort."

He turns to stare at me. "That principal looks at me the way my brother looks at a box of a dozen donuts. Felix inhales donuts. Not that I won't have your back if you and Principal Sinton throw hands, but I prefer to avoid that if I could."

"You think I'm going to fight for you?" I choke out a laugh. "Do I look like the type to engage in a physical altercation?"

He presses the hand holding mine to his rock-hard chest. "You wound me, sweetheart. Are you saying you wouldn't defend my honor and your claim on me?"

"I hope you're joking because this isn't the Regency Era. No one in Skylark is going twenty paces with dueling pistols. Besides, I'm certain you can handle Amanda Sinton."

He shrugs. "It would be kind of hot to see you do it though."

I laugh again and suck in a breath when he lifts our joined hands to his mouth and kisses my knuckles. "Why is that Casey chick your sister's maid of honor? Why aren't *you* her maid of honor? You're her sister."

"It's how Piper wanted it," I reply quietly. "She asked me to walk her down the aisle because she doesn't have parents to do it. The bridal party is made up of people her age."

"You're not exactly a senior citizen. You also *aren't* her parent. You're her sister."

"I know that," I mutter.

"Does she?"

"It's not a big deal. Party planning isn't exactly my area of expertise. I'm happy Casey is taking care of things. Piper's friends can be high maintenance. It's a relief not to have the pressure to ensure they have a good time."

At least that's what I've convinced myself at this point. When Piper first told me about her plan for the wedding party and who would play what role, my reaction might have been similar to Ian's.

I don't love that he can read me so easily, especially when not many people in my life bother to try.

"If our mother hadn't died, maybe we'd have more of a sisterly relationship, but there's no chance of that."

"There's always a chance to change things." His eyes are solemn as they track from me to his daughter in the pool. He's speaking as much to himself as me. I'm glad I'm not the only one finding hidden messages in casual conversation. "If you're willing to try," he adds.

What am I supposed to say to that? Most days I have more in

common with the water aerobics set than people my own age. This man has lived a big life and shares a child with one of the planet's biggest movie stars.

Big, bigger, and biggest. A common theme with Ian Barlowe. The Playmaker. Yes, he's in my little town *playing* house in my modest neighborhood when he could afford to buy the whole block. But for all I know—for all he knows—this is temporary. He's talked about looking at his next business venture, and as solid as his intentions are for raising Riva in Happy Valley, there's no guarantee that won't change.

I'm way too aware that life can change in an instant. And maybe my life is smaller than it needs to be, but I can handle this size. It means I don't get hurt. It's not my problem if people want more than I can give. I like expectations that I can manage without risk.

Didn't I take a risk loving Bradley for so long? Or at least pining after him? Look where that got me.

"I need to go home." I yank my hand from his. "The dog-school clients I have today need some socialization in the backyard before pickup." I stand and take Beast from him, trying to ignore the emotions choking me. "If you and Riva want to stay, I can ask Heather to give me a ride home. She won't mind."

"We can take you." He looks confused by my sudden insistence on ending a lovely afternoon, but doesn't argue.

He stands, again crowding my space. When I take an instinctive step back, my ankle catches on the corner of the lounge chair. Ian steadies me with his big hands and traces his thumb along the inside crease of my elbow.

Has my skin there always been so sensitive? Do I have any ability to control my reaction to him? Once again, he uses that patented X-ray vision to see right into me.

"We're not done, Sadie. Not by a long shot. And I don't care how other people see you. I don't care what you think this does or doesn't mean. I'm a simple man, and I want you," he says.

I suck in a breath and turn my head because if I meet his gaze right now, I might spontaneously combust.

"You've said you want me too, and I'm taking you at your word, sweetheart. If that changes, I'll respect your decision, but until then, this..." He draws his hand down until his thumb is resting over the pulse in my wrist, which is leaping at an alarming rate like I've just run a marathon. "...*We* are going to happen."

"Okay," I agree in a voice that sounds nothing like my own. I sound like I've been nursing a two-pack-a-day Marlboro habit for the past twenty years. "But I think I'll wait for the two of you out front."

He chuckles and releases me. "We'll be there in a few minutes."

I walk away, ignoring the stares of the other sun worshippers. Or trying to. But it feels like these people—mostly mom-age women—are staring at me like they can't figure out how I snagged a man like Ian.

If only they knew. No matter how much Ian is acting like it is–like it could be everything I want, this isn't real. And remembering that is what will keep my heart safe.

15

IAN

RIVA DOES most of the talking on the way home, and I let her joy wash over me. She's happy with her new friends and over the moon that Beast made such great progress in his anxiety.

This is the daughter I remember from when she was little. Before she understood that her daddy isn't half the man she believed him to be. Before I let my fear of disappointing her close me off and create a self-fulfilling prophecy.

I glance over at the woman next to me. What is it about Sadie Hart blowing hot and cold that makes me want her all the more? I don't think she's playing games. She's not trying to lead me on with that bottom lip between her teeth and the fire in her eyes when she doesn't think to bank it before meeting my gaze.

And no one has to tell me where her reluctance originates. I understand all too well. Sadie isn't a casual sex type of person, but that's all I can give her.

She wants me, I don't doubt that, but her desire can't possibly match mine. I bet she's got some three-date rule about hitting the sheets, too. And while it could be argued we've spent enough time together to take things to the next level, this isn't a relationship.

Because although it sure as hell feels like one, I don't *do* relationships. Not anymore. Not when my whole purpose is to give my daughter the stability she needs and convince her to trust me again.

To love me again.

I screw up relationships, and if I screw up with Sadie, it could affect Riva. Nothing is worth that.

Not even being on the receiving end of Sadie Hart's sweet smiles.

And though she's conflicted, she's now flat-out told me I'm not the type of guy she wants to date. You can bet money on the fact that I'm going to be watching for Captain Dan-O to pick up his wimpy dog. To see the type of guy Sadie would date if given the chance.

I'm not giving her that chance until after the wedding. I may not be the brightest bulb, but I understand claiming. My body is damn sure she's mine—at least for now.

Long enough to satisfy the need she's stirred deep within me.

According to the armchair pundits and sportscasters, one of my football skills was patience. That's why I was so good at finding opportunities to execute key plays. I didn't rush the ball, get flustered, or make a stupid throw or a Superman pass into heavy coverage.

It wasn't patience. My calm under pressure was a strategy, a hunger for victory that enabled me to see the whole field, analyze it, and then get the job done.

I can't say I totally understand this new field and the workings of a small town, but I'm going to figure it out. And make Sadie beg for more in the process. Because while this isn't a relationship, it's still something, I want all the things that come with it.

She gives me an odd look and I realize I'm smiling to myself.

"Whose car is that, Dad?"

Riva's question jolts me back to the present. I frown at the bright red Ferrari parked in our driveway. There's only one person ballsy enough to show up unannounced in a car like that.

I assume it's a rental. You don't drive a Ferrari across the country on the two-day trek from Cincinnati—where Felix lives. Particularly not when you're six-six like my brother and barely able to fold yourself into something so compact. But Felix is flashy enough to choose it over a nondescript SUV, the vehicle I'd prefer him to drive to my new hometown.

"Looks like your uncle's come for a visit."

"Yes!" Riva whisper-shouts in the back. "Uncle Felix told me he'd get me a dog the last time I saw him."

"As I understand it from your mom," I say, "she let Uncle Felix know that wasn't his call to make."

"But Mom's not here. This isn't her house. It's your house. She's not the boss of you."

Tense in the passenger seat beside me, Sadie manages a laugh. My daughter hasn't violated our agreement by coming right out and asking for a dog, but baiting me with my brother is the next best thing.

"Uncle Felix isn't the boss of me either."

I'm trying not to display the same type of nerves Sadie is exhibiting. I love my brother. He's one of the few people I told about my move to Colorado. But Felix is a big personality. He's always been larger than life.

I like this little bubble I've created where I'm still The Playmaker, but adjacent to who I was when I was training, competing and making deals. I'm Riva's dad in Skylark. I take the time to make pancakes for breakfast. Yeah, they're from a box, but I put fresh blueberries in them that I bought at the local organic market. I shop for myself instead of having an assistant or somebody from the team do it. Those things mean something.

I'm not the version of me Felix knows. What will he think of who I'm trying to become when he's still in his prime?

I don't even let myself consider what he'll think of Sadie. She's different than any woman I've dated or shown the slightest bit of interest in, all the way back to elementary school.

"Does he know about our deal?" she asks quietly.

"Dad, you can't tell Uncle Felix about you and Sadie." Riva meets my gaze in the rearview mirror, her eyes filled with alarm. "Uncle Felix has the biggest mouth on the planet. That's what Mom always says."

Monika isn't wrong, and I understand where her comments came from. Felix found the pregnancy stick in the bathroom when he visited me in LA.

I don't know why Monika took the pregnancy test at my condo instead of hers, or left it clearly visible in the trash can, if she didn't want somebody to find it. She claimed she hadn't decided what to do or whether she'd intended to tell me, but Felix made the decision for her.

"He's never going to believe we're dating," Sadie says.

"Of course he will. Why wouldn't he?"

She shoots me a look, and I give her one right back. Enough of this 'we're not each other's type' bullshit. I'm sick of it.

"I'm not going to tell Felix about the fake dating deal," I reassure my daughter.

I reach across and squeeze Sadie's bare leg, gratified at the now-familiar goosebumps along her thigh. "And he *will* believe it."

My brother will believe it because we might be fake dating, but the attraction between us is damn real.

As I pull into the driveway, Felix straightens from where he's sitting on the porch swing. I installed that thing myself and am impressed with how well it holds my brother's considerable weight.

Riva is bouncing in her seat, her excitement at a visit from her adored uncle—or f-uncle, *fun uncle,* as Felix likes to call himself—clear now that she's not worried about me messing things up with her and Sadie.

No doubt that was the cause of her alarm. If our true relationship status is made public, it could jeopardize her work with the Hart House of Dog, and neither of us are ready for this to end.

"Can I leave Beast in the backseat?" she asks. "I don't want Uncle Felix to scare him."

"Of course," Sadie answers.

"You're a good boy," Riva assures the dog before she bounds out of the car.

My brother scoops her into a bear hug, then quickly flips her upside down with Riva shrieking a gleeful protest. Sadie exits the car more slowly and leans into the backseat to pick up the dog. I'm still sitting in the driver's seat, letting the jumble of emotions I feel at Felix's arrival flow through me.

Happy because he's my brother and I love him, mixed with a healthy dose of trepidation because he's my brother and he knows me better than anyone.

"I should go home." Sadie's voice is nearly a whisper.

"You need to meet him first," I tell her. "If he's going to believe this, we both need to sell it. There's no chance I wouldn't introduce him to my girlfriend right away."

"Okay then." She nods and climbs out of the SUV with Beast in her arms.

"I found this kid trespassing in your yard," Felix calls as he dangles Riva high with one hand.

"Uncle Felix, all the blood is rushing to my head!"

He flips her onto his shoulder like he's going to carry her across the lawn firefighter style.

"Pipe down there, cutie," Felix tells a still squirming and shrieking Riva. He winks at Sadie, no reaction to her at my side other than his propensity for flirting. "You're going to scare this nice lady and her—" I try not to grin as he studies Beast. "Is that a chicken?"

"Beast's a dog." Riva twists around my brother's shoulder, patting his cheek. "And Sadie is Dad's girlfriend."

"I'm sorry, what now?" He swings my daughter up and then plants her on two feet in front of him. "You're not going to convince me the chicken dog lady is your father's girlfriend."

"Told you so," Sadie says to me under her breath.

I shift closer, snaking an arm around her waist before she can pull away.

Felix looks between us, his eyes wide. "There's no chance on the green earth of this planet that such a lovely woman, choice of pet notwithstanding, would choose to date my brother."

I breathe out a sigh of relief and feel Sadie relax slightly. Felix is a lot of things, but an asshole has never been one of them.

"Back me up here, Rivs," I tell my kid.

"It's true, Uncle Felix. They're dating, and I work for Sadie. I have an official job. It's important, and we need to check in with our clients right now."

"What kind of business?" Felix asks, one thick brow lifting.

"Pet sitting. You can talk to her later." Riva grabs Sadie's arm and starts toward her house.

I don't want to let her go, but I do. Sadie waves goodbye, looking relieved she hasn't had to utter a word.

"I'm not a little kid anymore, Uncle Felix," Riva calls over her shoulder. "You can't hold me upside down like that. Sadie's going to take me shopping for a training bra."

Sadie and I speak at the same time.

"She is?"

"I am?"

Riva ignores us as well. Pretty sure she inherited the selective hearing from her mother.

"Monika will love that." Felix grins at me then calls out, "Just remember, cutie-pie, if you need help chasing off the boys, your funcle is ready for action."

"She doesn't need help chasing off the boys," I grumble when the two of us are standing alone in the driveway.

I catch a flash of something in my peripheral vision. Across the street, one of the neighborhood moms stands at her front window with her phone raised in our direction, no doubt taking a picture to spread around town. Why not document two sports stars hanging in the 'hood?

"Come on." I chuck Felix on the arm. "Let's get in the house before your damn car alerts the whole damn neighborhood to your arrival."

"Right," my brother answers. "I'm sure you blend in like an average mountain-loving Joe around here."

I've already opened the garage door, but can't pull in because of Felix's damn Ferrari blocking my way.

"Is Monika aware your new lady love is taking on some mommy roles?" he asks as he follows me through the garage.

"She isn't taking on mommy roles. Monika met Sadie when she dropped Riva off at the house." Not an outright lie. "She's got no problem with this." That I haven't verified.

Felix is practically treading on my heels. He's always had a terrible concept of personal space. He might be revered for his size now, but in first grade, he was the tallest boy in the entire elementary school, and gangly as a baby giraffe.

Any time a kid doesn't fit the expected mold, it makes them a target for bullies, which is why I got suspended for the first time in third grade. No one messed with my little bro. Felix eventually learned to throw a punch, but wasn't born a fighter like me.

"Why didn't you tell me?" he demands. "I mean, for God's sake, if Monika knows..."

"Because I didn't want to hear your opinion on my life," I say, more put out than I should be. "You made your thoughts clear about me moving here."

"I don't understand why Colorado," he repeats, "when you'd have so many more opportunities in LA."

"I have more money than I know what to do with. Just like you. I already told you, I don't want to raise my daughter anywhere near Hollywood. Not with the built-in attention she gets from her mom."

He inclines his head and glances out the window toward

Sadie's backyard. Riva's head is just visible above the privacy fence as she supervises the dogs.

"She seems less pissed in general. But what does she think about you picking a home town based on an online article?"

"As you're well aware, she doesn't know why I picked Skylark. And she *is* happy. Sadie has a lot to do with it."

"Tell me again about this business that's run out of her home. Is pet sitting a G-rated way of talking about Only Fa—"

"Are you trying to get punched in the face?" I hand him a beer from the refrigerator. "Retirement doesn't change the fact that I can kick your ass anytime I want. I should, just on principle, for even hinting I might have a girlfriend who'd engage in a less than above-board business. Or that I'd allow my daughter anywhere near that kind of a woman."

"I was joking, and you know it." Felix pops the cap on his beer and takes a long drink. "We've both dated some real winners, and I don't think you'd let Rivs spend time with any of them."

"Sadie is *not* that kind of woman." My tone conveys how serious I am about that fact.

Felix takes a moment before responding. "I still don't understand why you didn't tell me."

"Which is exactly why I didn't tell you," I counter. "She's different." Also not a lie.

Felix looks like he wants to argue but asks, "Why does Riva say she's working for her?"

"Sadie runs a dog boarding and training business out of her home. Riva's nuts about dogs, so Sadie's letting her be the assistant trainer a few mornings a week."

"And afternoons," Felix points out, tapping the ostentatious gold Rolex encircling his wrist.

My brother loves flash, which had been his nickname in high school because none of the coaches could believe how fast he ran given his size. Now that moniker has come to mean something different in Felix's world.

"So it's more a nanny-core situation with some benefits?" He tips his beer in my direction. "I respect that."

I cut him off with a forearm to his throat, pinning him against the refrigerator. "I swear to God, Felix, if you don't stop running your mouth, I'm going to make sure the next word comes out of it through a fat lip. I'm not using Sadie for child care."

Not precisely true, but only because Riva loves being over there and I'm giving Sadie something in return. Even if I still think she could find a date the regular way.

Even Felix understood within seconds of meeting her how special she is, and my brother has worse taste in women than me.

"I got it," he says, toasting me with his bottle.

I might be the older brother, but Felix can hold his own.

"I didn't plan this." I stalk to where I left my beer on the counter and drain it in one pull. "Sadie and I aren't serious. She knows my daughter is my priority."

"The daughter who obviously adores her." Felix crosses his arms over his massive chest. In his sleeveless athletic top and basketball shorts, the guy dresses more like a teenager than a thirty-two-year-old who earned his first Super Bowl ring last season. "I don't see why there's an issue with the two of you getting serious."

"How about the fact that Riva adores her?"

I grab another beer from the fridge. I haven't had more than a sip since my daughter got here, and this will be my last one for the night. I need something to take the edge off these feelings, and well...I don't even want to call them feelings because I don't want to admit to Felix that I feel anything for Sadie Hart beyond this situation-ship we're in.

"You know I screw up relationships. I've tried. I've tried multiple times, and I've screwed up multiple times, just like Dad did, just like Uncle Charlie did, just like you do. It's—"

"The Barlowe curse." Felix finishes my sentence for me.

I shake my head because I've never been superstitious like a lot of athletes who rely on rituals and lucky routines. Blaming my failures with women on a curse is a weak excuse. We're all inherently dicks when it comes to relationships.

"It's who we are, but I don't want to hurt Sadie. I don't want to hurt any woman, and I sure as hell don't want my daughter to realize that's all her dad does. What if she thinks that's what all men do?"

"Dang, bro. You sound like Adam Sandler." Felix shakes his head as he stares at me dumbfounded.

"I do *not* sound like Adam Sandler. What does that even mean? Adam Sandler in *The Wedding Singer*? Or Adam Sandler in *Happy Gilmore*?"

"Adam Sandler in his recent movies where he's a dad." Felix is pacing now, jabbing his beer bottle in the air for emphasis. "He's kind of still a doofus. Then toward the end, at the critical part, he gets it together and says something brilliant. That's what you just did. You said something that made you sound like a father."

"I *am* a father."

"A good father." Felix clasps me on the shoulder. "Dad never once sounded like a good father."

"Thanks, bro. You want to order wings?" I ask before we crack open a bottle of brown liquor and end up blubbering like babies.

"Hell, yeah." Felix loves wings almost as much as he loves women. "All drummies, extra wet."

He does a ridiculous dance, shimmying his hips as he grabs another beer. "Is this how you and Sadie get—"

"Don't say it, Felix. For the love of God, don't say it."

"Chill, dude. It's all good. Sadie is a huge step up for you, and what a bonus Riva likes her. My niece is a great judge of character. Clearly, since she adores me. Order a few dozen extra and let's invite your lady love for dinner."

I can't help but grin. "You think Sadie's going to eat a few dozen wings."

Another patented Felix wink. "One of us will."

I've just logged on to the local wing shop app when Riva comes in through the back door.

"Riva!" Felix hollers, twisting her off her feet like he hasn't seen her in years. My brother's enthusiasm is contagious, and Riva's laughter makes my heart pinch.

I need to try harder to be fun, which doesn't come naturally to me. But the intense hyper-driven football star mask doesn't fit either. I need to channel my inner Felix. He brings all the fun.

"You finished early today." I start to pull my daughter into a hug but stop when she gives me a quelling look. A look that says it's okay for Uncle Felix to love on her, but not me. "We're ordering wings for dinner. Do you want to...Felix said we should invite Sadie?"

"She can't. She's dropping off the day school dogs now because she has an emergency book club meeting later."

Riva grabs a soda from the fridge while my brother and I both mull that over for a minute.

"On the plus side, your dad's new girlfriend is literate," Felix remarks. "That can't be said about every woman he's spent time with since your mom."

Riva giggles.

"Rude, Felix," I mutter, although I'm not sure he's wrong.

I finish up our order, still trying to figure out if I should be concerned about Sadie's last-minute plans. "Hey, Rivs, did Sadie happen to mention what constitutes a book club emergency?"

She shrugs and swipes a hand over her mouth. "Not really."

"Maybe there was a big plot twist or some character they didn't expect got murdered," I suggest, wondering why I care so much.

Felix nods. "Since I've never belonged to a book club, I can't begin to guess." His thick brows draw together. "Could book club be some sort of code word for hitting the bars or something?"

"Sadie doesn't hit the bars." Riva looks offended on our neighbor's behalf. "All she does is work."

"And go out with your dad," Felix adds.

"Yeah, they went on a date the other night," she confirms. "Her friends Sally and Trina babysat, even though I don't need a babysitter because I'm almost *thirteen* years old."

"You'll be thirteen in nine months," I remind her.

"You got a babysitter?" Felix gives me a strange look. "We spent entire summers as latchkey kids."

I bark out a laugh. "Look how we turned out. Do you remember the trouble we got into?"

Riva inches closer to me, and I reach a hand to ruffle her hair, which sticks out a million different ways. It makes me think of her as a toddler just up from a nap, and reminds me how much of her life I've missed. Will I ever be able to make it up to her?

"Your dad's right for once," Felix agrees.

Riva rolls her eyes like it's her job. "I'm going to go take a shower. All the sunscreen he made me wear is sticky and gross now." She walks out of the kitchen and we hear her bounding up the staircase.

"You even do sunscreen." Felix whistles. "You *are* a good dad. Maybe better than Adam Sandler."

I didn't realize before now that my brother was such an Adam Sandler aficionado, but I appreciate the vote of confidence. I can use all of them right now.

"A book club emergency isn't a thing, is it?" I wonder for a moment if she's actually going out on the town, or maybe even to Denver with her girlfriends, and she doesn't want me to find out.

But why? She doesn't owe me anything. I've been crystal clear on that fact.

"Maybe they found out one of their members folds the pages down instead of using a bookmark. That's a no-no with books." He stares at me stone-faced for a few seconds before a shit-eating grin splits his face. "I'm messing with you, bro. I'm sure you'll hear all about it at some point, but this just means more wings for us. You got extra ranch, right?"

"Yep. Let's watch TV until it arrives."

It's good to have Felix here to give me a break from my thoughts about Sadie.

"There's a great local ice cream shop in town," I tell him as we settle into the family room's extra deep sectional. "After dinner, we'll show you the Skylark sights."

"Big time," Felix says. Anyone else would think he was being sarcastic, but my brother loves ice cream. Felix loves all foods other than green vegetables.

"It's going to be wild," I confirm, reminding myself that Sadie's book club business is not mine.

16

SADIE

I slide into the booth at the back of my favorite local Mexican restaurant, Casa Rosa, and Iris immediately pushes a margarita in my direction.

"We got this for you," she announces. "Strawberry, frozen, no salt."

Wow. This emergency meeting must be serious if I need an immediate hit of fruity tequila-infused fortitude.

"We also ordered the giant nachos and two cheese quesadillas," Sloane adds with a smile that looks a little tight around the edges.

Cheese quesadillas are Sloane's favorite.

"Is anyone else coming?" I scan the faces of Sloane, Iris, and Molly, all seated and facing directly at me.

"Taylor is out of town at a library conference," Iris answers, "And Avah drove down to Denver for her parents' anniversary dinner."

I try not to focus my full attention on Sloane. It's only been a week since I ran into my friend at the farmers market, but I can't help my tendency to be on high alert, assessing every detail about her demeanor, the spark in her eyes, and how she's holding up. I assume the emergency involves Sloane, but refuse to venture a guess as to what more our friend might reveal. We've all vowed to support her however we can.

"We want an update on Operation V-Card," Molly chimes in. "You've been dating The Playmaker long enough that surely he's made some kind of *play*."

I've just taken a massive slurp of tequila and start choking as the ice-cold drink goes down the wrong pipe. So much for my worry about Sloane. Turns out, I'm the emergency.

She pats me on the back. "We were going to lead into the topic at hand in a more roundabout way. Like maybe after Sadie finished her drink." She gives Molly a pointed look.

The curvy redhead throws up her hands. "We need to get this show on the road, and not just because babysitters cost a small fortune these days. At least the ones willing to take on my twin terrors."

I dab at the corner of my mouth with a napkin and will my cheeks not to heat with embarrassment at how little I have to report. "Is there a deadline or reason I need to rush this?" I lean forward. "It's kind of a big deal, you know?"

Molly glances at Sloane out of the corner of her eye, then gives a meaningful shrug.

"What?" I demand. "What's that look about? There's something you aren't telling me."

Sloane shakes her head. "There's no hurry or deadline."

"Do you expect me to believe we're just here to discuss when I'm going to finally get a sex life?" I've had a lot of mortifying moments in my life, but this could be the pinnacle.

"I'm flying to Nashville next week," Sloane says slowly. "My brother has a friend who's an oncologist at the cancer center at Vanderbilt."

"I thought you were seeing a doctor in Denver."

She wrinkles her nose. "That was my plan, but Jeremy wants me seen by someone he knows and trusts. Chemo is the typical treatment, but they're doing some cutting edge stuff with immunotherapy and other targeted cancer drugs. I'm going to see what options I have."

"Are your parents meeting you in Nashville?" I ask.

Sloane's parents are archeologists and college professors who've been living in Europe for the past five years. She doesn't talk about her family much, but from the snippets she's shared, they worked and traveled a lot when she was growing up. They also refused to accept that Sloane wasn't interested in college. Because she didn't capitulate to their plan for her future—which included an Ivy League or, at the very least, second-tier Ivy university—her parents basically cut her off.

I get the impression she went a bit wild in rebellion. Lucky for us, her new adult adventures brought her to Colorado from the East Coast. The boyfriend she'd followed out here is long gone, but Sloane stayed and settled in Skylark, taking over and running the local bookstore with money from a trust set up by her grandma.

Her features stay neutral at my question, but she begins tapping an agitated finger on the edge of her water glass. "They're busy on a dig," she says. "Things changed too quickly for them to leave on such short notice."

That's some next-level crap right there. How could a parent not find a way to be with their kid during this kind of crisis?

"Let one of us go with you," Molly tells her.

"I'll go," I offer.

Sloane laughs. "What will the dog owners of Skylark do without their favorite trainer?"

"She's right." Iris nods. "I'm the mayor, and I can take time off more easily than Sadie."

"You matter more than any client, Sloane. I'm happy to do it."

Molly wraps an arm around Sloane's shoulder. "You can't do this alone."

Sloane draws in a long breath. "I'm not. My brother is meeting me in Nashville."

Iris snorts in obvious disbelief. "The brother you haven't spoken to in five years?"

"Five minutes is more like it recently," she says with a sigh. "Jeremy has decided he's going to make up for all those estranged years in one fell swoop. To be honest, I can't say no. My insurance doesn't cover the cost for some of the treatments they're discussing." She shrugs. "He's offered to pay for everything, but for whatever reason, the caveat is he wants to be with me."

We've heard stories about Sloane's brilliant brother. The textbook golden boy, according to her. Jeremy was the child who did everything their parents expected, including becoming mega-rich and successful by creating the backend software used by some of the world's most popular online shopping sites. I read an article that said Jeremy Winslow's net worth was pushing the billion-dollar mark. Not only can he afford to pay for her treatment, he can fund the whole hospital.

"How long will you be gone?" Iris asks. "Do we have time for a going-away party?"

Sloane leans her head against Molly's shoulder. "I'm flying out early tomorrow."

"Do you need a ride to the airport?" Iris asks.

"Jeremy is sending a car." Sloane smiles softly. "It's weird to see my Jeremy going full overprotective big brother mode, but I guess I'll take it."

"It's good he's stepping up." Iris holds up her glass in a mock toast to Jeremy.

"What do you need from us?" I shoot Molly a glare. "I find it hard to believe the primary concern right now is my sex life."

The waitress, who has just brought the plate of nachos, clears her throat. "How *is* sex with Ian Barlowe?" she asks, leaning in. "I mean, I've seen the underwear ads and how he fills out those boxers. It's got to be good, right?"

I turn my head to stare up at her. "I'm sorry, have we met?"

"Not officially, but my aunt boards her dog with you when

143

she's out of town. She's always going on about how great you are with Roscoe."

Roscoe is a seven-year-old dachshund with a penchant for eating his own poop. "He's a real sweetheart." I offer a smile because I can't afford to lose any more clients. "But I must have misheard because I thought you just asked me, a complete stranger other than an association through your aunt's dog, for details about my sex life."

The waitress, whose plastic name tag identifies her as Andrea, smacks her gum and shrugs. "No offense, of course, but everyone in town is talking about you."

"What are they saying?" I blurt the question then hold up a hand when Iris leans forward like she's going to cut the young woman off before she can answer.

"Most people assume that since you're neighbors, it makes sense you two would have a little welcome-to-our-town fling. But no one thinks it will last. I'm sure he can find a better—"

"You should stop right there," Iris interrupts, ignoring my hand. "And get us another round of drinks instead. Coping with your propensity for oversharing is thirsty work, Andrea."

The waitress frowns like she doesn't quite understand the mayor's subtle censure.

"Real thirsty work," Molly adds. "For the record, Sadie is the perfect person to welcome Ian to town."

Sloane chokes out a laugh, and I concentrate on the triangular chip sitting on the plate in front of me. How fantastic...another new pinnacle. My head is woozy from the altitude on this mountain of mortification.

"I don't mean in any sexual way," Molly clarifies. She points a finger at Andrea like she's calling out a misbehaved child. "We should not be talking about Sadie's sex life with you."

"Stop saying the word sex out loud," I mutter.

"How are those drinks coming?" Iris makes a shooting motion with her hand.

Andrea blows a small bubble with her gum and turns away with a flounce.

"We've all seen the underwear ads," she says over her shoulder.

"Why can't people get over the damn underwear ads?" I ask no one in particular.

"Um...let's assume that's a rhetorical question." Molly fans a hand in front of her face. "But just in case it's not, the reason is because they make The Playmaker look like sin on a stick."

"And they don't look photoshopped," Iris adds with a soft laugh.

I take a sip of my margarita then place it back on the table, contemplating my next move as I meet Sloane's concerned gaze. It's humbling that she can be facing cancer and still manage to show concern for my little problems. Or, not so little in Ian's case.

"Is it important to you that I lose my V-card before you start chemo or immunotherapy or whatever?"

She squeezes her eyes shut and laughs. "I don't think so. Cancer sucks either way."

"Which is why you need a distraction," Molly says, giving me a pointed look. "Checking things off the bucket list challenge, for example."

"Then move on to the next person," I suggest, trying not to sound peevish before turning to Iris. "Who happens to be you. What's on your list?"

"Skipping to the next person isn't how it works," Iris insists. "We can't change the rules we made. Sticking to a commitment is important. But if you don't want to do this..."—she lays a comforting hand on mine—"no one is going to force you. It's okay."

The waitress returns with the drinks, and I quickly finish my first one.

"I do want to have sex," I admit after she disappears again, glancing over my shoulder to make sure we're not overheard, "but I'm scared. Especially at the thought of sex with Ian. I've seen the underwear ads too. Those boxer briefs weren't stuffed with socks."

"How do you know?" Molly asks with a wicked laugh. "Are you holding out on us?"

"I'm trying to keep some dignity here," I argue. "I should have just picked something like skydiving or climbing Mount Everest. Those would have been easier options."

"The point is to do something that takes you out of your comfort zone in a meaningful way," Sloane reminds me. "To be afraid but take the action anyway. Trust me, I understand being afraid."

I press a palm to my forehead. "Oh God, I'm sorry, Sloane. My paltry fear is nothing compared to what you're dealing with. I know that."

"We're all dealing with our own challenges," my sweet friend assures me. "Nobody gets to decide which of them means more or less."

"I think we decide that," I continue, pointing a chip in her direction. "Cancer is more."

Iris and Molly nod in agreement, but Sloane shakes her head. "I don't want it to be more. I want it to be something I can get over, just like you can overcome the fear of your first time with a man. Kristen Quinn wrote that it's not the size of the lessons that make a difference..."

"It's how we learn from them," Molly chimes in. "Ian is the perfect guy for this lesson," she assures me. "He can be your training-wheel bike."

Sloane snorts. "Having sex with The Playmaker is prolly not going to be like riding a bike with training wheels. More like a fancy e-bike that does all the work for you."

"You said it's not serious," Iris reminds me. "He's just helping you for the wedding, so it's okay to do whatever. You guys are the definition of no strings attached."

I don't answer, and my friends stare at me, the food and drinks forgotten for the moment.

"Oh, sweetie," Molly murmurs like she's comforting one of her kids. "Don't say you're falling for him. You told us there was no chance of falling for him."

"I haven't," I lie. "But he's my neighbor, and what if I'm bad at the bedroom stuff, which is highly probable since I've never done it before? I'll have to see him still, and that'll be more humiliating than never having done it in the first place."

"Sadie, honey..." Molly shakes her head. "You're making sex a bigger deal than it is."

"Sex is a big deal," I say in a louder tone than I intended. The woman at the next table turns to stare. I wave at her then focus again on my friends. "It should be. I think I want it to mean something."

"You don't have to do this if it doesn't feel right," Sloane tells me. "Not with Ian or anyone. Bucket list or no, you need to take care of you."

"I want to do it. I just didn't expect it to be so complicated. Women have random one-night stands with guys they meet in bars all the time. And there are a gazillion apps that facilitate meeting someone, but I don't have a single profile. I'm hopeless."

At this point, I'm not even sure why I chose this as my bucket list activity.

"You could be right." I nod at Molly. "I've made this too big of a deal in my own head. I want to get rid of this stupid V-card. There's being a late bloomer and then there's..."

"Being a real-life forty-year-old virgin?" Iris suggests with a grimace.

"Rude." I elbow her hard in the arm even as I laugh. "I'm in my mid-thirties." The protest sounds weak to my own ears.

I take another healthy swig of margarita, grateful for the warmth it sends spiraling through my chest. "Maybe I should knock on Ian's door when I get home or text him for a booty call. He's made it clear he wants me, and even if it's for the reasons Andrea suggested—I'm convenient and a sure thing—who cares. They're both the truth."

I toast Sloane's glass with mine. "If you can face down the big C, I can handle...well, me."

"It'll be great," Molly assures me. "And if not, it will be over quickly enough."

Iris nods. "Besides, there are always battery-operated options to fill in the gaps."

There's a beat of silence at the table, and then we all dissolve into laughter. Leave it to Iris to remind us that we can take things into our own hands. My friend the mayor is the most self-sufficient woman I know. And apparently, that applies to all facets of her life.

Wiping some stray tears of laughter from my cheeks, I turn a more sober eye to Sloane. "Does the rest of the book club know?"

She nods. "I called them once I knew who was going to be able to make it tonight. I really wanted to tell you all in person, and I appreciate your support so very much." She flashes a sheepish grin. "I also appreciate you're not giving up on your bucket list item, Sadie. It's not exactly the same thing, but it helps to know somebody else is struggling. Misery loves company and all of that."

Molly kisses Sloane's temple. "I hate cancer," she whispers. "But you've got this, girl." Her soft green eyes track to me. "You've both got this."

Iris squeezes my hand. "And we're here for you every step of the way."

17

SADIE

Because I'm a lightweight when it comes to drinking and finished nearly two whole margaritas, Sloane drives my car home while Molly follows us.

I do my best not to cry when I hug her and wish her good luck in Nashville, but it's not easy. No matter how brave of a face Sloane puts on or the bottomless bank account her brother has to make sure she gets the best care possible, cancer is cancer.

It's real and scary, making my fear feel paltry in comparison. But sex is a big deal for me, no matter how much I want it to be easy-peasy. Maybe if I'd dated or done it when I was younger, it wouldn't have built up in my head like this.

My mom also didn't instill in me the best impression of men. She refused to speak about my father other than to tell me he hadn't wanted anything to do with either of us, and she didn't date when I was younger. At least not until she met Piper's dad.

Harold had been great for the first couple of months. He doted on Mom and taught me to throw a ball and put a worm on the end of a fishing hook—the kinds of things in my make-believe world that good dads did.

Then Mom got pregnant with Piper, and Harold disappeared before the first ultrasound.

At first, I'd been angry at my unborn sister for messing up my chance at a family with two parents. But Mom blamed him—men in general, to be honest—so I did too, eventually. Throughout my teen years, she muttered, "They won't buy the cow if they can get the milk for free," so often I almost gave up ice cream, even Rocky Road.

Ridiculous in retrospect, because why blame innocent ice cream on a jackwagon willing to walk away from his kid?

That could be why I went all in on my Bradley Carlson crush. He was safe. We were friends, but he dated cheerleaders and popular girls with shiny hair and short skirts.

Even in high school, I dressed more for function than fashion, and I'd been scared half to death of sex—not just the act, although that's part of it.

I'm scared of what it means. How intimacy leads to heartache. At least it did in my mom's experience, which is what informed my feelings about relationships the most.

On my way into the house, I glance toward Ian's, but the inside is dark. It's only eight-thirty, and the long summer day is just starting to give way to night, so I highly doubt he, Riva, and his brother have turned in early.

Although he's big and intimidating, I liked Felix on sight. It's hard to imagine the kind of trouble those Barlowe boys got into when they were younger.

I still can't quite believe the kind of trouble I want with Ian.

There are two dogs boarding with me this week, and I let them and Max into the backyard to do their evening business then head upstairs for a shower. I spend longer than usual standing under the hot water, washing away the anxiety about my life and Sloane's future, how big Ian might actually be and what that will mean for...everything.

When the shower runs cold, I dry off, then open the top

drawer of my dresser and run a finger along the lace edge of one of the panty sets Iris had sent to my house.

That's right, I'm an adult, but my friend had to buy me decent underwear. I should be more embarrassed than I am. Mostly, I'm grateful to have something nice to wear the weekend of the wedding.

I assume that's when Ian and I will do the deed, if I don't chicken out. And I won't, despite my fear. More recently, the worry isn't as much about the physical part as my feelings for Ian.

I shouldn't have feelings for my sexy neighbor other than physical attraction. My heart shouldn't thud every time his glacial blue eyes meet mine or the corner of his mouth tips up into that hint of a smile I don't see him give to anyone else. Feelings are dangerous. They open me up to being hurt or abandoned, and I'm not willingly inviting either of those prospects into my life.

MAX IS the only dog allowed on the furniture—another perk of being mine. He and I settle in for a night of *Friends* reruns while Millie and Mo, the Bernedoodles staying for the week, curl up on oversized dog beds in the family room.

Headlights illuminate my front window as a car pulls into Ian's driveway, and I hear muffled voices from next door. He must have taken his brother and Riva out for dinner. The girl laughs and then squeals, and I can imagine Felix picking her up again. He seems to enjoy tossing her over his shoulder, and Riva obviously adores him.

I should work harder at lightening the tone of my relationship with Piper. We talk and text plenty, but I'm always in the big-sister-playing-mom role. My baby sis is an adult now, about to be married, and it's time I start treating her as one.

My phone pings a minute later, and I stupidly hope it's Ian checking in. It's a dumb expectation, because while we've gotten into the habit of texting, it's most likely because he's bored, and I'm one of his few friends in town. But tonight he's got his brother and is probably not so bored.

Piper's name and a photo of her with Max when he was a puppy pops up on the screen.

> Piper: How's my boy tonight? I'm missing his doggy snores.

Piper almost always starts a chat asking about Max, which is sweet. But now that Ian has pointed out that there's more to me than the dogs in my care, it feels odd that she rarely asks what's going on in my life. Maybe when things calm down after the wedding, the two of us can plan a girls' trip and start to change our dynamics a bit.

> Me: Picture of Max laying tummy up on the couch, snoring peacefully.

> Me: Missing you as always.

> Piper: 😍

I want to create something new with my sister, a relationship where we're friends and she treats me like her sibling—not a stand-in mom, but a sister.

Three blinking dots appear, then vanish several times, and I sit up straighter.

> Me: Everything okay?

At the same time, her message comes through.

Piper: Why didn't you ever have a boyfriend when I was younger? Was it because of your feelings for Bradley?

The words hit me like a punch, and I suck in a breath. It takes a minute to think of how to reply, but my fingers tremble too hard to hit the right keys.

I tap the call button under Piper's name instead. She picks up on the first ring.

"Hello?"

"Why would you ask me that?"

"Are you mad?"

"Shocked is a better term. What's going on to bring this up now?"

There's a long pause, then a sniff like she's holding back tears. "Bradley says I'm acting strange. He says you were always weird about guys and dating. He thinks we both have man issues and blames Mom."

I press a hand to my thudding heart. Bradley Carlson can fuck right off with his arm-chair psychobabble. "Everyone has issues," I assure my sister. "We're doing just fine, Piper."

At least I can say I've gotten better at picking friends in the years since high school and college. "I'm not hung up on Bradley. I'm dating Ian, Piper. I told you that. I sent pics. He's coming to the wedding."

She laughs softly. "Right. My blend-into-the-wall sister is going to overshadow me at my own wedding with her famous boyfriend."

"I'm not trying to overshadow you," I snap. Hell, this all started for her benefit. "And blend-into-the-wall is a little rough."

"I'm sorry." I hear the remorse in her tone. "I'm all spun up. People get nervous before they walk down the aisle, and I want to marry Bradley. We've come this far. I think he still wants to marry me."

"You think?" I sit up straight. "What is this about, Piper? Bradley is damn lucky to be marrying you."

"You're just saying that because you're my...sister."

I hear the pause and understand her hesitation. It breaks my heart for both of us. I've been functioning as Piper's only parent for nearly as long as Mom was alive. It's no wonder our dynamic is messed up.

"Stop it, Pip. If you and Bradley are having issues, or you're having second thoughts, all you have to do is say the word, and we'll cancel the wedding. But you aren't going to make it about me. You're not in high school where you could use me to get out of doing stuff with your friends."

"You offered to be my scapegoat when I needed one."

Sometimes I forget that my sister is only twenty-two and not that far removed from her teenage years. "I know, but this isn't the same thing."

"He says Mom hated men," she tells me in a rush of breath.

I'd like to kick Bradley Carlson in the shin.

"Mom didn't hate men."

"She hated your dad and my dad."

"She didn't hate *all* men," I amend. "Neither you nor I hate men." Although I might hate Bradley.

"He's worried I'm not committed enough."

"How is planning a wedding not committed?" I demand, my voice rising. Now I want to kick Bradley in the nuts.

"I think he's nervous, too, and this is how he's trying to tell me he's afraid to be vulnerable."

I choke back a snort. It sounds like he's telling my sister he's an asshole. I'm uncomfortable stepping in because if she calls this off based on something I say and then regrets it, that's on me. I'm not sure she'll ever forgive me.

Our relationship might need some work, but I love Piper. She's the only family I have and means the world to me. She's been my world, literally.

"Does he make you happy?"

"Of course," she says, almost too readily. "We have similar goals. We want the same things. We're suited, Sadie."

"None of those sound like the happily-ever-after you deserve."

"Does dating an ex-NFL star make you happy?" she fires back. "You, who wants everything understated and practical. You don't even like people looking at you. It's a given that people are looking at The Playmaker, especially in Skylark. I can't talk to one of my friends without hearing about an Ian Barlowe sighting in the grocery store or the farmers market or wherever."

I swallow, and adrenaline shoots through my veins as I think about how to answer.

"Are you happy, Sads?" she repeats.

"Yes." I'm shocked to realize how true it is despite everything. "Being with Ian makes me happy, and I don't care about all that other stuff. Let people look. It's about time they see me happy."

She's quiet for a long moment. "Good for you. I'm sorry about what I said about you overshadowing me at the wedding. I'm excited to meet Ian. Not because he's famous, but because he matters to you."

"Thanks, Pip. I meant it when I said we can handle any second thoughts about marrying Bradley."

"I want to do this." She sounds more confident, but I'm not convinced. "He does make me happy, and I love him. It's just nerves on both our parts. If I had it to do over again, maybe I'd choose to elope."

I blow out a laugh. "There's still time."

"I'll be arriving in Vail on Thursday." So much for eloping. "You're coming up Friday morning, right?"

"First thing."

"And Ian is okay golfing with the groomsmen?"

"He's planning on it."

"Okay, then. Ignore my wedding jitters. I need to go."

"I love you, Piper. We can make it through anything. You and me. Always."

"I love you too, Sads. Give Maxie a kiss for me."

"I will." We disconnect, and I reach out and rub the dog's soft belly. "I'm not sure she'll ever find anyone who loves her like you," I tell him. He yawns because that's old news for our old boy.

The doorbell rings, odd at this time of night. Millie and Mo pop up with a barrage of woofing, and Max rolls off the couch in a more dignified manner. The four of us move toward the door, and my breath catches at Ian in all his handsome bigness, smiling at me from the other side.

18

SADIE

"Is everything okay?" I study him in his white T-shirt and low-slung jeans, searching for clues as to what could bring him to my doorstep in the dark. And working hard at not letting my lady parts run rampant with the hope they have something to do with it.

"Everything's fine, Sadie."

"Is it Riva? Where is she?"

He flashes a smile. "She's in bed. Sleeping, I hope."

"What about your brother?"

"Watching an Adam Sandler movie in my basement. He's a huge fan, apparently. I had no idea."

Ian reaches out and touches the ends of my damp hair. "You're also ready for bed."

I only have the door open part way so the dogs can't escape. He takes a step closer and bends to pat the three heads poking out in greeting.

"I was watching TV and talking to my sister."

He nods. "How is she?"

I sigh, suddenly grateful for someone to share my worries with. "Stressed. Bradley is acting weird, and she's nervous. Pre-wedding jitters, I guess, but I'd like to throat-punch her fiancé. He's stressing her out."

Ian inclines his head. "Bradley is an asshat." His words are more fact than opinion.

"You aren't wrong."

I poke my head out and glance toward his house, because looking into his eyes for too long feels like staring at the sun. It leaves me disoriented and dizzy, like a hit of dopamine directly to my heart, but I know I could so easily be burned. "Did you come over just to hang out on my porch and chat in bare feet?"

He looks down and wiggles his toes. "I came over here to say when."

When his gaze meets mine again, it's changed. Gone is the teasing light, banked into a deeper, hotter flame. One that sends chills all up and down my body, even though I'm the opposite of cold.

"When, what?" I ask slowly. My mind can't seem to process the meaning, hindered by my body's reaction to him.

"Earlier at the club, you asked when we were going to have sex. That's what I'm here for, to tell you that this is when."

"Tonight?" I swallow.

"Is that a problem?"

I'm unable to answer for so long, he finally waves a hand in front of my face. "You doing okay, sweetheart?"

I manage a nod. "I'm not wearing good underwear."

He laughs, then moves forward, crowding me like he's in the habit of doing, until I step back into the house.

"I couldn't give a rat's ass about your underwear." He shuts the door with his foot, then takes a minute to greet the dogs to their satisfaction. He links our fingers together and lifts my hands above my head as he spins me until my back is against the wall. "All I'm thinking about is getting you out of them."

He leans in and kisses my neck, edging my chin up for better access. Need rockets through me, but anxiety tamps it down before things spiral out of control

Did I shave my legs tonight? Yes, praise the Lord. Although smooth skin doesn't mean everything else will go smoothly.

But I'm committed. I want this. And more importantly, I want it with Ian.

"Sadie, are you still with me?"

Am I?

My body is all in, but I can't shake the fear that my heart might be as well. It doesn't change me wanting this. Wanting him. And not because of punching my V-card or some bucket list commitment I made. It's because of Ian and me and this connection between us that can't and won't be denied.

I'm sick of letting fear about the consequences rule my life. I'm sick of letting fear, in general, have control over me.

I nod. "I want this." Although the words are shaky, I don't hesitate to speak them.

The relief in his eyes is the answer I need to know I've made the right decision.

Still holding my hands above my head with one hand, he trails his other over my breast. When my nipple hardens against the palm of his hand, a small moan rips from my throat.

"No bra," he whispers, and I choke out a laugh.

"I wasn't expecting company." I wasn't expecting any of this.

He reaches under the hem of my shirt, but I make a noise of protest. "The front curtains are open. We can't do this here."

Releasing my hands, he scoops me into his arms, but pauses at the base of the stairs.

"Will the dogs be okay on their own for a while?" His voice sounds rough, like his desire is causing him physical pain.

I suddenly find it hard to stop my heart from melting even further at the thoughtfulness of his question.

"The dogs are fine." I wrap my arms around his neck.

He flashes a lopsided grin. "Thank fucking God."

"I can walk," I say, in case it's not clear.

"I've been looking for an excuse to get my hands on your ass for weeks." He keeps moving, taking the steps two at a time. "I'm not giving that up now."

I want his hands everywhere, so much that it should be terrifying. Now that it's happening, all I feel is desire. Except I've spoken too soon, because when he deposits me on the bed, those nerves take flight again.

I've never had anyone share my bed other than Piper, who had nightmares for months after Mom died. What do I do now? Do I get undressed or wait for him to handle it?

I start with the obvious. "The blinds..."

I gesture toward the window facing the house's front, and he walks over and closes the wood slats.

"Not an exhibitionist, I take it." That draws a laugh from me.

"I hope you're not too disappointed."

Ugh. Those words feel more significant than I want them to.

"Nothing about you could disappoint me," he answers without hesitation, and I resist the urge to blurt, "Hold my beer," like this is some kind of a joke.

"What about the lights?" I ask as he moves toward me again.

"Oh, no." He shakes his head. "It's just you and me, sweetheart, and I plan to memorize every inch of your body."

I nearly choke as the breath leaves my lungs in a whoosh. The truth is, I'm planning the same thing. Because I have the distinct impression that being with Ian is going to ruin me for whatever and whoever comes next.

I pull down the sheets and try to quiet the voices in my head that still want to convince me I'm going to ruin everything with my inexperience and insecurity. Ian knows what he's doing. I can trust that. I trust him, certainly more than I trust myself.

"Do you have a condom?" I ask when his knees bump the side of the bed.

He nods and takes his wallet from the back pocket of his jeans, then tosses a foil packet on the nightstand. "And I've been tested," he tells me. It takes me a minute to realize he's not talking about his charcuterie making skills.

"I'm good, too," I answer, obviously not for the same reasons. What would he say if he knew? Would he stop or...

He lifts his T-shirt over his head, then undoes the row of buttons on his jeans with a flick of the wrist.

His upper body is broad, with muscles forming smooth, sculpted lines. Muscles I didn't even know existed. And those underwear ads do not do him justice.

The skin on his chest is golden, covered by a dusting of dark hair that adds to his rugged masculinity. His chest rises and falls slowly with each breath he takes, offering a sense of calm that I certainly don't feel.

This is no big deal, or at least he makes it seem that way.

I suppose I should do the same—take off my clothes—because that's how I'll end up. But I can't move. I can't do anything but watch with a hammering heart as Ian pushes his jeans and boxers down over his hips, his erection springing out.

Another wave of panic tries to battle its way through my clouded brain fog. He's so big. Every part of him, but especially...

He watches me watching him and smiles. I blush, averting my gaze.

"I like how you look at me, sweetheart, but if you comment on my retirement Dad bod, I might get a complex."

I lick my lips because my mouth has gone dry. "You're hot as hell and I'm sure you know it. For sure we should rethink leaving on the lights before I take off anything." I'm still staring at his chest and lower and—

"You're beautiful, Sadie." The sincerity in his tone interrupts my thoughts, and I feel warmth spread through me.

He puts his hands on the bed and tugs on my legs until I'm lying under him.

"You're real and perfect. God, I want you so much." He buries his nose in the crook of my neck. "I can't promise I'll last as long as I'd like this time. It's been a while, and I swear if you bite down on your lip one more time, I'm going to lose it."

"It's all good," I say automatically. I might not know much about sex, but I'm an expert on offering reassurance.

He hooks his thumbs under the edge of my shirt, pushing the soft fabric up my body as his calloused hands trail along my skin, leaving fire in their wake. When I feel cold air on my breasts, I shiver, then cry out as Ian takes one hard nipple into his mouth. He sucks gently while rolling the pad of his thumb over the other.

I squirm beneath him, but he holds me steady with his muscular thighs, and I feel his big—or a more appropriate word would be giant—cock against my leg.

This is it, I think. He's going to slam into me and take what he wants. I won't be a virgin, and maybe I can pretend it doesn't matter.

We're two people—unlikely friends—having sex. I can't help but brace myself slightly, waiting for the pain I know is coming, willing myself not to react in a way that he'll realize I haven't done this before.

But he doesn't slam into me. What he does is continue the exquisite torture he's inflicting on my breasts with his teeth, his tongue, and his hot, sweet breath. He doesn't seem in any hurry to move on to the main event, and I'm so caught up in the sensations he's producing in my body that I forget to be nervous.

I would have bet my life Ian is so caught up in what he's doing he can't possibly notice the subtle change in my body, but he hums in approval.

"That's right, Sadie, relax. We're in no hurry."

I'm in a hurry. I'm in a damn hurry to release the pressure building inside of me—the ache that's pleasure teetering on the edge of pain.

"Lift your arms, darling," he commands softly, and I do it without question.

A moment later, he pulls my shirt over my head and flings it to the side. I'm left with him staring down at me bare-chested. Even though I can still feel the heat of his mouth on my breasts, I fight the urge to cover myself with my hands.

"I knew it," he says, and kisses me long and slow, deliberate. "I knew the first time I saw you blush that your whole body would turn that delectable shade of pink when I touched you."

"I don't think you know enough yet to claim it's my whole body."

Oh, my god. Where did that come from? Who spoke those words? Certainly someone with a hell of a lot more self-confidence than me.

I can tell by the way Ian's eyes flare with satisfaction that he appreciates my paltry attempt at sexy talk. I wish I had more to offer, but lose all ability to speak once again when he shifts lower, pulling my pajama pants and plain pink cotton panties down over my hips.

Here we go, I think, but Ian doesn't move. He stares at me—all of me. My most private parts.

"You still with me?" I repeat his question from earlier.

"So. Damn. Beautiful." He says every word like it's a complete sentence.

It makes my chest, as well as the soaked center between my legs, clench with longing.

Sure, I'm girl-next-door cute, but Ian is looking at me—touching me—like he's a man who's spent weeks in a desert, and I'm the first oasis he's stumbled upon.

Instead of crawling back up my body like I expect, he draws my knees apart and puts his mouth on me.

I just about buck off the bed from the shock and pleasure of it. This isn't what I expected. It's too much, too intimate. Sex is one thing, but this...

I'm open to him in a way that makes me feel vulnerable. But my God, the things he's doing with his tongue as he swirls and sucks. A voice is crying out for more. A moment later, I realize that voice belongs to me.

Ian seems to love the noises I'm making. When I clamp my mouth shut and cover it with one hand, he lifts his head, his eyes dark and wonderful.

"Tell me more, Sadie. Tell me what you want, what makes you happy, what gets you off. I want to hear everything, and I want to feel you come against me."

As if I could deny him. It's not easy for me to make my needs known when I barely understand what makes me feel good. Not like this. When I take matters into my own hands—or vibrator—it's quick and efficient, but this is totally different. It's luxurious and lustful, and holy crap, how have I been missing out for so long?

"Yes. There. Harder." I manage breathy words as the pressure continues to build in me.

When my climax hits, Ian holds me steady, true to his word that he wants to feel all of it, all of me. I ride the wave, and as lost as I am to sensation, I never for one moment lose my awareness that this amazing, wonderful, out-of-my-league man has brought me to the peak of pleasure.

I haven't even caught my breath when Ian places one more gentle kiss on the hair at the top of my mound, then reaches for the condom on the nightstand.

"I can't wait any longer." His voice is low and tight. "I have to feel you around me."

He spreads my legs again, and I'm still delirious with the afterglow as he leverages himself above me. He wipes his mouth on the back of his hand, then kisses me as he nudges forward, and I'm shocked at the taste of my own desire on his lips.

Then I'm even more shocked when he pushes inside me in one forceful thrust.

I should be prepared. I know it's coming, and I can't be more relaxed after that bone-melting orgasm, but a strangled cry escapes my lips as pain slices through me.

"Fuck," Ian whispers. "Sadie, are you okay?"

He lifts his head to look at me, but I follow him up, wrapping an arm tight around his neck and fusing my mouth to his. My body is adjusting already, and I roll my hips, testing out the weight of him inside me. It feels different, but good.

"Fuck," Ian mutters again, then begins to move.

19

IAN

A BETTER MAN would have realized her innocence was more than a propensity to blush.

At the moment, I can't be that man. Not when I'm sheathed inside her warmth, and she's plunging her tongue into my mouth, mimicking the motion of how I want to drive myself inside her.

She's inexperienced, but Christ, so irresistible.

Despite my need for release, I move slowly at first, giving her every chance to stop me.

If anything, she holds on tighter, and the strain I felt when she let out that first yelp dissolves. The sweetest, sexiest little sounds of pleasure come from her throat, and a shudder pulses through me.

I'm still careful. Not to sound like a cocky bastard, but I've been in enough locker rooms to know I'm a lot to take.

And she's a virgin.

She *was* a virgin, my stupid brain reminds me. Not anymore. Not thanks to me.

There'll be time for regret and recrimination after. Right now, all my focus is on Sadie, and this moment. Making it special for her.

We find a rhythm that works for both of us, like we've done this dance a thousand times. Well, one of us has, but it's never been like this. I caress her soft skin, wanting to touch her everywhere. To learn every inch of her. Our kisses are deep and warm, but I pull back to look into her eyes, wanting her to see what she's doing to me. How much it means that she chose me for her first time.

Just when I think I can hold on a moment longer, she climaxes again, and I follow her over the edge, my body clenching with its release. I hold her tight, astounded and humbled to be the man she trusted with something that means so much. I'm blown away by the emotions that rush through me like a wave.

Blown away that no one has claimed her before now.

My first experience with sex was with a high school senior. I made varsity as a freshman, and she was making her way through the team as a dare from her friends.

I don't think I've ever been with a virgin, and the protectiveness that surges inside me is more than shocking. It terrifies me. Because I can't ignore how much I've been fooling myself into believing things between Sadie and me could remain uncomplicated.

I wish I knew what to say. How to act. How to avoid making this weird or awkward. To make her understand I'm worthy of this gift and the trust she's placed in me.

Except I'm not. I can't be.

"I'll be back in a minute," I tell her as I pull out.

She gives me a wan smile, and, oh shit, tell me that's not a tear hovering in the corner of her eye.

I grab my boxers from the floor and head to her bathroom, making quick work of the condom. There's a stack of thick washcloths in her linen closet, and I refuse to meet my own eyes in the mirror as I wait for the tap water to turn warm.

After soaking the washcloth, I return to the bedroom, planning to help her however I can. The condom had traces of blood on it, and even though she had to be expecting it, I hate that I've hurt her in any way.

But the bedroom is empty, and I hear Sadie's voice downstairs talking to the dogs. I quickly pull on my T-shirt and jeans, buttoning them as I move.

There's a breeze coming from the open slider. She's wearing a fuzzy polka-dot robe and rubber clogs, standing in the backyard while the dogs explore the shadows cast from the porch light.

Max trots over to greet me, shoving his snout in my crotch. I scratch behind his ears, then walk toward her, grateful for the wisp of a smile the dogs have brought to her lips.

"The stars are pretty this time of night."

She's staring at the sky, and I have trouble pulling my eyes from the creamy column of her throat, illuminated by the moonlight.

It's too dark for me to notice for sure, but I swear there's beard burn on her perfect skin. Another way I've marked her. As much as my brain regrets it, my body and heart seem unwilling to get on board with my better self.

"The sky's a lot bigger here than it was in Atlanta," I remark, and she breathes out a small laugh.

"Go big or go home," she says. "That should be the tagline for the Rockies. I still don't know how my sister was able to move away. I can't imagine not having the mountains to ground me."

As I take another step closer, she wraps her arms around her chest, a silent cue to keep my distance.

"Sadie, we need to talk about what just happened."

She purses her lips and continues star gazing.

"It was great," she says conversationally. "For me, it was great. I don't have a lot to compare it to, but... I mean, you are The Playmaker, so..."

"Don't do that." I rub a hand over the back of my neck. "Don't make a joke out of it. If I'd known, Sadie—"

"What?" She turns to me now, her gaze fiery. "You would have said no, I imagine."

"Have people—men—said no to you?" I can't imagine a world where I could deny her, even if I had known.

"I haven't gotten that far with anyone else."

She's killing me with the honesty.

"I wouldn't have said no. But I would have been more careful with you." I bite back the urge to apologize and ask for a do-over. I don't regret it, but I sure as hell would have done things differently if I'd known.

"Maybe I didn't want careful," she counters, her voice fierce. "Maybe I wanted exactly what happened. So, thank you. I barely expected one orgasm, let alone two."

Hell, I'd like to give her ten or twenty. I'd like to keep her in bed for days—preferably mine since it's a king. So long that we both figure out precisely what she likes. I'll give it to her over and over until mine is the only name she can speak.

"It's all good, Ian."

She finally takes a step toward me. "We're friends with a heck of a benefit. Thank you."

"Would you quit thanking me? I don't know if you clued into this part, but I had a good time, too."

She shrugs and gives me a quick once-over. "I always thought men were guaranteed a good time."

I grit my teeth, because the thing about Sadie is, she isn't trying to be a smart ass. She means it. Like she had nothing to do with the most mind-blowing orgasm of my entire damn life. I want to grab her again and show her that it wasn't a fluke, and it isn't all just me. I want her to understand what she does to me.

Damn it, as much as I want to learn all the things that get her off, I want her to know the same about me. I've never wanted to give a woman any power over me. Definitely not sexually.

But Sadie can have it all—anything to prove I deserve what she gave me.

"I need to get to bed," she says. "I have a trio of dogs being dropped off early tomorrow."

The clear message is that she needs to get to bed alone. Not that I expect or want to stay with her, but being so casually dismissed chafes. I'm not used to it. Just like the old saying, Sadie is a riddle wrapped in a puzzle inside an enigma. Only that's my usual role.

It's comical the number of women who have tried to get me to spend the night or commit in a more significant way than I'm willing to give them. I haven't had a serious relationship since Monika. Now I'm wholly invested in a fake relationship with a woman who is basically giving me a boot in the ass when I don't want one.

At least one of us has some common sense, and it sure as hell isn't me.

"Felix wants us to go out to dinner tomorrow night. He made reservations. A place in town called 1200 West. Have you heard of it?"

She's nearly inside the house, the dogs trailing behind her like she's the canine Pied Piper. Her hand pauses before reaching for the slider's handle.

"It's the nicest restaurant in Skylark."

"Is it good?"

She gives me an odd look. "I've never been there, Ian. You know my life by this point. It doesn't involve fancy dinners."

"It does now," I tell her.

"I have a busy day tomorrow."

"I can help you hike the pack in the morning."

"I'm not asking for your help."

"I'm offering it anyway because you're my girlfriend. At least as far as my brother is concerned, as far as everyone is concerned. We slept together." Why won't she let me in? Let me help.

She holds up a finger like I'm a naughty schoolboy she's scolding. "One doesn't have anything to do with the other, and you know it."

Do I?

I bite back my frustration. This isn't the time or place for it. "The reservation is at seven. I hope you can make it. Either way, sweet dreams, Sadie."

Regret for so many things, including the way I mucked up this moment, courses through me as I head toward the gate. The only answer is the sound of her patio door whooshing shut.

Thankfully, Felix has gone to bed by the time I return home. In addition to my worry over Sadie, I've got a niggling suspicion my brother's surprise visit is more than just a friendly check-in to make sure I'm adjusting to retired life.

AFTER A SHITTY NIGHT'S sleep spent tossing and turning, I wake up to a call from my agent, Phil, telling me he's booked me for a paid appearance at a charity event.

I'll need to get my ass to Los Angeles the day after the wedding, which pisses me off. Phil isn't dealing well with the fact that I'm becoming more selective in the events I agree to. I have half a mind to call him back and explain, once again, that asking for approval before accepting a gig on my behalf wasn't a suggestion. It's a requirement for our continued partnership.

When Monika had Riva full-time, I couldn't have cared less about my schedule. All I wanted was to train and play and make money.

It's different now that I'm a full-time dad. I can take Riva with me, but I promised her a normal life, so I need to stop relying on gigs that require me to travel, especially once the school year starts. I'm going to need to get my ass in gear and figure out how I'm going to fill my days here in Colorado.

Because if I don't, I'm liable to spend most of them pining after my next-door neighbor, and I'm not a man who pines.

"What kind of bug crawled up your ass and died with its stinger lodged in your sphincter? You're a bigger ass than normal today."

I line up for my drive on the third hole of the country club. "Sphincter is a pretty big word for you," I shoot back.

Felix and I had an eight o'clock tee time, so the sun shines on us from a cloudless blue sky. There's a slight breeze, and the smell of freshly cut grass mixes with the woodsy scent of the pine trees that line the fairway. The morning is perfect in every way, except for my lingering frustration about how last night with Sadie ended. It's like I'm dragging my own black cloud along with me on a kite string.

"Let's just say your chocolate starfish is especially tight today," Felix says.

I swing, and the ball sails down the fairway, then cuts sharply to the right, landing smack dab in the middle of a sand pit.

Felix whistles under his breath. "The Playmaker is losing his touch. I should have put money on this round."

"I'll still kick your ass," I tell him. "And the only thing lodged in any part of my body is your voice droning on in my head."

"I figured you'd be mellow and chill this morning after sneaking out for some booty call action last night."

"How would you know?" I demand as he approaches the tee box. "You were busy busting a nut in the basement with Adam Sandler."

"Because I know you." He flashes a shit-eating grin. "Are my Spidey-senses already tingling with trouble in paradise?"

"Nothing is tingling, dumbass." I think about bashing him over the head with my golf club. Instead, I take a deep breath and slide it into the bag. "Speaking of trouble, it's about time we get down to business. What are you doing in Colorado, Felix?"

He swings and the ball wings down the fairway but, unlike mine, lands on the center of the course. "Displaying my superhuman athletic prowess."

"Come on, man. Out with it. You aren't built for secrets." He slides his club into his bag, and we hop in the cart.

I'm sure the golf pro wanted to round us out into a foursome, but I tipped extra to ensure we'd have some privacy. I'm not up for being social today.

"Ronnie and I broke up," he says after a moment of weighted silence.

Veronica Bolton. Mega influencer and star of a hit reality show. They'd been dating for the past six months—an eternity for Felix. And practically a lifetime commitment if you factor in my history.

"Got sick of holding her purse?"

"Fuck you, Ian," he says with enough fire to make me blink. "Do you honestly think I have a problem with dating a successful woman?"

"It's a joke, Felix. You've never minded sharing the spotlight."

"She cheated on me," Felix says, then quietly adds, "with Russ."

I mutter a string of curses under my breath that would make a sailor blush. "Was it a one-time thing?"

He shrugs. "Does it matter?"

"No. How could Russ do that to you?"

Russ Farmington is the quarterback in Cincinnati, and Felix's best friend. They won a national title together in college, and although Felix had been drafted to the Cincinnati Cougars right out of school, Russ played a few years in Buffalo before being traded. That trade—their reunion—became lightning in a bottle. It propelled both of them to marquee status. Russ more so than Felix because of his position as quarterback, but Felix's flash both on and off the field makes it hard for anyone to look away. Russ is introspective and serious. A perfect straight man for Felix's over-the-top personality.

"I don't see them being each other's type."

"Yeah, well, me neither. Except I came home four days ago and found my best friend balls-deep in my girl. They have at least one thing in common. Both of them are lying cheaters."

I don't know how to respond and Felix continues, "She says I'm too shallow and I don't take things seriously. This coming from a woman who makes her living hawking sunglasses and face masks on social media. The worst part is, I love her. Loved. I thought she was the one."

I blink at that. "You thought Ronnie was the one?"

"Why not? We had fun together. It was easy not having to dive into all the deep shit. She's like me. I thought we'd be happy cruising along and enjoying the ride. But like you said, Barlowe men aren't built for relationships. Even if we think we want it, it just ain't in the cards for guys like us."

I agree, but I also don't like hearing the pain in my brother's gravelly voice. We might have beat the shit out of each other growing up, but I've got his back, and he has mine. Nobody gets to hurt my baby brother.

"What about Russ?"

The relationship between a quarterback and his star receiver isn't anything to sneeze at. There's a bond everyone can feel between the great pairings. My brother and Russ Farmington have that bond.

Or, they had it.

Felix has a heart as big as the rest of him, and I wonder how he'll fake it on the field or in front of his teammates, never mind with the press next season.

"I don't know, man. I've seen Russ's naked ass a thousand times in the locker room over the years, but I can't eradicate the goddamn image of him pumping into Ronnie from my brain."

"That's beyond awful, man." I clap him on the shoulder and pull the golf cart to a stop at the edge of the fairway.

"That's why I'm here. I need a distraction. I need a place that doesn't make me think of either one of them for a while."

"You'll get through this. I'm here for whatever you need."

"Appreciate it, bro. Right now I want to concentrate on kicking your ass."

"This is not your fault, Felix," I call over my shoulder as I head for the sand trap.

But I know it'll take more than my words for him to get over it. It's hard to outrun the pain you carry around inside. Physical scars heal. The rest, not so much.

20

SADIE

If being with Ian is sensory overload, the two Barlowe brothers together are a force of nature that almost pushes me over the edge. Ian pinballs between being enigmatically guarded and endearingly sweet, but Felix is the polar opposite. Every fiber of his being acts like a magnet, drawing the attention of anyone and everyone in his orbit.

For this dinner, he's wearing a robin's egg blue silk shirt in a polka-dot pattern with a chunky gold chain around his neck, cargo pants, and bright orange high tops that I'm sure cost more than all of my shoes put together.

He pumps hands, slaps backs, and poses for selfies like he revels in the fame that comes with his superstardom in the football world. It's hard not to get caught up in that kind of energy. And it's obvious that both Ian and Riva are used to it.

Ian is doing his best to let his brother take center stage while he fades into the background like he's just another Skylark local out for dinner with his family. Riva sticks close to his side, and I can tell she appreciates her dad's more laid-back demeanor even as she giggles at Felix's outlandish jokes and posturing.

We're all laughing, and I'm grateful to Ian's brother for

being the best buffer imaginable. It's needed as I scramble for footing in this fake dating arrangement that no longer feels fake at all.

"What got you into the dog training business?" Felix asks as the main course is served. He and Ian each ordered a bison steak while Riva's having sweet-potato gnocchi and I'm dining on the salmon special.

"To be honest, I've always liked animals more than people," I say, earning an appreciative chuckle from the brawny receiver.

"You're one up on this lug over here." He points his fork at Ian. "He doesn't like people or animals."

"I like people," Ian argues, "and I like animals."

Riva snorts. "Name your favorite animal, Dad."

"Grizzly bears."

"Right." Felix nods. "That tracks. An animal that would just as soon claw you to death as walk on by."

"I respect grizzly bears." Ian defends his choice even though it's obvious neither Felix nor Riva are buying what he's selling. "They're powerful and strong and know their own minds."

Felix chortles. "What the hell do you know about the mind of a grizzly?"

"I like Max," Ian says instead of answering his brother's question.

"Max is my sister's dog," I explain to Felix.

"He's the best boy," Riva confirms.

"Your sister lives here in town?" Felix asks.

I shake my head. "She just finished nursing school and works at a hospital in Kansas City. She's getting married this summer in Vail."

"Sadie's taking Dad to the wedding." Riva winks at me. "Because he's her boyfriend."

"Yeah, kid, that's how it works." His bemused gaze tracks back to me. "Does your sister bring her dog to visit on the regular?"

"Oh, no, Max lives with me. He's ten, and Piper is busy with her job, so Max stays here. He was her dog growing up. We got him after our mom died."

"So he's your dog," Felix insists. "If your sister was that dedicated, she'd find a way to have him with her."

"She checks in on him almost every day," I say, even though he's right. I offered to drive Max out to Piper when she graduated from college so she wouldn't be alone. At that point, I didn't realize she'd already started seeing Bradley and they'd moved in together. Bradley wouldn't pretend to like animals, not even sweet Maxie, for my sister's benefit.

I feel Ian's warm hand on my leg and feel the backs of my eyes sting. Max means the world to my sister—I know this—and it breaks my heart that she's marrying a man who won't love her first four-legged love.

"Max is the perfect ambassa-dog for Sadie," Riva tells her uncle. "He helps the anxious dogs get comfortable when they first come to her for training. He's a total sweetheart."

"It would take one to warm up to your dad." Felix chuckles. "When we were kids, he got chased by almost every mutt in the neighborhood. He emitted suspicious pheromones. Still does. Or maybe it's that grizzly-bear energy. Look at me wrong and I'll swipe you with my claws."

"Or try to scare you for no good reason," Riva chimes in.

"I'm not scary," Ian says quietly, prompting more laughter from Felix and Riva.

He looks surprisingly uncomfortable as his brother and Riva continue to share the joke at his expense. Not fragile, exactly—no part of him could be described as fragile—but there's a sense of vulnerability there. I can tell he doesn't like being the butt of a joke, but just as clearly, he's not going to defend himself.

I've understood from the beginning that Riva is the quickest way to expose her father's soft underbelly, but now I realize he's just as vulnerable with his younger brother. I do the same thing with Piper, but in a different way.

"Grizzly bears have a lot of positive attributes," I announce to the group. "They're strong, independent, and fiercely protective of their cubs."

I offer Riva a smile. "Just like your dad. And you can't deny that Max is discerning in his affection." I turn my gaze to Felix. "Max's most notable trait is the habit of greeting certain people with an enthusiastic sniff between the legs. But he saves this special hello for humans he really likes. He doesn't just shove his snout into any old crotch."

The three of them laugh at my joke, and Ian's shoulders relax.

"Are you saying my brother's crotch is special?" Felix asks, then quickly holds up his hands when Riva makes a sound of disgust.

"That's so gross, Uncle Felix. She's saying that Max likes Dad."

"If he likes my brother, then I'm guessing that dog would camp out with his head firmly lodged between my legs."

We all glance up at the strangled noise the waitress who just approached the table makes.

"Oh, hello," Felix croons in a tone that is clearly meant to sound like a caress.

Her brown eyes widen. She definitely heard his comment. Hell, half the restaurant probably heard it. Felix Barlowe doesn't have much of an inside voice.

"I wouldn't be too sure," I tell him. When I notice the waitress lick her lips as her gaze turns flirty, I shake my head and nod toward Riva. "Can we see the dessert menu, please?"

She blinks then nods and hurries away. Ian mouths *thank you* to me across the table, and I smile in response. This is more like it. Back to the dynamic I'm used to with him.

Until his gaze lowers to my mouth, and I'm once again a bundle of nerves and desire. Like a ball shot through an arcade game, pinging from side to side with no clear direction.

Get it together, I command myself, but my body refuses to listen.

The waitress brings the dessert menus, and Felix orders one of everything. It's the kind of casual excess that reminds me how different my world is from the life of the Barlowe brothers. I live on a set budget, one that includes eating out twice a month, and never at a restaurant as fancy as this one.

I'm not claiming they don't work hard or aren't good guys, because they clearly are. But I'll never be entirely comfortable in their world.

Of course, that doesn't stop me from sampling a bite from every one of the desserts.

Crème brûlée is my favorite. Mom would sneak a ramekin of it from the kitchen at the country club on special occasions or to celebrate a good report card.

I close my eyes as I savor the creamy and crunchy bite, the perfect amount of vanilla giving the sweetness an extra depth. When I open them again, Ian is watching me, and the intensity of his gaze makes me blush.

After dessert, Ian and Felix banter over the check the waitress leaves on the table between them, each insisting on paying.

Riva, ever the peacemaker, suggests they settle it with a thumb war. There's a lot of muttered trash-talking as they link fingers and begin, but they're both grinning boyishly.

I know they're closer in age to each other than Piper and me, but watching them have fun together makes me yearn again for that kind of lightness in my sibling bond. I really need to change the tone of my interactions with her.

I want more fun in general. I've learned plenty from Ian in these past few weeks, but that might be the most important takeaway.

Felix wins and slams his palm on the table in celebration so hard, his wine glass tips over, the last bit of the red liquid splashing onto my dress. "Oh shit, Sadie, I'm so sorry," he says immediately.

"Nice work, numbnuts," Ian says while Riva covers her mouth with her napkin to smother a laugh.

"It's fine," I say, but Felix is already reaching out with his napkin to dab at my chest.

"Get your hand away from her." Ian's voice carries a warning tone.

Felix drops the napkin and pulls back like a referee tossing a flag onto the field.

"It's fine," I repeat, mostly for Ian's benefit. "I'm going to run to the bathroom and see what I can wipe off while it's still wet. I'll meet you at the host stand."

I'm somewhat successful with a damp towel, removing most of the wine stain, and I'm sure I can rinse out the rest when I'm home. As I throw the paper towel in the trash, I glance up at myself in the bathroom mirror. I barely recognize the woman looking back at me. My hair is down around my shoulders, and although I only wear a hint of mascara and lip gloss, my skin shines and my face practically glows with vitality.

I look relaxed, and, I can't believe I'm saying this...beautiful.

Is this what great sex does for a person? Who knew? I should probably work harder at separating my feelings for Ian from our mutual physical attraction, because the benefits part of our unlikely friendship is doing me a world of good.

I walk out of the restroom and find Felix waiting for me. He gives me a sheepish smile. "I'm really sorry, Sadie, and I'd like to tell you that's the first glass I've ever tipped over with my enthusiasm, but it's kind of my thing."

"No worries at all," I assure him, scanning the restaurant. "Where are your brother and Riva?"

"She saw a girl she met at the pool. They want to have a sleepover and dragged Ian over to meet this new friend's mom."

"Did you catch the girl's name?" I ask, intrigued. Not that I know everybody in town, but I might recognize her.

"Tamara Green is the kid's name, so I suppose Mama Green is the mother's name."

"It's Lillian," I correct him. She's a few years older than me, but arguably the it-girl of Skylark for more than a decade. Bradley and half his friends had major crushes on her, and they made a huge deal about spotting her around town during summer and winter breaks when she would come home from college.

"You guys might have friends in common with her." I shrug. "She was a Grizzlies cheerleader for a few seasons before she had kids. She moved back here, but divorced her husband a couple of years ago. She works at a popular salon in town."

Lillian was one of my first clients, and the first to leave when Dogapalooza opened. Although other customers have come and gone over the years, Lillian's desertion hurt because I'd mistakenly believed we were becoming friends.

The rumor around town is that she's blown through the settlement she got from her ex and is looking for a candidate to become husband number two. How convenient for when my time with Ian is over.

The thought of him moving on shouldn't bother me, but my heart feels like someone's squeezing the life out of it. I'm in big trouble.

"Divorced, huh?" Felix wiggles his thick brows. "I might be due for a cut."

The shock at his words must show on my face because he reaches out and squeezes my arm. "Bad joke. Sorry, Sadie. I'm a total fucking idiot. I don't need a haircut, and I wouldn't try to bag the mom of one of Riva's friends."

He scrapes a hand over his jaw. "I also shouldn't use the word bag when it comes to being with a woman. Shit. Please punch me in the face to shut me up."

"It's okay, Felix." I give him a quick hug, hoping to offer the comfort he obviously needs. That we both need at the moment. "You're not a total idiot. Just a bit of one."

He hoots in pleasure and lifts me off my feet in a tight hug. "Let's go rescue my brother. Something tells me he needs it."

I mentally wrestle the green-eyed monster as I follow Felix to the front of the restaurant. I have no right to feel jealous at the possibility of Ian someday dating for real in Skylark. If this were a thumb war, I'd be losing. But there's no reason to feel possessive over Ian. He's given me more in this arrangement than I ever could have imagined, and I'm not just talking about the toe-curling orgasms.

I'd have allowed Riva to work with me even without the fake dating part. She's a great kid and excellent with the dogs. I hope she'll want to continue helping even after her dad and I stage our big break up.

But, just like Ian—like almost everyone in my life—there's a good chance she'll move on to bigger and better things.

Suddenly Felix stops and turns to face me, grasping both of my arms to stop me from plowing straight into him. "You're okay, right?"

His words break into my spiral of self-pity. "Totally," I agree with a smile I hope doesn't look as fake as it feels. "I've had this dress forever. It's no big deal if the stain doesn't come out."

He proceeds to disabuse all stereotypes I have about football players full of ego and swagger when he offers a gentle wink. "I'm not talking about your dress. I'll buy you a dozen just like it. I'm talking about women like Lillian trying to put the moves on my brother. The two of you are good. Trust me, Ian likes you. He's different around you, Sadie. Relaxed in a way I haven't seen in years. To be honest, I don't know if I've ever seen him this relaxed. It's good for him, and it's good for my niece. I can guarantee he's not interested in the moves any thirsty moms in this little town make on him. You're the only cool drink of water he wants."

I'm taken aback by Felix Barlowe's insight into my insecurity and his ability to say precisely the right thing to give me hope. Despite knowing the risks to my heart, I appreciate the reassurance.

"It might be having you here that's relaxing him," I suggest. "The two of you are like a sibling stand-up act."

He runs a hand through his thick hair—which could use a trim—a thoughtful expression crossing his face. "You know what they say about comedians, right? They're some of the most messed up people you'll meet. All that funny business is a defense mechanism. Ian and I have the routine mastered. That's for sure."

He chucks me on the shoulder. "But you make him happy for real, and my brother deserves a boatload of happiness after too long of not letting himself have much. I get the impression you do, too."

"I'm glad you came to town, Felix," I whisper, my throat tightening with emotion.

"Me too, girlie. Now let's go rescue your man."

My man. It might not be the whole truth, but I like the idea of it. Way more than I should.

21

SADIE

The morning before we head to the mountains, Sally shows up with an armload of dresses for me to try on. She's borrowed the lot from Trina, the fashionista in their relationship.

"She can't wear them while she's pregnant. Not that she has a lot of reasons to wear cocktail dresses and ball gowns in Skylark anyway."

"I don't think I need so many outfit changes," I argue, even though protesting is futile when Sally has her mind set on something. "We're only going to be in Vail for a couple of days, and I have my sister-of-the-bride dress for the ceremony and reception."

Sally grimaces then heads past me toward the stairs. Once in my bedroom, she drops the dresses on my bed and pulls a garment bag from the pile. "We can do better. I have options, but one in particular will be perfect. By the way, Trina's sorry she can't be here for the fashion show, but her troll of a boss wouldn't let her out of the staff meeting this morning."

"What's wrong with the dress I have?" I ask as she unzips the cloth cover shielding what is probably a very expensive article of clothing I would never buy for myself.

"Not one Golden Girl, even Betty White, rest her soul, would be caught dead in that travesty of a dress."

I open my closet door where the dress I bought on clearance at a mall in Denver hangs. It's an admittedly boxy design, and the color can only be described as cement gray. But it's comfortable and has pockets. Plus, Piper approved it via a FaceTime call from the dressing room.

"Pockets," I remind my friend.

"The pockets are a bonus, but you're thirty-three, not ninety-three. You've got a rocking body, even though hardly anybody realizes it because of the baggy clothes you insist on wearing. I'm not letting you walk down the aisle at your sister's side with everybody thinking asshat Brad is marrying the hot Hart."

"He's not marrying Piper because of how she looks, although—"

"Do not start with the crap about Piper being the pretty sister. You're gorgeous."

"I never said I wasn't pretty, and this isn't a competition. I don't even want Bradley anymore."

"Thank God for small miracles," Sally agreed. "I can't figure out what Piper sees in him. The guy peaked in high school, and he was a schmuck back then."

Before I can respond to that jab, my eyes catch on the fabric of the dress as she pulls it out. "I can't wear that," I whisper.

"Of course you can. It's Trina's wedding dress, and she insists."

When Sally and Trina married five years ago on the top of Skylark Mountain, Trina wore a unique pale blue gown, similar in shade to Ian's glacier-hued eyes. The dress has an ethereal, fairy-tale vibe with a fitted silhouette that gently flares at the thighs, creating a sense of delicate movement. The fabric is a shimmery silk with layers of tulle that add depth and dimension. A designer Trina is friends with created it just for her, and I can't believe she'd want me to wear it to my sister's wedding.

Sally holds up her phone and hits play. Trina waves at me from the screen. "Hey, Sads, I'm recording this message because I know what you're thinking, and I insist you wear the dress. Ian Barlowe won't know what hit him. He's going to fall head over heels."

Sally tosses the phone onto my bed. "She made me promise to text her pics."

"I'm not trying to hit Ian with anything."

"I know," she agrees. "That's my wife's hopeless romantic streak. She's convinced the two of you have all the makings of a classic nineties rom-com."

"We don't." I cross my arms over my chest to keep from reaching for the gown. "Besides, he already knows that I have—as you would describe it—a rocking body."

Sally frowns as she studies me like she's searching for traces of a scarlet V. "You did it? The big it?"

"You could show a little enthusiasm," I tell her, fidgeting under the scrutiny. I touch a finger to the center of my chest, which feels inordinately tight, then grab the dress and turn for the en suite bathroom, mostly for a moment to collect myself. Sally knows me way too well to hide my emotions.

"Did you do it because you wanted to or because you felt the pressure of the book club bucket list?"

"What's wrong with wanting to have sex?" I demand as I pull off the tank top I'm wearing. "You had sex with plenty of people before Trina, even a guy. If it's okay for you to have a penis inside you, why isn't it okay for me? I actually like penises."

I hear gagging noises from the bedroom. "I still don't believe anybody likes the one-eyed wonder weasel."

"Ick. Not when you call it that."

Her laugh is defiant. "Yes, I had plenty of sex before Trina, even once with a dude. I blame another dude—Jack Daniels—for that lapse in judgment. Once I fell in love, it was different. Sex means something to you, Sads. That's not wrong."

"So why does it sound like you think I made a mistake? Let's remember, you were the one who told me about the underwear ads."

"Sure, Ian Barlowe can fill out a pair of boxers. But you're special and you deserve to be treated that way. I want to make sure it wasn't just some throwaway. A couple of hot and heavy minutes to check off a non-existent box."

I open my mouth to tell her there's nothing wrong with checking off boxes. Sally's kept a planner with a to-do list for as long as I've known her. She's the queen of checking off boxes. Okay, Iris might be the queen, but Sally's pretty good at it, too.

Unfortunately for me, I won't—can't—lie to my best friend.

"I wasn't just checking off a box," I say as I emerge from the bathroom in the gown. "Which makes me a bigger idiot than you and your night with Jack Daniels and the weasel."

Sally opens her mouth, then shuts it again. She whispers, "You're so beautiful," and wraps her arms around me. "And you've fallen for him."

Even though I need her hug like I need my next breath, I pull away. If I start crying now, I might be a blubbery mess for the rest of my life. And I'm not dripping tears on this fantastic dress.

"Nobody can know, Sal, not even Trina."

"You heard her. Trina wants you to fall for him."

"Not if he doesn't fall in return, and there's no chance of that. He doesn't do relationships." I shake my head. "His ex-girlfriends give interviews about how he's got no heart, but I don't believe that."

"Maybe he hasn't found the right woman to unlock it. That's how it was with Trina and me."

"I'm not a princess, Sal. This isn't a fairy tale."

"You look like a princess in that dress," she answers, a warm smile on her face. "And why shouldn't you have the fairy tale? No one deserves it more. You gave up everything when your mom died."

"You would've done the same thing," I reply with a shrug. "I had great sex, okay? I don't regret it, but that's all it's going to be."

"It could be more if you put yourself out there." Sally's tone is gentle but firm. "But not because Ian Barlowe is a magic pigskin prince who'll carry you off into the sunset. You don't need a white knight. You saved yourself and your sister. And back in high school, when I didn't know how to handle who I knew I was, you saved me with your friendship."

"You got me through calculus," I tell her with another hug. "So we're even."

"Hardly." She pulls back and cups my face between her hands. She smells like coffee beans and vanilla syrup, a comforting mix I always associate with Sally. "You've been the hero in your own life for a long time. You have to see that. But even heroes need a break. They're allowed to rely on other people and open themselves up to love." She gently pats my cheeks. "You deserve to be loved for exactly who you are."

I press my lips together when they start to tremble and give her a shaky nod. "Maybe I'll be ready for love when I figure out exactly who I am." It's a question that's been keeping me up at night lately. That and the fact that my recent dreams always star Ian...and he's *always* naked.

She sighs, and I step away from her hold, smoothing a hand down the front of the dress. "But right now, I'm going to take your lovely wife up on her offer. I don't want Bradley Carlson, but I also don't want to look like a Golden Girl."

"It's a start," she concedes with a wink. "Let me take some pics for Trina and I'll get the next outfit ready."

"Do I need other outfits?"

"I texted Piper about the itinerary, and Trina gave me strict instructions about what you should be wearing. We expect proof-of-outfit selfies as you go."

I laugh and head for the bathroom to change. It feels odd, but kind of nice, to have somebody taking care of me. Making me the star of my own show, at least.

We spend the rest of the morning trying on outfits, doing my makeup, and testing out a curling iron Trina sent along that neither Sally nor I know how to use. It's so far outside my norm, but it's fun to play.

How have I let my life become so not fun? I went into survival mode when Mom died. My entire focus became acting like the competent adult Piper needed me to be. That became my safe place. But now I realize how much it held me back.

And, yes, it will hurt when Ian and I have our fake breakup—because my feelings for him are all too real—but I won't let that stop me. Before him, I hadn't been on a single date in the past decade, which is pathetic. But also fixable. With some time and effort, I can fix the broken parts of me.

"I think I hoped Piper would come back for a little while after she graduated college," I tell Sally as I lead her to the door later in the afternoon. "So we'd have a chance to redefine our relationship. Growing up, I didn't want her to feel like I put a man before her, ever. She'd dealt with too much loss already."

I hold up a hand when she shakes her head. "Yes, I lost my mom, too, and I understand I'm not Piper's mother. But I'm just starting to accept it."

My best friend hugs me tighter than before and we both swipe at our cheeks before she leaves.

"Time for a potty break," I tell the dogs and begin the process of letting them out in small groups.

What I'd like to do is climb into bed with Max and watch *Friends* reruns all afternoon, but that isn't an option with my business, especially as it stands at the moment. I don't regret the career I've made for myself, or running the business out of my home. It allowed me to be here for Piper when she needed it.

Max hangs back like he knows I need the company. I'm grateful Bradley agreed to make him the ring bearer for the wedding. It would have broken my heart if they hadn't included Max.

Maybe the asshat will change his mind about animals in general, although it would also break my heart to lose Max in addition to Piper.

I've just finished letting in the last of the dogs when there's another knock at the door. My heart thuds, wondering if it might be Ian. We don't have plans to see each other tonight, but he's childfree with Riva at a sleepover, and I'm childless, so...

I open the door to find Mona Davenport looking eight kinds of nervous on the other side.

I haven't seen Mona, who used to work as my full-time assistant, since she failed to show up on a Monday morning two years ago. Then she ghosted me for weeks before a client spilled the beans that Mona had taken a job as a manager at Dogapalooza.

"Hi, Mona," I say, trying to keep my voice steady. "I was just heading out." She should realize that's a lie since I'm standing barefoot in a tank top and athletic shorts with dogs nosing into the backs of my knees.

"I need your help," she replies urgently. "I've been calling, but it goes straight to voicemail."

"Because I blocked you."

She doesn't react other than a conciliatory nod. "Okay, but there's a situation at the ken...canine experience factory."

I can't help but snort. "What in the world is a canine experience factory?"

"That's what the corporate marketing materials instruct us to call the facility," she explains. "It offers a friendlier tone than a kennel or doggy daycare."

"That's the dumbest thing I've ever heard. You're running a doggy daycare."

"It's going to be a doggy disaster if you don't help me," she continues, her tone desperate. "A fight broke out when one of the reactive dogs got into the big playroom. There's an injured animal in the corner, but I can't get to her because the other dogs are so freaked out. Several of them lunged at me when I tried to enter the room."

"How many are in the room?"

She grimaces. "Around forty."

"Are you joking?" I'm truly shocked at that number. What are they thinking?

"It's a busy week, and we're under strict instructions not to turn away customers."

"At what cost?" I demand, then continue before she can answer. "Tell me you didn't leave the dogs unsupervised to come over here."

"There's another canine experience facilitator with them."

"Stop using the corporate marketing speak. You sound ridiculous."

"You have to help me, Sadie."

"I don't have to do anything, Mona. Don't forget that I hired and trained you when no one else would because of your police record. I let you set your own hours while you cared for your dying mother. And a week after her funeral, you ditched me for the competition."

Mona's forehead puckers at my rebuke, like she's shocked I have the nerve to call her out on how she deserted me without a sliver of explanation or apology.

With a start, I realize there's a reason I expect people to leave me. So many people I've cared about or depended on already have.

She glances at her watch and then lifts her hands in prayer. "Please, Sadie. I need these dogs under control before their owners pick them up. We've had two incidents already this quarter."

"What kind of incidents?" A sense of foreboding presses at my gut, making my stomach tighten.

"It doesn't matter right now," Mona insists. "We've managed to keep them under wraps, but if this gets out, it could be..."

Terrible for Dogapalooza and a boon to my business.

Dog trainers don't take an oath like doctors with the old "first, do no harm" rule. But the good ones, the trainers I studied at the start of my business and who I like to think I honor in the way I care for dogs, put an animal's health and well-being first. As much as I'd like to slam the door in her face, I can't ignore an entire facility full of agitated animals.

I kennel my dogs, then follow her to the Dogapalooza building. It takes nearly two hours to defuse the situation, and somehow, Mona convinces me to sneak out the back door when the first owners come to claim their pets for the day.

For all of Sally's words of wisdom about claiming my own power, I realize the practice of being the hero of my own story is easier said than done.

By the time I get home, I'm irritated with myself and the rest of the world because it's easier to blame stuff outside of me than take responsibility for being treated like a doormat for most of my life.

As I wait for the garage door to open, my gaze tracks to Ian's house. Since he convinced Felix to return the rented sports car shortly after arriving in Skylark, Ian had to drop his brother off at the Denver airport today. He should be back by now, but the house seems too quiet to have somebody inside. Not that he's going to be hosting a rager just because his daughter is at a sleepover with Sally and Trina.

I secretly hoped he might ask me on a real date, something more official than a barefoot booty call, but I haven't heard from him. I know I'm being ridiculous to think that one night together had the power to change our arrangement. He doesn't owe me anything—not until we start our weekend charade.

I told myself that losing it before the wedding would make the weekend easier. Nobody will look at me and think, "definitely a virgin." Although I don't have any reason to believe people were looking at me like that in the first place. Who would think a single woman in her thirties would be so inexperienced?

And thanks to Ian, I'm not anymore.

After the last daycare dog leaves, I take Max for a walk around the neighborhood. We go slow because that's his speed these days. I try not to think about the fact that, like everyone else I love, Max is going to leave me, too.

I need to put these morbid musings aside and slap on a happy face for the weekend. I'm glad Piper is happy, and I want her to see that I am, too. Because damn it, I am.

Well, I will be, anyway.

Rome wasn't built in a day, and my identity won't be either. I'm not giving up on any of it, even the fairy tale.

22

IAN

I BLINK AWAKE, staring up at an unfamiliar ceiling. It feels like a heavy metal band is rocking out inside my brain. I lift my fingers to either side of my forehead, hoping to turn down the volume.

No matter how hard I press, there's no relief. What in the hell happened? I force myself to sit up, then lay back again when the room spins.

Snippets of memories flutter through my mind like confetti raining down after a national championship win. I mentally grasp them and try to put my thoughts together.

After dropping Felix off at the airport, I was heading home when one of my former teammates texted. Phil Johnson saw the photo my dumb-fuck brother posted on Insta before I made him delete it. Since moving to Colorado, I've maintained a low profile and intend to keep it that way.

But Phil, who'd been traded a couple of seasons earlier to Denver, was a friend at one time, and I agreed to stop by his house for a drink—just one.

Only it hadn't been one, and it hadn't been just Phil. Most of the Grizzlies O line was partying at his house last night. For a few hours, I got swept back into the me I used to be—the guy who only cared about having fun off the field. But I'm not a complete idiot and have no intention of falling back into that life. I don't even want it anymore.

I swear I only had a couple of Jack and Cokes, but I feel like I partied for four days straight on some billionaire's yacht in the south of France.

I pat down my body, which is shockingly in one piece. I'm fully dressed, also a small miracle at this point.

My phone is on the nightstand next to the bed. I grab it, then bolt upright, pounding head be damned. Sadie and I are supposed to leave for Vail in twenty minutes, and I'm still an hour away from Skylark. I sniff my pit. Shit, I could use a shower.

A blender whirs from somewhere in the house. Stumbling out of the unfamiliar bedroom, a little weak in the knees, I head downstairs to find Phil in the kitchen, something green, thick, and nasty-looking spinning in his Vitamix.

"What the hell happened last night?" I yell over the sound.

He turns off the machine and grins. "I'm making a hangover cure, Playmaker. It'll make you right as rain in no time."

I scrub a hand through my hair, "Why do I have a hangover? I had two drinks. What the fuck was in them?"

His smile turns sheepish. "Yeah, the new punter is a practical joker."

"Did he roofie us?"

Phil cringes. "Roofie is a strong word, but something like that. It's harmless. The headache will fade, and you won't fail a drug test."

"I don't drug test anymore, dumbass. I'm retired. My girlfriend and I are driving to a wedding this morning, and she's going to be pissed as hell when I'm late to pick her up."

At least, I assume as much. I'm pissed as hell. Although calling Sadie my girlfriend out loud takes the edge off my frustration. It has a nice ring to it, a long-term ring that feels right.

"Oh, sorry, man." Phil looks legitimately remorseful. "But I'm sure she'll understand."

I shake my head. "Christ, Phil, I barely understand. What the hell is wrong with a kid who would secretly drug his own friends?"

"More talent than sense, I guess."

I study my former teammate. "You don't seem that worse for wear."

"Oh, buddy, I learned last season to drink like a college girl on spring break. Only what I open myself, and I never put it down. Hell, I've mastered the one-handed piss."

"Could have used that info last night."

"You'll know for next time."

I don't bother telling Phil there won't be a next time. If this train wreck of a night has taught me anything, it's that I'm done with the football party lifestyle. There isn't a damn thing I miss about the off-season antics. Why had I tried to fool myself into thinking there was?

"Let me pour you a hangover cure to go."

"No." I rub a hand over the back of my neck. "I'll see you later, Phil. Good luck this season to you and the guys."

"See you, Playmaker," a voice calls out as a hand lifts from one of the plush leather couches situated around the fireplace of the open-concept main floor.

"Later, Barlowe." Denny Craig, the team's star offensive lineman, waves from a recliner.

"You weren't the only one messed up," Phil tells me with a shrug.

"Kellerman's a douche," Denny shouts, then lets out a groan and grasps his head with giant hands.

"A douche and a half," I mutter and walk toward the front door. I stop and turn back before heading out into damage control mode. "Tell Kellerman that what he did last night isn't cool. If I catch wind of him pulling that shit again, either with guys on the team or anyone else, I'll come back down and personally break every toe on his kicking foot."

Phil visibly swallows. "Got it, Playmaker."

"Also, tell him I'll be calling Coach, just for more incentive."

"Dang, Barlowe, you sure you need to do that?"

"Come on, Phil. This isn't Vaseline in somebody's jockstrap. It's serious shit and not okay. I've got a daughter. You might have a daughter someday. Would you want a guy like Kellerman anywhere near her?"

"Fuck no. I'll relay the message, man."

Thank God my keys are still in my jeans pocket. I jog to my car and start to call Sadie, but what the hell am I going to say? The kind of night I had is evident in my voice. Hopefully, I'll feel more human by the time I return to Skylark.

I text instead, apologizing that I'm going to be late, using the excuse of an emergency with a friend in Denver.

Her response is immediate.

> Sadie: If you've changed your mind, you don't have to go to Vail.

Shit. I don't want her to think that.

> Me: I haven't. I'll be there as soon as I can.

It kills me that I've hurt Sadie when it's the last thing she deserves. Maybe I can explain away a night I barely remember, but not the underlying truth. Even when my intentions are good, I hurt people. My dad always had the best intentions to put down the bottle and not raise his fist to Mom. It never worked that way.

My behavior is nowhere near as bad as his, but I'm still his son. How can I trust myself? It's enough of a struggle to be the dad my daughter needs. I'm not sure how I'll handle that once this weekend ends and Sadie breaks off our arrangement.

If I can hurt her when it's supposed to be fake, the thought of what I might do to her if I let myself truly have feelings is terrifying.

Interstate traffic is light, and I make good time home. The house feels empty without Riva, but I'm glad she stayed with Sally and Trina last night. I don't want her to see me like this.

After the quickest shower known to man, I throw some clothes in a duffel bag, grab my suit from the closet, and text her I'm ready.

"I'm sorry," I say as she emerges from her house. Max trots down the steps to greet me, and I shift to guard the family jewels.

"It's fine, Ian. I appreciate you coming with me." Her tone is way too formal. "I know it's a lot."

"It's not." I pick up her suitcase and place a hand on her arm. She stiffens but doesn't pull away, which I take as a good sign.

"I didn't mean to stay out all night. It's a long, stupid story. Let's just say I got a bit of not-quite food poisoning, but something incapacitated me."

She lifts a brow, and I can only imagine what she's thinking kept me from coming home, but I don't offer more of an explanation.

"This weekend is going to be fun, Sadie. Promise. I'm glad I'm coming with you."

The headache has worn off, and now that I'm with Sadie, I feel more like the man I've become over the past few weeks. A guy I like a lot more than The Playmaker.

"Me too," she agrees, with a sigh like she wishes she wasn't.

We load Max and her luggage into the car, and we start the drive to Vail. I could explain exactly what happened, but instead, I let her think the worst. I'm bound to disappoint her—if not now, at some point. Maybe it's smart we go into this weekend with what I can and can't give in the forefront of our minds.

"Other than your sister and Brad-ski, who else important to you will be here this weekend?"

She gives me a funny look. "Max might be the only other wedding attendee I care about. But you saw Piper's best friend, Casey, at the country club."

"The maid of honor," I answer and she gives a terse nod.

"You might recognize a few of Bradley's high school friends still living in Skylark. Amanda and that group."

"I can't wait," I say with a smile that feels tight at the edges.

"You'll meet his parents. They retired to Arizona a few years ago. Of course, I've known them forever."

I glance at her as I merge onto I-70 West. It's hard to read her expression behind her tortoiseshell sunglasses. "What do they think of their son and your sister as a couple since you and B-man were such close friends growing up?"

She grips the door handle as we come around a particularly tight bend in the highway heading into the mountains. I'd bet the reaction has more to do with her nerves about the weekend than my driving.

"They were always nice to me, but I was never the kind of girl they wanted for Bradley. According to Piper, his mom didn't approve when they first started dating, but she's come around."

"I'll believe that when I see it."

"Agreed," she murmurs. "Although I wonder if anyone would be good enough for Connie Carlson's adored prince. Guarantee she still thinks Dr. Bradley should have aimed higher than a twenty-two-year-old nursing grad."

"If she's anything like you, your sister's a catch."

Sadie laughs like I'm making a joke. For the record, I can't imagine a woman who could hold a candle to my fake girlfriend.

"I hope I'm wrong and Piper's right," she says. "The whole damn Carlson family is lucky to have her, Bradley especially."

"The more I hear about this guy, the more I'm convinced he's a royal tool."

Her grip on the door handle eases as she laughs again. "Mega tool. I can't believe I was blind to it for so long. I hate that Piper thinks she's the lucky one."

"She grew up knowing him as your friend," I offer, giving her sister the benefit of the doubt if not B-Rad. "You liked him, and he probably seemed safe and familiar. Starting out after college in a new city where you know no one isn't easy."

She lowers her sunglasses and looks at me. "Even when you arrive in that city as a first-round draft pick out of college?"

"Someone's been doing her homework."

A blush rises to her cheeks as she shoves the sunglasses up her nose again and faces forward. "I figure I'm going to be inundated with questions about my boyfriend, so I did my Playmaker homework."

Hearing Sadie call me her boyfriend makes my heart hurl itself against my ribcage like it's trying to escape my chest. Shit, I've got it so bad for this woman.

"Your career is impressive."

"And over," I mutter.

"You're impressive," she amends.

Is that enough of a foundation to convince her to turn our fake relationship into a real one after this weekend?

"I still don't believe we're going to convince everyone you're head over heels for me."

"They'll believe it," I say simply. I don't add because it's true.

A complete shock, but so very real. Over the past several weeks, I've let Sadie into my life and heart in ways that surprise even me. At first, it was watching her connection with Riva. Seeing the warmth and support she brings to my daughter's life and realizing she shines that same light on the dark corners of my well-guarded heart.

She's a woman with a huge capacity for love, and the feelings I've caught for her are far from fake. Although it might have started slowly, the way I feel now hits me like a ton of bricks. I'm in love with Sadie for so many reasons.

She's lovely without the need for superficial glitz and glamour, but it's more than just physical. Her genuine kindness makes her refreshing to be around, especially compared to the transactional relationships I'm used to. I can be myself with her, and she anchors me to what's real and valuable—things I had a tendency to lose sight of in the chaos of fame.

She gasps as I overcorrect on one of the sharper bends along the winding highway through the mountains. "Sorry," I mutter.

I never expected this, and I don't want to scare her away or stress her out before this weekend.

Last night is a reminder that I'm capable of making dick moves, but I'm going to do better. She's absolutely perfect, and I'm damn lucky to be at her side this weekend, even if she thinks we're still pretending. I still don't trust myself not to hurt her, which is the last thing I want.

So I'll keep these feelings to myself a little while longer. If I have anything to say about it, Sadie and I will have plenty of time to explore our connection. Maybe even the rest of our lives.

"What kind of music do you like?" I ask as I hit the power button for the radio.

"Whatever you want," she answers without thinking about it, but I shake my head.

"Everyone has faves. Tell me yours."

I want to know everything about her, as much as she's willing to share. Even though it'll hurt more in the long run if things don't work out the way I want, I can't seem to stop myself.

"It's embarrassing." Her cheeks turn a rosy pink, and my body reacts, remembering the blush that colored her entire body when she came apart in my arms. "Sally and Trina make fun of me all the time."

"You're killing me, Hart." Somehow I know whatever she says is going to make me happy. Everything she does makes me happy. "Just spill it."

"Yacht rock," she whispers.

"Are you serious?" I throw my head back and give a deep laugh. "You're a fan of saccharine sentiment and bell bottoms. I love it."

"Don't forget chest hair," she tells me with a wink.

I tug on the collar of my shirt. "I've got chest hair."

She giggles. "And a pretty hot chest underneath it."

"I kind of love the Kenny Loggins vibe." The word love has me swallowing the sudden lump in my throat. I'm not sure Sadie notices. I sure as hell hope not and grab my phone to cue up a playlist.

"You're not going to make fun of me?"

"Not on your life. If I'd known, you can bet I'd be wearing my skipper's hat twenty-four-seven. Shall we start with Gordon Lightfoot?"

She grins back at me. "Yes, please."

Suddenly, everything is right with my world again. All because of Sadie Hart's smile.

23

SADIE

THE MOMENT we pull into the hotel parking lot and I see Piper waving from the front entrance, the bulk of my worries about the weekend fade—not totally away, but at least into the background.

Her fitted T-shirt has *bride* emblazoned across the front in shiny gold script. And while Piper is a few inches taller than me and has always been thin, I swear I can see her hip bones jutting out under her black leggings. I get that plenty of brides lose weight before their wedding, but I want to feed my sister. Food has always been one of our love languages.

Her hair, a lighter blonde than her natural shade, is piled on top of her head in a messy bun and her smile looks a little wobbly around the edges. I can relate, as tears prick the back of my eyes. I've missed her, and hate that we won't have much private time to catch up this weekend.

Especially when I have the feeling she needs my support more than ever. The urge to protect and mother Piper is part of me, always. Plenty of people have questioned the sacrifices I made for her, but I'd do it all over again—every challenging, lonely minute.

After Mom died, I needed my sister as much as she needed me. I needed her light and love to get me through the sorrow and grief of losing my only parent. Taking care of Piper meant I wasn't alone in the world. It gave me the strength to keep our little family going.

Max perks up in the back seat when I reach around and lower his window. He might be more excited than me to see her, which melts my heart.

"I'll drop you off and then park," Ian offers like he's reading my mind again.

I squeeze his arm. "Thank you for everything this weekend."

He grins. "I haven't done anything yet."

But he has, and I'm not talking about two spectacular orgasms. Just by being here, even if this morning was a bit of a stress shitshow, he's made me feel not alone in a way that's as vital to me right now as the bond I share with Piper.

I don't have too much time to consider my feelings, or the fact that I've failed at controlling them, because Piper rushes to the car as soon as he pulls under the portico in front of the hotel. I climb out, ready to embrace her, but of course my sister heads straight for the back seat, ignoring both me and Ian.

"Maxie," she coos, and Max answers with a yelp of delight. She opens the door, and he bolts out like he's a renegade puppy, not a dignified senior. "Who's my good boy? Did you miss me like I missed you?"

She crouches down and wraps her arms around his body. Max isn't one for full-on hugs, but he'll happily endure the affection for Piper.

"Do you have any hugs left over for me?" I ask, hoping my voice sounds amused and not hurt. I'm joking, but also trying not to be upset that I'm a distant second in the race for my sister's affection.

"Of course." Piper straightens and hugs me tightly.

I breathe in her scent, but it's different than I remember. "You're wearing a new perfume," I say as we pull back.

She rolls her eyes. "Bradley said my old vanilla sugar was

'cloyingly sweet'." She uses air quotes and looks like she's trying hard not to roll her eyes again. "I've upgraded to something French. Do you like it?"

"It's classy." Honestly, it smells like cat pee, but I don't mention that.

"I'm so glad you're here, Sads. I just want to come to your room and chill out. Casey is all intense about every dumb detail. Between her and Bradley's mom..."

She holds out her hands, and I cringe at the nails that have been bitten to the nubs.

"It's a good thing I'm getting a manicure tomorrow, because I can't stop gnawing them."

"Oh, sweetie." I hug her again. "Weddings are a lot of work, but I'm here now. We've got this."

"Maybe we could duck out after tonight's dinner and have a sleepover?"

I shake my head. "That's going to be a little cozy with Ian in the room."

The flash of disappointment in her hazel eyes sparks a flare of guilt in my chest. I can't remember ever denying my sister anything she needed. But she'll have to deal with sleeping arrangements on her own tonight.

When she first told me about the plan for a Vail wedding, I offered to rent an Airbnb and come up a few days early. Some sisterly bonding time sounded nice. But she insisted she wanted to be in the thick of the action with her groom and the bridal party.

Only boring old me cared about recapturing the way things used to be with movie nights and the two of us together. Boring gets a bad rap sometimes.

"Yeah, of course. I can't wait to meet him. Everybody can't wait to meet him." She scratches behind Max's ears. "I hope it's okay that this guy stays in your room."

"Um, sure." I frown as Max looks up at me with the word traitor in his dark chocolate eyes. "But I thought you wanted to spend your last couple of nights as a single woman with the first love of your life."

She sighs. "Kristin was supposed to get a room with her boyfriend, but he broke up with her and then cleaned out their bank account, so she's staying with Casey and me. Annie got jealous that we're all together and canceled her room. So there's four of us in my room, and Annie is allergic to dogs."

"You have four people staying in one room the night before your wedding? Are you getting any sleep?"

"Here we go with Sadie, the wet blanket." I grit my teeth but plaster on a smile as Bradley joins us. "How do you always manage to sound like an overbearing mother even when you're not?"

Ouch. I can't even pretend that question doesn't hurt. What a dick.

Max moves closer and settles his back end on my foot in solidarity. No crotch love for Bradley. I don't blame the dog. You couldn't pay me to get near that thing.

"Come on, babe," Piper says in a voice I barely recognize as hers. Talk about cloyingly sweet. "Sadie just wants me to get the rest I need to look my best on our wedding day."

"Of course you're going to look your best. You're the hot sister." Bradley casually rattles off the compliment slash insult like he's discussing the weather.

It's hard to believe I ever considered this asshole my friend.

Piper winces and I start to turn away, but a heavy arm wraps around my shoulder.

"Well now, *Brian*, that was a real asshat thing to say." Ian points at Piper. "No offense, because you're lovely, but my heart beats double every time your sister smiles."

"Sadie has a great smile," Piper agrees, sounding somewhat dumbfounded. I can't decide if it's a reaction to Ian's overwhelming masculine perfection up close—it's a heady thing for sure—or hearing someone compliment me. I'm still unaccustomed to it. "It's our mom's smile," she whispers as if just now realizing that.

Ian drops a kiss on the top of my head. "Sadie is beautiful in so many ways. I could spend this whole damn weekend telling people about them."

He could? Damn, Ian Barlowe is better at this boyfriend thing than I imagined.

My sister looks surprised but genuinely happy at Ian's praise. "Except this weekend is about Piper," I say quickly. Flattery and I have a tenuous relationship, and even if Ian's laying it on thick as part of the arrangement, I could come to rely on the way he makes me feel.

I make introductions as Piper's gaze continues to dart between Ian and me like she can't quite believe what she's witnessing. Join the club, sis.

"Congratulations to both of you," Ian offers. "Brian, you're a lucky man."

"It's Bradley, but you can call me Brian if you want," Bradley says as he thrusts out a hand. I smother a snort.

Based on the way Bradley's wide grin fades, Ian might be squeezing just a bit too hard as they shake.

"I'm sure you didn't mean to insult my girlfriend, right?"

"Oh no, bro." Bradley shakes his head and extricates his hand from Ian's grasp. "Me and Sadie go way back. I'm sure she told you. She followed me— I mean, we went everywhere together in high school and undergrad. It's like we're already family."

"Sure it is, *bro*." Ian turns his attention to my sister. "I've heard great things about you, Piper." He leans in to give her a one-armed hug, not releasing his hold on me.

Her eyes widen as she looks at me around his arm. "Wow," she mouths.

Precisely what I'm thinking. Five minutes, and Ian's already more than paid his non-existent debt to me.

Piper studies Ian, and some of the initial star-struckness

disappears. "Most of what I know about you is from my fiancé since my sister dislikes sharing details of her life. I look forward to getting to know you better this weekend."

"I like to share my life," I mutter under my breath. I simply don't have much practice at it because I'm so used to focusing on everybody else.

"Sadie's the best," Bradley adds, nudging Piper out of the way so he's standing directly in front of Ian. "The guys are excited to have you on the links with us tomorrow, Playmaker. Excited to have you here in general. Hell, if we didn't already have a minister, I'd ask you to get ordained on one of those internet sites tonight and do the honors yourself."

He turns to Piper. "That's not a bad idea. Think about it for the pictures. Me and The Playmaker."

"How about we focus on you and your bride," Piper says, her voice tight.

"Yeah, but you're a given."

Ian holds onto me tight when I start to lunge at Bradley, and offers a patently fake smile. "Let's pump the brakes on the idea of me being involved in your ceremony."

"Right." Bradley grins. "You're here for the party."

"It's also weird as fuck," Ian mutters.

His hand starts making circles on the small of my back, helping me keep my frustration and anger in check. This is Piper's life, and I need to let her make her own decisions, even the bad ones.

"Sadie..." Ian squeezes my shoulder. "How about we head up to the room? I could use a little *rest* before dinner."

"Yeah, big drive up from Skylark, right?" Bradley nods like a bobblehead on crack. "I've heard you're the talk of the town. We should send the chicks in with the luggage and grab a beer at the hotel bar."

Ian winces. "I don't think so, bro." He glances down when Max softly whines.

Even the dog knows Bradley's a tool.

"Sadie, you need to get that thing groomed before the wedding."

"I just bathed him, Brad. Or should I call you Brian?"

A soft giggle escapes my sister's throat, and Bradley shoots her a glare.

"I don't want it shedding all over my tux."

"He's not an *it*, Bradley. He's my Maxie." Piper bends down again, pressing her face into the dog's soft neck.

When she glances up at me, I swear she's blinking away tears, and it about breaks my heart.

"Let's take Max for a hike tomorrow morning before we're due at the spa. Just you and me."

She smiles as she straightens.

"Wear sunscreen and a hat," Bradley says.

"Isn't that cute?" Piper links her fingers with Bradley's, although I'm not sure he notices. "My groom is worried about me."

"Worried about having to pay the photographer to photoshop out a sunburn. Playmaker, I'll take a raincheck on that beer. Seriously, if you don't have plans before dinner, the guys would love to meet you."

Ian pulls me a little closer to his body. "We'll find some way to occupy our time. Don't you worry, B-Rad. We'll see you guys at dinner."

I'm not sure if Bradley picks up on the way Ian's voice has gone deep and gravelly, but my lady parts practically tremble in anticipation.

"Leave Max with me," Piper offers. "I'll take him for a walk." She grabs the leash that's poking out from the top of the tote bag on the ground next to Ian.

"Seriously?" Bradley holds up his hands in a lame kind of protest. "I wanted you to meet my cousin, Kyle."

"Thanks, Piper," Ian says with a smile. "I'm looking forward to getting to know you, too."

A blush rises to my sister's face, which I totally understand, because when Ian Barlowe puts his full attention on you, it's like being bathed in warm sunlight.

All three of us ignore Bradley as Piper hooks the leash to Max's collar and heads away from the hotel. "See you later," she calls over her shoulder.

Bradley mumbles something under his breath.

"You're a lucky guy." Ian chucks him on the shoulder with enough force that my future brother-in-law stumbles back a step. "I hope you realize that."

"Sure," Bradley agrees, rubbing his shoulder. "See you at dinner."

Ian grabs our luggage while I pick up the tote bag, and we head into the hotel.

Neither of us mention the obvious fact that my sister is about to marry a complete asshole, but my mind is racing with worries about Piper's future happiness.

Not enough that I overlook the hotel staff and guests staring at us. I can't imagine getting used to the attention. I checked us in online, and we don't bother stopping at the reception desk since the digital key is on the app. Ian offers a few waves as we move through the lobby, but it's clear he's on a mission to get to the room.

"Bradley seems like a real catch," he says when the elevator doors slide closed behind us.

"I don't think he was that insufferable when we were younger."

"Or maybe you were just too nice to notice."

Too lacking in self-esteem is more like it. "I haven't seen him since I left college after Mom died." I shake my head. "I understand that he was someone Piper knew in a new city, but my sister is amazing. You met her. She's gorgeous and kind. She's a pediatric nurse and has a huge heart. Why is she marrying that..."

"Douche canoe?" Ian supplies.

I laugh, even though it's not funny. "I always knew he didn't like pets. I volunteered at a shelter during college, and he'd complain he could smell the animals on me even after I'd showered. But Max is family to Piper, and he doesn't want her anywhere near him."

My voice catches as the doors whoosh open, and before Ian can answer, I hurry down the hall toward our room. Am I going to be relegated to the same fate as my sister's dog? What if they have kids? Will I even get to see my nieces and nephews? Will Piper ever come back to Colorado to visit? Will Bradley let her? How is she marrying someone who might not *let* her?

I stop at the room as emotions roll over me like a tidal wave. My phone is in my hand, but I can't move.

If I move, I might burst into tears.

What would my mom think of Piper marrying that dick? She'd hate it just like I hate it. And I hate that there's nothing I can do to stop my sister from making a huge mistake. All those years of taking care of her, and now I'm about to fail to protect her from what I have no doubt will be a lifetime of unhappiness.

24

SADIE

"I FAILED MY SISTER." I realize I said the last words out loud and wish I could swallow them back. They expose me and make me feel too vulnerable.

Ian doesn't respond, but takes the phone from my hand, holds it in front of my face to unlock the home screen, and then opens the door to our room and ushers me inside.

"I'm sorry," I say automatically. "I'm sorry for bringing you into this."

"Sweetheart, stop." He deposits our bags on the floor, then wraps his big arms around me. "You don't have to apologize for anything, especially not the behavior of people you have no control over."

He rests his chin on my head, and it feels natural to tuck into the crook of his neck. "For the record, I'm the one who should apologize—in advance. There's a decent chance that tomorrow I'm going to shove a five iron up your soon-to-be-brother-in-law's tight ass."

I laugh against the soft fabric of his shirt, breathing him in. The mix of his soap and the heady male scent that's unique to Ian relaxes me, and at the same time, it makes my head spin.

"If I thought it would make him a better man, I'd beg you to. Although, based on Bradley's reaction to meeting The Playmaker in person, he'd probably have that golf club removed, then hang it on his wall like a trophy."

Ian's laugh rumbles deep in his chest, and I snuggle in tighter. There's something powerful about feeling like I'm not alone, even though I know the reason he's here is because of our fake dating deal.

He smooths his rough hands over my hair, then tips up my head and kisses me. It's gentle and chaste as kisses go, but my body hums to life.

"Thank you," I tell him as he rests his forehead against mine. "You want to take a nap, so I'll be quiet and let you—"

He adjusts his hold on my face so that his thumb is covering my mouth, quieting me.

"When did I say anything about taking a nap?"

"You said you wanted to rest, and I figured you had a late night, so..."

"I said I wanted to come up to the room and relax with you. To be clear, by relax, I mean naked with you screaming my name. Quietly, of course, because we don't need you to get a reputation among the wedding guests. Or do we?"

I choke out a laugh, "A reputation? Me? As if."

"As a screamer," he clarifies.

Oh, well. Wouldn't that be something? "But I'm not a screamer."

He steps back and crosses his arms over his chest. I could melt into a puddle of lusty goo at the intensity of his gaze.

"I take that as a personal challenge." He cocks his head and offers a half smile. "You have to know I'm dying to be with you again."

I shake my head, which feels fuzzy, like it's filled with cotton candy. "I thought after you realized our first time was my first time, you wouldn't be interested again."

"Are you joking?" His laugh is rough. "Sadie, look at me. I mean, look south." He uncrosses his arms and cups the obvious erection straining against the front of his cargo shorts. "Just the thought of a couple of hours alone with you in this hotel room has me harder than the damn Rock of Gibraltar, whatever that is."

I jab a hand in the air, momentarily distracted because I know this one. "It's a limestone monolithic promontory on a peninsula between the United Kingdom and Spain." I'm talking way too fast and not making any sense, but it's the nerves, and I can't seem to shut up. "I got into monkeys one semester as part of my pre-vet undergrad classes, and Gibraltar is home to over three-hundred Barbary macaques. Betcha didn't know that."

Ian shakes his head, his grin widening. "A guy's got it bad when hearing his woman talk geography and monkeys and shit revs his engine."

"I rev your engine?" I ask instead of blurting something about being his woman and how that plays into our future after this weekend.

"Like a fucking Ferrari." He takes a step closer to me. "I need a good, long *rest*, sweetheart. So can we move onto the non-nap portion of the afternoon?"

"Yes, please," I whisper. I may not be experienced, but I'm also not a fool.

He lifts the fitted white T-shirt I'm wearing up and over my head, then reaches around and deftly flicks open the clasp of my bra. Shivers trail along my spine as he drags it down over my shoulders, then cups my breasts in his hands.

"I dream about you like this. I dream about you every night, Sadie. I swear I'm like a damn fifteen-year-old boy taking myself in hand for some relief, but it isn't the same."

My nipples pebble as his thumbs stroke over them, and shimmering heat pools at my center.

"There's that flush," he says as he bends forward and draws his tongue along the base of my throat. "Are you wet for me already, girl?"

I whimper as an answer, and that seems to be exactly what he's looking for because he goes to his knees in front of me and yanks my cotton shorts and panties down over my hips.

Then his finger is inside me, exactly where I want him to be.

"More," I command, even though I'm half afraid my own knees will give way. Waves of pleasure roll through me, and I give myself over to them.

He adds another finger, then runs his tongue along my folds until he sucks my clit into his mouth. Crying out from the exquisite sensation and shock of it—the sparks that flicker through me— I welcome the zing of pain, which only adds to my desire. I just don't know how I'm going to take much more of this and not fall to the ground.

As if he's aware of how close I am to losing control, Ian stands and lifts me into his arms. It's only a couple of steps to the bed. He draws back the covers then lays me on the crisp white sheets— gently, like taking care of me is the most important thing. He's certainly a man on a mission and doesn't waste any time spreading my knees apart and putting his mouth on me again.

I don't know what Ian Barlowe majored in at college, but meeting a woman's needs must have been part of the curriculum.

I'm moaning now, gasping for air as he licks and sucks, his tongue drawing lazy circles around my sensitive center. Letting instinct take over, I reach down and roll one of my nipples between two fingers. My whole body is a live wire, and touch is the only way to ground myself. His touch or mine, I don't care.

"Yeah, sweetheart, that's the way. Touch yourself for me." His breath is hot against me, and I can't do anything but obey.

He takes me to the edge for what feels like hours, until I'm on the verge of screaming, begging, doing whatever it takes for Ian to give me my release. I can't believe I'm letting him—anyone—have this kind of control. I'm the one who takes care of people, but being on the receiving end of his sexual attention is a different kind of power.

It's a choice to let go, to trust and believe that I deserve this.

Ian's fingers pump inside me, an unwavering rhythm that builds until I cry out as the first wave hits me. To be honest, you might even call it a scream. Wave after wave of pleasure rolls through me until I finally return to earth...and Ian.

While my body settles, he climbs off the bed, shucking his clothes in efficient movements. I'm blissed out but still want more. I want him, the two of us. Together.

I sit up and take the condom packet out of his hands, which seem to be trembling slightly. "God, you make me crazy," he says as he climbs back onto the bed.

I want to make him crazy. I want him to feel what I do. I want everything he'll give me. Mostly, I want it to last longer.

But wanting and wishing are for little girls. I'm a grown woman who's going to enjoy this moment and not worry about the future.

He's kneeling over me, but I sit up and push him to his back on the sheets. He lets me, his blue eyes hooded as I reach for his erection. I wrap my hand around the thick shaft, stroking once, then trace the pad of my thumb along the pre-cum at his tip.

He moans and my body responds with its version of a hallelujah chorus. I sheathe his impressive length, then straddle him slowly, lowering myself to take every inch of him. I'm tight, and although the pain isn't sharp like the first time, it takes a few moments for my body to adjust.

A muscle ticks in Ian's jaw and sweat beads on his forehead. "Take your time," he tells me, his voice gruff. "I could stay here all weekend."

I lean down and run my fingers up his defined abs and over his chest, then start to move. My body knows more than my brain about what feels good, so I let it be the guide.

Ian threads his fingers through my hair and lifts enough to

claim my mouth. I taste my desire and his as the kiss deepens, and I move faster, sliding over him as his hands inch down my back.

His nails graze my sensitive skin, and I arch forward when he squeezes my ass. He takes the opportunity to draw one of my taut nipples into his mouth, swirling the tight peak as I ride him faster.

He's urging me toward release, but I'm unprepared for the power of it. Sparks seem to rain over me in a dazzling downpour. I shatter in his arms, and Ian flips me to my back like I weigh nothing, then drives into me.

I wrap my legs around his hips, wanting him deeper, reveling in his frenzied movements like I really am making him crazy. Like he's as affected by our coupling as I am.

A low growl hums in the back of his throat as he finds his own release. This is mind-blowing sex, but also something more—a level of trust I didn't think I'd ever experience. And it means the world to me. He means the world to me.

His hands grip the sides of my head as if he needs me to ground him, and I wrap my arms tight around his neck and kiss his heated skin. It tastes like salt and sweat, and I'm definitely ruined for any other man.

Realization dawns in a jarring flash, like a crack of thunder close enough to make the ground shake beneath me. Because I'm truly, madly in love with Ian Barlowe, my fake boyfriend.

The one thing I knew better than to do. The one thing I promised myself I wouldn't do.

For better or worse, there are no takebacks. As impossible as it felt at the beginning to convince people our fake relationship was real, I'm going to have to work just as hard to convince my heart that these very real feelings don't matter. It won't be easy to put them aside when this ends.

Ian doesn't seem in any hurry to disentangle himself from me, and I blink back the tears that spring to my eyes at the thought of letting him go. Not just now, but when I have to say goodbye to this part of our relationship.

Can we still be friends? Before this summer, I would have said yes. I was so good at hiding and putting aside what I truly wanted to make everybody around me more comfortable. Can I go back to the person I was before?

I don't know that I want to.

Eventually, he pulls out and walks to the bathroom. I watch him go, admiring the view. But as perfect as his body is, that's not what draws me to Ian the most.

It's him and how amazing he is. It's how he makes me feel about myself—like I matter. I spent too long not mattering in my own life.

As the bathroom door clicks shut behind him, I quickly jump up and throw on a pair of shorts, my bra, and T-shirt. I'm too exposed and vulnerable in this moment to stay. We've already established that I have zero poker face, and I don't want to think about what Ian will read in my eyes if I don't get out of here. Now.

The bathroom door opens, and he frowns as his gaze rakes over me.

"Going somewhere?" he asks as I grab a pair of sneakers from my duffel bag.

"I'm going to find Piper and Max," I tell him, my voice casual, like I'm not running away.

"Sadie."

I hear the disappointment in his voice but pretend I don't. Pretending is second nature for me, so this shouldn't feel as hard as it does.

"We're good, Playmaker." I lift up on my toes and press a kiss on his cheek. "I just want to make sure my sis is, too. She needs me this weekend."

He looks like he wants to argue, but nods instead. Because he's a good guy at his core. Good and kind and sexy as sin. And definitely more than I deserve.

"I'll be back before dinner," I promise, still willing myself not to cry.

He doesn't stop me when I slip out of the room, even though the part of my heart I've locked away for too long wishes he would. But wishing and wanting aren't for me.

25

IAN

I'VE HAD some level of fame in my life since I led my high school team back in Oklahoma to a state championship my freshman year. I was recruited to a big college program, earned a national championship and a Heisman nomination, although not the actual trophy. Then onto a successful and lucrative career in the NFL.

Not once, until this summer and Sadie Hart, did I slow down long enough to appreciate the pleasure of being a regular person. I love Skylark, and don't mind admitting that I occasionally pat myself on the back for choosing my new home based on a Buzzfeed article about the happiest towns in America. Happy is awesome. Maybe those articles have more merit than people give them credit for, even if they're mainly used as clickbait.

I've been used as clickbait enough times, but I'm moving past that part of my life. So far, this weekend has been a revelation.

Mountain towns are used to hosting celebrities on a bigger scale than a former football player. Monika might even be able to go incognito here, not that she'd want to. I understand people recognize me, and while Bradley is a douche of the highest level, most of the wedding guests and other visitors at the hotel have left me alone.

But I like being Sadie's plus one. I want to hold her hand and rub her back, leaning in close to smell the sunshine scent of her skin. I like talking and laughing with her and not worrying that she's going to take a picture of my naked ass while I'm asleep or showering and post it on the internet.

I like having sex with her. A lot. And I hate the thought of Sadie with another man, even though the protectiveness swelling inside me is terrifying.

My body and heart have decided she's mine, and there isn't a damn thing my brain can do to convince them otherwise.

Is it time to tell her I don't want our fake relationship to end? What would she say if I told her my feelings are real? What would my daughter think, given that Riva is well-aware of the Barlowe curse?

I appreciate that Sadie is special to her, but she means something to me too, and I don't want to let her go. I like who I am with her, and I'm not ready to let that go either.

We had a pleasant enough dinner with the bridal party last night, although it's weird how Piper and her friends treat Sadie like she's middle-aged. The dress she wore, with a low-cut V neckline and a slit up the thigh, wasn't at all matronly. Although more power to the matrons who want to rock out the midlife sex appeal.

Sadie's body is sexy as hell, and last night, I spent hours worshiping every inch of it. She slept in my arms, and I even convinced Ms. Modest to forgo pajamas and snuggle up skin to skin. It made for a hell of a way to wake up, and I played the best round of golf in my life. Hell, if Sadie and I continue dating for real, they might recruit me for the Senior PGA Tour.

In contrast, the groom got more frustrated with every shanked shot and sand trap he hit. I don't think I'm the only member of the wedding who took pleasure in watching good ol' Bradley pitch a baby fit on the fairway.

But when he ordered a second round of tequila shots at the hotel bar, I did an Irish goodbye. I've already screwed things up with Sadie once because of bad choices while drinking, I'm not going to ruin this weekend for her.

I walk around the corner of the building, and like my heart summoned her, Sadie sits on one of the log benches that borders the trail surrounding the property. Her back is to me, and I take a moment to appreciate the long line of her neck. Her dark blonde hair is piled on top of her head in a messy bun, the ends damp and curling.

As I move closer, I realize she's holding her phone in front of her on a video chat with someone. I don't want to interrupt or infringe on her privacy, so I start to step away but stop when I hear my name. Several oversized SUVs in the parking lot separate us, hiding me from view as I draw closer.

"It's not a big deal, Sloane."

There's an answering laugh on the other end of the line. "Sadie, my days are currently filled with tests and talk of stem cell transplants and chemo. And even I can still appreciate that sex with Ian Barlowe is a big deal. Of all the guys to punch your V-card with, you picked the cream of the crop."

"Only because I knew it would be a better story for you and the book club."

The words hit me like a blindside tackle I never saw coming. The betrayal tightens my chest and makes my gut churn, leaving me breathless and stunned.

"It's the gift that keeps on giving...to all of us," Sloane answers. "I want to hear every juicy detail. Because as vivid as my imagination is, I'd bet money the real deal is even better."

A sick feeling settles in the pit of my stomach, like watching a missed field goal in the last seconds of a playoff game. So close to winning, but now just as empty and hollow as watching a game clock wind down to the end.

I spin on my heel and stalk toward the front of the hotel, not wanting to stand there like a creeper and eavesdrop on my performance in *deflowering* a woman. My inclination is to grab the keys, get in my car, and drive home. Or punch a fist into something just for the satisfaction of the crunch of my knuckles against a rock-hard surface. The physical pain might give me some relief from the mental agony I'm feeling at the moment.

I truly believed Sadie was different from every other woman who wanted something from me, to use me somehow.

How could I have been so stupid?

It's like Felix says—Barlowe men are shit at love. No matter how much I want to be, I'm not the special snowflake exception.

Shit. Do I even have a right to feel this angry and betrayed?

Our relationship was fake from the start. We were each getting something, but that felt different because it was between us.

And I thought things had changed.

I thought Sadie's feelings changed because mine did.

What an egotistical idiot.

I think back to the previous night, the two of us wrapped around each other in the soft sheets. My body runs hot, so I usually kick off the covers before morning. For all I know, Sadie snapped photos of me without me even knowing. Of course I don't believe she would sell them to a tabloid like my previous girlfriend. Yet the fact she might show her friends, or even her sister and the women in the bridal party, makes my stomach turn. But hell, if she's looking to connect and fit in, why not share a laugh over The Playmaker's flaccid dick pic.

I might have been somewhat indiscriminate with the partners I chose, but I'm old-fashioned in my belief that sex is private, something between two people, not to be shared. I've never sent any woman a photo that could be considered sexual or racy. I never took part in locker room chatter, or shared anything about my partners with anyone, not even Felix.

I thought Sadie was the same as me. And I hoped she'd fallen in love the same as me.

Based on the excruciating ache in my chest that's splitting me in two, she isn't going to be easy to get over. Thank God I have a hell of a poker face, because no way will Sadie—or anyone—know how much this hurts. Not that anyone would believe it from a guy like me anyway.

But how do I go back to just being neighbors when my daughter adores her and my heart knows she's the piece that's been missing from it for so long?

I put all of those future worries aside as I quickly shower and dress for dinner. Walking away now would reveal too much. It would show her that she hurt me. The one lesson my dad instilled in me with his fists and cruel words was that the best revenge is not letting someone know you care.

I came too close to letting Sadie in for real, but I'll take that secret to my grave.

I text her on my way out of the hotel, thumbs jamming the phone's home screen like the device insulted my mother.

> Me: I'll meet you at the restaurant.

I'd planned to be at her side during the ceremony rehearsal, which is taking place on the lawn behind the hotel, overlooking several of Colorado's majestic mountain peaks. Instead, I'm taking some time to pull my shit together to put on the show we've agreed to. I'm used to playing injured and under pressure, but never has faking something felt so hard.

Within seconds, she texts back.

> Sadie: You okay? I hope spending the day with Bradley and his buddies wasn't too much. 😔

The smiley face emoji she includes with the message does me in. I have only my own stupidity to blame.

The bar I walk into near the resort is already half-full—not unexpected on a Friday afternoon—and in my dress shirt and sports coat, I don't exactly blend in. Which is fine, because I don't want to. I slap backs and accept drinks from people who aren't my friends and don't know me as anything other than The Playmaker.

This is a different kind of cloak of invisibility, and it's easy to fall back into the persona of the excess-loving athlete. I offer a charming smile to a table of women in their early twenties, and the opening gives them the courage to approach and ask for a picture. I drape my arms around the two flirtiest girls in the group, encouraging them to lean in and plant sloppy kisses on my cheeks.

"Be sure to tag me and our location," I tell them. Several of Piper's friends seem the type to stay glued to their social media feeds.

I'm not doing anything wrong or against the rules of my arrangement with Sadie, but I'm not doing anything right either. And that's just how I want it. She changed the game and I'm the one left watching from the sidelines with a busted heart, anger the only thing left for me to hold onto.

26

IAN

PLAYING the womanizing jock helps ease the pain in my chest the same way slipping into a pair of comfy sweats always relaxes me. Or it could be the alcohol lessening the sting of feeling the connection I trusted slip through my hands like an interception that should have been a perfect pass.

Everybody wants to buy The Playmaker a drink, and I want to numb everything inside me. Win-win.

I can hold my liquor fine, but by the time I exit the bar and head toward the restaurant after two texts from Sadie, I'm feeling fuzzy but no less pissed both at her and myself.

"Playmaker," Bradley calls as I walk into the private dining room of the steakhouse where the rehearsal dinner is being held. "How you doin'?"

"Never better, never better. You ready to be shackled to the ol' ball and chain tomorrow?"

Bradley laughs and gives me an awkward thumbs-up while Sadie's head whips around to stare at me.

"Better you than me." I chuck one of the single groomsmen on the shoulder. "Am I right, Rosin?"

"Hell, yeah," he agrees.

At that moment, a line of waitstaff enters the room, plates in hand, distributing them to the guests. I saunter over to Sadie, who's sitting at a table with two older couples.

"Ian." She grabs my arm in a vise grip. "I'm so glad you're here."

"I bet you are, but there were some important things I needed to take care of first."

One of the bridesmaids sitting at the table next to ours snorts. "Important like multiple rounds of shotskis at the bar two doors down."

The platinum-blonde is wearing a tight dress with a low-cut neckline. She leans forward to give me a better view of her ample cleavage. I manage a smile, but God help me, I need to escape. Unfortunately, playing the part of a dick doesn't come naturally to me anymore.

I wink and point a finger at the bridesmaid. "Right on the money, baby."

Sadie yanks on my arm and I fold myself into the chair next to her. She smells delicious and looks beautiful with her hair falling in waves over her shoulders, which are bare thanks to the strapless dress softly draping over her curves. A bead of sweat drips between my shoulder blades as I remind my body that we are moving on. My body gives me the middle finger in return.

"You remember Bradley's parents, Barry and Connie, from last night, and I'm not sure if you met his aunt and uncle. They arrived earlier this afternoon."

The two couples stare at me. My smile widens. "Barry and I golfed together earlier. You gave yourself an extra stroke on the fourth hole, Bar. Cheaters never prosper and all that."

The uncle chuckles. Sadie gasps as Barry turns beet red. "You must be mistaken. I wouldn't cheat."

"Sure, sure. Let's go with that."

Sadie turns to look me straight in the eye. "What's going on with you?"

"Nothing, sweetheart. Just here for the lolz."

My chest tightens at the look of confusion and hurt she gives me. I need to rein it in and stop acting like a complete jackass. She kept up her end of the bargain with Riva, and no matter how I feel after overhearing her conversation, I owe Sadie. I'm not going to go back on the promise I made, even if it kills me.

"White or red?" A waitress appears at my side and leans in closer than necessary, her breast grazing my arm.

"I'll stick with water for now." Time to switch to a brooding grump versus an outright dick.

Sadie starts talking a mile a minute, as if she can compensate for my sullen attitude. I have a difficult time not inserting myself into the conversation when it's obvious that Bradley's parents are rude, arrogant asswipes who think far too highly of themselves and have no intention of giving Piper or Sadie the respect they deserve.

We've almost made it through the meal when there's a shriek of horror from the other side of the room. I realize it's coming from the table where Piper and Bradley are seated.

"Is there shrimp in the pasta sauce?" Piper shouts. Sadie is out of her chair in a second.

I glance over to see Bradley's mom and dad sharing an eye roll, and then quickly follow Sadie.

"You're going to be okay, Pip. Where's the EpiPen?"

Piper glances around then back to Sadie, her eyes panicked. "Damn it. I left my purse on a bench behind the hotel."

She looks horrible. Her cheeks are red and blotchy, lips and eyes swollen. Bradley lets out an exasperated sigh. "You need to be more responsible, Piper."

"Shut up, Brad," Sadie commands. When he opens his trap to snap back at her, I shift closer and my glare shuts him up. Not as unequivocally as a sharp right, but it's a start.

"I'll get it," I offer. "What does it look like?"

"White with crystal beads," Piper says, her words slurred like maybe her tongue is swelling. That can't be good. "It's on a bench near the wedding arbor."

Sadie reaches for my hand. "She's going to be okay. Her reaction to the allergy isn't anaphylactic, it just looks bad. But please hurry."

"I'll sprint both ways." I might be pissed, but this isn't the time to be petty.

I race back to the hotel, which is less than a quarter mile away, and give a silent prayer of thanks that the purse is still sitting on a bench in the fading light.

One of the bridesmaids, not the blonde, stands just inside the restaurant's entrance when I get back. "They're in the women's restroom." She points toward a hall visible past the main dining room.

I haul ass through the steakhouse, and burst into the bathroom. Sadie grabs the purse from my hand as Piper murmurs, "Thank you," her words slightly garbled.

Bradley and his mother are standing near the bank of sinks, looking equally horrified.

Piper pulls up her dress and Sadie stabs the EpiPen into the skin of her upper thigh, then pulls her sister into a tight hug, reassuring her, "You're going to be okay."

Bradley sniffs. And just when I thought the guy couldn't be any more of a jackass, he shifts into full power-tool mode. "She was going to be okay anyway. The swelling would have gone down on its own or with some Benadryl."

Sadie rounds on him. "Look at her, Brad."

"Bradley," his mom corrects.

"Whatever," Sadie mutters. "We need to talk to whoever scheduled this dinner and oversaw the menu. Obviously, you told them about her shellfish allergy."

"I wouldn't exactly call it an allergy," Bradley says, and I reach for Sadie just in case she's tempted to go after him. He's not worth it.

"That's exactly what it is."

"I always thought of it as more a personal preference," the mother of the groom says, averting her gaze from Piper.

While Sadie now seems rooted in place, I keep hold of her just in case. And because I don't want to let go.

Although Bradley and his mom deserve a good swift kick or a throat punch—whatever fits the bill.

"There's a reason I don't eat at your house," Piper says. Her eyes and lips are looking a tiny bit less puffy, like the EpiPen is already starting to do its thing. "You use a base of fish sauce for every dish."

"It gives the recipes a deeper flavor profile. Umami is all the rage on cooking shows." Connie holds up her hands. "I always thought it was a bit rude that you wouldn't even have a bite."

"I can't eat shellfish." Piper points to her face. "This is what happens."

Sadie jabs a finger at Bradley. "Did you not alert the chef to Piper's allergy?"

"Bradley told his mom," Piper says to Sadie. "This isn't his fault."

But Sadie focuses on Connie Carlson, whose lips looked tighter than a sealed envelope. "Did you tell the restaurant no shellfish?"

Connie sighs and glances at her son. "We know Piper doesn't like shrimp."

"Our paella includes shrimp." A man in a white chef's coat has appeared in the bathroom's doorway. "I apologize for not leaving it out, but we weren't alerted to any allergies and…" He offers Piper an apologetic shake of his head. "The manager specifically asked."

"What the actual fuck is wrong with the two of you?" Sadie asks through gritted teeth.

I might curse like a sailor, but Sadie dropping an F-bomb is serious business.

"Is there anything I can get you?" the chef asks.

"A sharp butcher knife," Sadie answers, taking a step toward B-Rad and his mom. This time, I let her have at it.

The chef takes a step back, letting the door swing shut as Piper reaches out and grabs Sadie's arm. "This isn't Bradley's fault," she insists

Connie crosses her arms over her chest. "For the record, he and I selected the menu together."

"Thanks, Mom." Bradley loosens his tie and looks up at the ceiling like he's hoping for a spaceship to crack open the roof and beam him out of this shit show of his own making. "A lot was going on, and paella is the chef's most popular side dish. I figured you could eat around the shrimp."

"That isn't how a food allergy works." Piper straightens her shoulders. "You're a doctor. You know that. And this is our weekend—our wedding. I'm about to become your wife. I need to know you have my back. The way Sadie has my back."

Bradley massages two fingers against his forehead like this whole thing is giving him a headache. Poor guy. "Oh, right. Saint Sadie. Your favorite protector. You don't need to blow this out of proportion, Pip. You have the EpiPen. Who knows if it even was the shellfish. Maybe there was something else that triggered this reaction. You could have been stung by a bee."

"I'm not allergic to bees." Piper's tone displays way more patience than her douche fiancé deserves. "And I wasn't stung."

"Pretty sure it was the shellfish, Brad-ski," I tell him. "I'm going to remind you again that talking shit on Sadie won't end well for you. Not while I'm around."

Which won't be for long, but I don't mention that. I hate being angry with Sadie, especially when my instinct is to take her into my arms and find a way to make this better. Having Bradley and his mom step into the villain role gives me an excuse to focus my temper on someone else.

Brad-ski moves his hands up and down in front of Sadie and her sister like he's settling a couple of naughty toddlers. "You seem okay now. Let's finish the meal without fuss, then belly up to the bar. The Playmaker has a head start on all of us, so we've got some catching up to do."

"I want to go back to the hotel," Piper says.

"You're going to take her to the hospital for a follow-up, right?" Sadie asks Bradley.

"She's fine. And I'm sure you can handle it, *sis*," Bradley counters. "This is your big chance to swoop in and rescue somebody. You love that."

Ignoring the fact that Brad's a complete dick, he's not entirely wrong. Did Sadie swoop in and rescue me? In a lot of ways, yes, but none that I care to admit at the moment.

"Stop talking shit on my sister," Piper snaps. This is the first time I've heard her—or anyone—defend Sadie.

"It's fine," Sadie mutters, although it's not fine at all.

"Yes, it's fine," the douche canoe in a suit mimics. "Have your little Maxi Pad sister reunion, and I'll entertain our guests." Bradley throws up his hands as he stalks out of the bathroom.

I cringe, because there are assholes, and then there's Bradley Carlson.

"I'm sorry you don't like shrimp," his mother says before following him out.

Piper looks at herself in the mirror, then half-laughs and half-sobs. "This isn't the greatest start to a marriage, is it?" she asks no one in particular.

I take a step toward the door. "I'm going to head out."

"Please stay," Piper whispers as she turns to face us both. "I want to thank you."

Sadie shoots me a wary glance. Maybe she can sense that my shitty mood has returned in full force.

"Thank you for getting the EpiPen, Ian." Piper takes a deep breath. "More importantly, thank you for being the kind of guy my sister deserves in her life."

"Piper, you don't have to—" Sadie begins.

"Let me say this. You always put other people first. Seeing you with someone who puts you at the top is nice. You guys give me hope for love, although I'm not sure I'll find it with my fiancé. But hey, I have eighteen hours to decide." The laugh that spills from her mouth sounds slightly hysterical, but I can't fault her at this point.

"You'll be okay," Sadie murmurs.

Piper swallows hard. "He was right about one thing. Mom did make us believe that men are horrible. Maybe that's why I picked Bradley in the first place. He's safe and familiar. Yeah, I love him. I've known him all my life. I thought I could fall in love with him. I thought safety would protect me from being hurt. It's practical on paper." Piper shrugs and then inclines her head toward us.

"Just like on paper the two of you don't exactly match. In real life, what you have is so special. It's what I want for myself and—"

"Stop." I hold up a hand, unable to listen to one more word about how perfect Sadie and I are. Not when I've been perfectly played. "Your sister and I aren't special. We're not even a couple."

"Ian, what are you doing?" Sadie's brown eyes widen in obvious horror.

I can't stop the words that trip and fall in their need to get out of my mouth. "Come on, Sadie. I know why you picked me. Let's face it, I only agreed because it benefited my daughter. We're both getting something we wanted, but I'm sick of pretending."

Piper's dark brows scrunch into a confused line. "What does that mean?"

"This whole thing—the emotional bond you think you see." I flap my fingers between Sadie and me. "It's fake. Your sister's friends put her up to it. I'm her fake boyfriend for this weekend and...well..."

"Ian." Sadie's voice is dull, empty. It makes me want to take her in my arms, but I'm fresh out of comfort to give.

I make a show of letting my gaze rake down her body. There's that damn blush again, and it infuriates me, mostly because my heart still lurches in response.

"I didn't know quite how far you were going to take using me, but I guess I can't blame you."

Before Sadie or her sister can respond, a voice behind me asks, "Oh my God, is Sadie paying you to date her?"

All three of us turn to see Amanda Sinton standing in the bathroom's open doorway. If things weren't a mess before, they definitely are now.

27

SADIE

Piper reaches for my hand. "Are you okay?"

Amanda steps into the bathroom, and if my knees didn't feel like they were about to give out, I'd walk over and slap the smirk right off her face. "Did you pay for a date to this wedding?"

"No, of course not." I drop my gaze to the floor, wishing it would swallow me whole. I can't breathe. I can't think. Most of all, I can't believe Ian has broken not only my trust but my heart.

"She didn't pay me," he says slowly, no emotion in his words.

Piper holds up a hand when Amanda starts to speak again. "Amanda, get out and keep your mouth shut, okay?"

"Of course, mum's the word," Amanda says. "Ian, we'll talk once we're back in Skylark," she adds before leaving. Her tone is so smug, but as much as I want to smack her, I'd like to smack myself even more.

"Sadie, why?" Piper moves closer to me.

Why? Isn't that the big question? Big—how funny that word seemed in relation to The Playmaker when everything started.

Why did I think I could do this?

Why did I think I could manage not to fall for Ian?

Why did I let him into my heart?

Because now he's broken it. Or maybe I'm to blame.

"It's fine, Piper. It seemed easier, and I didn't...I don't..."

I swallow and try to collect my thoughts and emotions into something that will make sense to either of us. "It started one way, but it's not like that anymore."

I risk a glance at Ian, who is glaring at me so hard I feel like I might throw up.

"I heard you on the phone with your friend," he says. "Talking about your book club bucket list and my part in it."

"Oh, God." I shake my head. Regret makes my limbs heavy. What the hell have I done? I know what I said to Sloane and can easily imagine how it must have sounded to Ian.

Those words were a lie, but at the time, they felt easier than admitting I lost my virginity to a man I fell in love with even though he's so far out of my league it's comical. Sloane has enough to worry about without adding the potential of my broken heart to the list.

How can I explain my convoluted logic now that Ian's revealed there's truly nothing between us? I can't tell him I've fallen in love with him. Would he believe me anyway? Or even care?

It's clear from the set of his jaw and the way his hands are clenched at his sides that he's going to walk away.

He's going to leave me just like everyone leaves me. And the worst part? This time around, it's my own fault.

"I don't believe you." Piper is standing at my side, but she's speaking to both of us. "Sadie, I've never seen you so happy. You can't tell me this isn't real. I don't believe either of you is that good of an actor."

I feel the weight of Ian's stare like he's waiting for my answer.

"At the start, it was for you," I tell Piper. That much is the truth. "I didn't want you worrying about me or to be one more thing that added to your stress."

She blinks a few times, like she's trying to hold back tears, then shrugs. "Since I'm about a hundred percent sure there isn't going to be a wedding, you don't have to worry about my stress. It would have been simpler to talk to me about how you felt. I'm not a little kid anymore. You don't have to protect me or sacrifice your happiness on my behalf. That's never what I wanted."

"I'll move my stuff out of the hotel room," Ian tells me, his voice tight. He's pretending to look at me, but his gaze is focused somewhere past my left shoulder. No emotion. No eye contact. Nothing. "Piper can stay with you tonight. I'll be heading to LA after I pick up Riva. I might even take her to Disneyland for a couple days. Long enough for things to settle down."

"It won't settle."

I won't settle.

I swipe a hand over my cheeks where a few wayward tears have fallen. "Amanda isn't going to keep quiet, so you don't have to worry about staging a break-up scene back in Skylark. The town gossip will be more than enough to keep their tongues wagging."

"That's not how I wanted this to go," Ian says.

Now he's looking at Piper, as if she's the one who needs the explanation.

Why can't I tell him I was lying to Sloane because admitting the truth made me feel too vulnerable? Because I don't know if that would even make a difference, and my pride—no, my heart—can't take any more.

Piper puts an arm around my shoulder. "My sister deserves everything I thought she was getting with you."

He doesn't argue. "She does and more. You also deserve a hell of a lot better than Bradley Carlson. Remember that." Without another word to me, he turns and walks out of the bathroom.

"Do you think we can sleep in here?" I ask Piper with a watery laugh. I'm trying hard not to completely break down, because this weekend is still about my sister. "It might be easier than facing the wedding guests. At least for me."

"I need to call off the wedding," Piper murmurs. "Officially."

She sounds less traumatized by the idea than I'd expect. "I can help with that. For the record, no one would think you should marry Bradley based on how he's been acting. Was he always that much of an asshole? How did neither of us realize it?"

She lets out a sigh. "He had you throughout high school and college, and that also made a difference for me. You make people better, Sads."

"Not *The Playmaker*," I counter. "All I did was manage to make him hate me."

She checks her reflection in the mirror. Her cheeks and eyelids are still pink, but most of the swelling has subsided. "I'm not convinced. After you two started dating—or fake dating if you want to keep telling yourself that—I read up on him and watched his old interviews. The Ian Barlowe who showed up at your side is way different than the man I expected to see."

There's a knock at the bathroom door, and an older woman who isn't part of the bridal party peeks in. "I really need to pee," she says apologetically.

"Come on in." Piper nods. "We were just leaving."

My shoulders tense, but she takes my hand. "I've got you, Sads. Let me be the strong one for once. You're not in this alone. Let's get out of here."

As much as my pride hurts at being outed to Amanda and her grown-up mean-girl posse, my heart has taken a bigger hit. But Piper's words and calming presence ease the ache ever so slightly.

I should be the one comforting her at the moment, but it feels nice to take a break from being the perennial caregiver.

I've always believed that if I wasn't taking care of people, I couldn't offer any value. As if just being me would never be enough. Perhaps it's not for some, but by not opening myself to receiving support in the same way I give it, I've cut myself off from more meaningful connections with the people I care about.

And thanks to my unwillingness to outwardly risk my heart and tell my friends I'm in love with Ian, I've also lost any chance I had with him.

Even though I don't say the words out loud, Piper seems to realize I'm one well-placed side eye away from losing it. We might have that in common, although she's remarkably composed. Were her pre-wedding jitters masking legitimate second thoughts?

Slipping out of the bathroom, she leads me down the hall away from the main dining room. We exit into the alley behind the building. It smells of pine, like the nearby forests, and the scent of cooking from the steakhouse kitchen.

I feel like this beautiful mountain town is ruined for me forever. I won't be able to return without remembering this night and how I torpedoed my own life with my cowardice and dishonesty.

Piper and I are silent as we return to the hotel, but continue to hold hands like we used to when I came back to Skylark right after Mom died. Like we're each other's tether to the world.

I stop at the edge of the hotel property. "Do you think Ian's gone already? I don't know that I can handle seeing him, and I'm fairly certain he doesn't want to see me."

"We'll be fine. You'll be fine," she assures me.

For possibly the first time in my life, I let someone else take control.

My body and heart grow heavy now that the adrenaline and shock of Ian's revelation—and Amanda witnessing it—starts to wear off. I slump against the wall of the elevator and catch the scent of Ian's clean, spicy scent.

Did he take this same elevator down as he left? Would it have changed anything if I'd told him I love him? Does it even matter now?

We enter the room with the digital key on my phone. The bed is made, and the room shows no sign that Ian Barlowe was ever here.

Not even the faintest whiff of him lingers in the air now.

It's hard to believe I spent last night in his arms right here, not to mention the things we did to and for each other before and after sleeping. The desire and tenderness seem like a dream to me now.

I move forward, thanking my legs for carrying me despite the unrelenting weight of my broken heart, and flop onto the bed, covering my face with my hands.

"Do you need anything?" Piper asks as she stands over me.

I shake my head but don't look at her. "I need a do-over on the past hour."

I hear her moving around the room. "What about the past couple of weeks? Would you make the same choices? I can't believe you faked a relationship for me."

"I'd do anything for you, Piper."

"I know, Sadie, and that's a problem. You need to start doing things for yourself."

Not to be crass, but I did Ian for my own pleasure, and look where that got me. I laugh and remove my hands from my face just as Piper tosses a T-shirt toward the bed.

"Change out of that dress. We'll watch a movie while I text Bradley and my bridesmaids. Casey will love handling the drama of a cancelled wedding. Do you want me to order food?"

I shake my head. "I feel sick already. Do we need to discuss the wisdom of calling off your wedding via text?"

"Hell to the no," Piper declares as she undoes the knot at the nape of her neck and shakes out her shiny blonde hair. "It's what Bradley and his mom deserve."

"I'm proud of you, Pip."

"You didn't raise me to be a complete doormat," she says with a wink.

Might be time for me to learn that same lesson.

We both change into comfy clothes. Piper's wearing one of my T-shirts like she used to on visits home from college. Then we climb under the comforter and sheets and move toward the center of the bed until our arms and legs touch.

"I wouldn't take it back," I tell her. "It was wrong and stupid, but I liked being Ian Barlowe's girlfriend, even if it was fake."

"Was it fake, Sadie?"

"No," I admit quietly. "None of it was fake. At least not for me. What a fool I've been to believe his feelings were as real as mine."

She reaches out and links our arms.

"He's a fool for not falling," she tells me.

I turn onto my side so I'm facing her. "Not as much of one as Bradley Carlson."

She glances over at me, but I can't read the expression in her gray-green eyes. Then she rolls her eyes. "What a dick."

"Complete dick." I kiss the tip of one finger and trail it along her rosy cheek. "Let's pretend reality doesn't exist tonight. Tomorrow will come soon enough."

She grabs the remote from the nightstand and flips on the hotel room's television.

"Love you, Sads," she whispers as she scrolls through the channel guide.

"Love you too, Pip," I answer, and we settle in for the night.

28

SADIE

THERE'S an insistent knock at my door Monday morning after the debacle of the wedding weekend.

Piper and I are on the couch, each with a bowl of our favorite sugary breakfast cereal, halfway through season three of *The Gilmore Girls*—which I'd argue is the show's finest.

I've canceled my daycare and training clients for the next twenty-four hours, citing a family emergency. The point could be made that outright humiliation doesn't count as an emergency, but it sure feels like one to me.

I'd argued to no avail that Piper shouldn't be embarrassed about calling off the wedding. Anyone who spends five minutes in Bradley Carlson's company will understand he's transformed from a harmless lout who thought too much of himself to a low-key intolerable asshat.

She doesn't seem to take comfort in the fact that she dodged a Bradley-sized bullet, and annoyingly counters that even though Ian and I started out fake dating, anyone who spends five minutes with us will know neither of our feelings were completely pretend.

We eventually agree to disagree, and since this is our only day to avoid the world together, we focus our attention on Lorelei and Rory.

Tomorrow, Piper drives back to Kansas City and begins looking for a nursing job at a hospital where Bradley doesn't have privileges. And I return to LBI.

Life before Ian. It's a lonely, dull prospect. I thought my life was fine—good even. But he showed me what I was missing, and I want the brightness he gave me. The way he made me feel perfect and loved, even if he never said those words. My heart felt it, and I don't know how to let go.

On the plus side, I'll have plenty of work to keep me busy. My phone has been pinging nonstop with potential bookings. Apparently, taking a few days off hasn't pushed my clients into the waiting arms of the canine experience managers over at Dogapalooza. Even some of my original customers who deserted me for the flashy national chain have been calling to book their dogs.

When the knocking becomes too much to ignore, I abandon our storybook escape, ready to face the music. I half expect to see Sally and Trina on the other side of the door, waiting to lecture Piper and me since neither of us has returned their messages. Instead, Penelope and Daniel, the pilot, stand on my porch.

"Hey, guys." I frown as I notice the two of them holding hands. Penelope has Princess cradled in her other arm, and Beast is staring up at me from a small crate sitting on the porch.

"Did I forget to message you? I'm not working today."

"We need you to take the dogs," Penelope says, more a command than a request.

"Not working," I repeat.

"Permanently," Daniel adds.

"We're moving to London." Penelope gives Princess a little squeeze. "We can't take them."

"My sister doesn't run a shelter," Piper yells from the sofa.

"You love Princess and Beast," Penelope insists.

I see the curtains across the street flutter and step back into the house, waving them forward.

"Since when are you two dating?"

"We met at pick up a couple of weeks ago." Daniel looks a bit sheepish. Maybe Riva hadn't been wrong about him flirting with me. A discerning guy...good to know.

"It clicked from the start." Penelope bats her caterpillar eyelashes at him. Yikes. Those lashes are really something. "Like it was meant to be. You know." She cringes in my direction. "Or I guess you wouldn't since you paid a guy to be your boyfriend."

"I didn't pay Ian," I say through gritted teeth.

"He likes her for real," my sister insists, hitting the mute button on the TV.

Penelope and Daniel share a look but don't argue.

"I got offered a position I applied for months ago. It's at my firm's London office," Penelope explains. "I've always wanted to live in England. I'm a huge fan of the royals."

"She doesn't mean the baseball team," Daniel explains.

"I got that," I tell him.

He smiles at Penelope, and despite my current outlook on love, the affection in his dark eyes seems genuine. "I put in for a transfer to Heathrow, and the airline approved it this morning. We're moving at the end of the week."

"Together," Penelope clarifies.

I blink at the dog cradled in her arms. "Without Princess. Why don't you take her with you?"

"I'd planned on it," she says, looking a tiny bit embarrassed, which is not nearly as ashamed as she should be in this situation. In my opinion, there's a special place in hell for people who treat dogs as disposable. "But we want to travel, and I wouldn't trust her to anyone but you, Sadie. Besides, I don't think she'd like the food in England."

Piper, who's gobbling up cereal and watching this interchange —I gather it's far more interesting than whatever's going on at

Luke's diner—snorts out a laugh. "Dogs are a lifetime commitment," she says. Max is draped across her, blissfully uninterested in any other human or canine while he has Piper's undivided attention.

Penelope's gaze hardens as she glances toward Piper. "You're the runaway bride sister, right? Too young and flighty to commit."

"Ouch," I mutter. "That's not how it went."

"Sadie told me that Max was your dog," Penelope continues, undeterred. "But you left him here instead of taking him with you even though you're done with college and working a steady job."

"This is Max's home," Piper says quietly. "It's my home, too."

I'm not sure if she believes her own words, but they warm my heart.

"Maybe you can arrange for Ian Barlowe's daughter to adopt Princess," Penelope suggests. "You know, since she already tried to steal her."

Ah, yes. Just what I need—a reminder of how my current mess got started.

"The point is, we can't take either of these..." She frowns at Beast's crate as if reluctant to put him in the same category as Princess, but finally relents when Daniel squeezes her hand. "Either of these dogs. Please, Sadie. We can't drop them at the pound. Who would adopt Beast?"

Over the years, I've helped several families re-home dogs who weren't a fit, but I've never agreed to take responsibility for one myself. However, having been so recently rejected, I can't bear to do that to another creature, man or beast. Or, in this case, Princess or Beast.

"I'll keep the dogs. But only until I find good homes for them," I tell the unlikely couple.

"Thank you so much." Penelope sounds equally relieved and shocked that I didn't put up more of a fight. Story of my life. She leans in as if to hug me but transfers Princess to my arms.

"Thanks, Sadie," Daniel echoes.

"Get the stuff from the car," she commands, and he snaps to attention like a soldier taking orders. "Quick," she whispers, then winks at me. "We wouldn't want Sadie to change her mind."

"I won't change my mind."

"Even though she should," Piper calls out.

Max finally sits up to check out the new arrivals, then yawns and lays back down on Piper's lap.

"I don't care what people say about how pathetic you are." Penelope crouches down to open Beast's crate. "You're a good person, which is what counts."

An interesting, if backhanded, compliment.

"Of course, you're going to have clients queued up around the block after that video," she tells me, crossing her arms over her chest.

Panic grips my chest. "What video?" More like, what new fresh hell is this?

Penelope ignores my question. "Queue is how they say line in England."

As my scrambled brain tries to process what video she's referencing, Daniel comes through the front door with a giant clear tub of dog accessories that appear perfect for Penelope's pampered pup. The box contains an assortment of bows, floral-patterned bandanas, and frilly dog dresses in shades of pink, lavender, and baby blue. And of course the fuzzy sweater Princess usually wears on cold days.

"If you take her picture, make sure she's wearing pink." Penelope picks a dress out of the tub. "It's her best color. She's sure to be adopted wearing pink. As far as Beast—"

"My mom loved him," Daniel interrupts, a hint of warning in his tone.

"Of course she did, bless her heart." The words roll off Penelope's tongue with the lilt of a Southern accent, even though she was born and raised in Colorado.

I decide to ignore the canine fashion advice. "What video?" I repeat. My heart clenches, wondering if someone recorded and then posted the humiliation I endured this weekend.

"The one of you breaking up the dog fight at Dogapalooza. You did your whole dog whisperer thing and calmed those two menacing animals."

"They were scared, not menacing," I clarify.

"Whatevs." Penelope waves a hand. "Somebody filmed the whole thing and posted a highlight reel to Insta. They tagged Dogapalooza, and I heard a ton of people have canceled their contracts."

Daniel's phone beeps. "Babykins, we gotta go. The realtors are at my house."

Babykins? I try not to make a face like I'm smelling a fresh pile of dog poo.

Daniel holds out a hand to high-five me. "I've got a bidding war on my hands. Only owned the house three years, and it's almost doubled in value. You could make a ton on this place."

"I'm not looking to sell." I leave him hanging on the high five.

Penelope grabs his hand and links their fingers. "We're renting a flat in Mayfair. It's the neighborhood for polite society."

"Like the Bridgertons," Piper interjects, her tone dripping with sarcasm.

"I'm sure it's lovely." I glance over my shoulder toward Piper, who's on her phone—checking out the reel, I assume. "I didn't realize anyone was filming me."

"It's got ten thousand likes." Piper's eyes widen as she stares at me. "You've gone viral, Sads."

"Babykins, gotta go," Daniel repeats.

Penelope pats her dog's head and blinks back tears. "Be Mommy's good girl. Remember, you are royalty." She glances up at me and swipes a hand over her cheeks. "It's true. She comes from royal bloodlines. You should put that in the adoption notice."

Beast rolls onto his back and lets out a whispered fart.

"Good luck," Daniel says with a grimace. Then they turn and walk out, shutting the front door behind them.

"You should see these comments," my sister says. "You're a hero. And there are at least a dozen companies interested in a collab."

"I don't *collab*." I kiss the top of Princess's soft head. "I don't want that kind of publicity. I don't want any publicity."

My phone rings again, and I switch it to Do Not Disturb. I'm famous on social media and infamous in my town. This should give the neighbors something to talk about for the rest of the summer.

There's another knock at the door. Beast barks while Princess wiggles in my arms. Max still won't move.

"Piper, can you take them out back to do their business?"

She groans and hugs Max's neck. "I didn't agree to take in somebody else's rejects.'"

"They aren't rejects," I tell her as I walk to the door, still holding Princess.

She sounds just like she did back when she was a moody teenager, which almost makes me smile. Not quite, but almost.

Penelope probably left the jeweled collar collection in the car. But when I open the door, Iris, Molly, and Taylor stand on the other side.

"Is that Penelope Frecker's dog?" Molly asks. "I don't think I've ever seen her unaccessorized. That dog has more outfit changes than a Cher concert."

"She's embracing the natural look." I breathe out a laugh that ends as a sigh. "This isn't a great time, guys."

Taylor holds up a box of cupcakes. "We came to commiserate and make a plan for your next big move."

"I'm out of moves."

"Are you sure?" Iris turns to look at the house next door. "When Ian comes back—"

"Who knows if he's coming back?" I counter. "Maybe our joint humiliation was enough to convince him to stay in LA."

Iris shakes her head. "He has to come back. A picture with The Playmaker is the big draw at the fun run fundraiser for the elementary school next week."

Great. That will give Amanda a perfect opening to make her move.

"Are you going to invite us in?" Molly asks, her smile gentle.

"You're invited," Piper calls, pushing Max off her lap and getting up off the couch.

She waves to my three friends. Her smile is only tight at one end, which is an improvement. "Nice to see you all." She steps forward and takes Princess from my arms.

"I'm going to take these guys out for a potty break."

"Sorry about your wedding." Molly reaches out to give Piper a quick hug. Molly is a hugger. "Bradley Carlson is a doofus."

"That's a kind word to describe him. Good riddance and all that." She disappears through the back of the house, and I hear the sliding door open and then close behind her and the dogs.

"This is hitting her harder than she's letting on," I tell my friends.

"What about you?" Iris gestures to the set up in front of the TV. Lorelei Gilmore's face is frozen on the screen. "I reserve binging Stars Hollow for desperate times."

"I'm not worried about how ditching Bradley affects me. I just want Piper to be happy."

"I don't think Iris was talking about Bradley," Taylor says.

"It's fine," I lie. "The whole business of people thinking I paid Ian to date me will blow over eventually. Did you see the Dogapalooza video? Maybe going viral as the Skylark dog whisperer will work in my favor."

I grab the empty cereal bowls and carry them to the kitchen as my friends follow me.

"Sweetie," Molly says gently, "we're not talking about the scandal or the gossip."

"Who's up next on the bucket list?" I desperately want to change the subject. "Is it you, Iris?"

She comes up behind me at the sink, takes the sponge out of my hand, and spins me around. "We're talking about your feelings for Ian."

What am I supposed to say? "It was always going to end. That was the agreement. He lived up to his part of the bargain, and he didn't mean for Amanda to overhear him explaining the situation to Piper."

"You like him." Taylor places the box on the counter and opens it, handing me a chocolate cupcake with a swirl of white icing. "We've seen you two together. He likes you, too."

I'm gripping the edge of the sink so hard my knuckles are turning white. I force myself to take the cupcake, trying not to completely lose it. "I did something really stupid."

I unwrap the dessert while glancing out the back window. Piper paces across the yard, the dogs following, eyes fixed on her back. I smile as I remember how she used to help me with the training. She had a knack for it, even though she didn't want to admit it. But she has even more of a gift with people, which is why nursing is the perfect profession for her. I hope the fear of running into Bradley doesn't stop her from pursuing the career she's wanted since elementary school.

"I video-chatted with Sloane from Nashville the night of the rehearsal dinner. I was outside, and I thought I was alone. She kept questioning me about the bucket list and checking it off with Ian."

I take a small bite of the silky icing. Although the sweetness hits my tastebuds with a rich, buttery flavor, I place the cupcake on the counter. I don't want to enjoy anything right now. Not with how badly my heart hurts.

"I told her having sex with him didn't mean anything. That I picked him because it would be a better story for the book club. Ian overheard me."

"But you didn't mean it," Molly says.

"I said it, and he doesn't know any better."

"Tell him you were lying." Iris picks up my discarded cupcakes and digs in.

"So he can reject me for falling in love with him? That sounds like a great idea. Great way to—"

"It's not about saving face, Sadie. It's about finally growing up and taking responsibility for your own life." Taylor speaks quietly, but the words land like she screamed at me.

I throw up my hands. "Responsibility? I've been responsible for my life and my sister's for a decade."

"You use Piper like a shield," Iris says. "You have a big heart, and you're there whenever anyone needs you. I don't know how you ended up with Penelope's dog and that other...whatever that creature is, but no doubt it's because of your kindness."

"She's right," Molly agrees. "Your kindness comes at the price of your happiness. If you're not being true to yourself, no one will know the true Sadie."

"Why would they want to?" I counter. "If I wear the mask people expect to see, they get what they want, right? My sister is here so I can support her through the wedding disaster. I've taken in two dogs that I shouldn't have. I'm best when I'm helpful Sadie. Why would anyone want something other than this version of me?"

"Because we love you," Molly tells me, "and we want you to be happy. Not to only make everyone else happy. And you can't know what Ian wants if you don't give him a chance to tell you."

"Sadie, honey." Iris wipes a hand across her mouth. "If you don't give us a chance to love you for who you are, not who you think we want you to be, you'll never be loved that way."

"It's scary." Taylor tilts her head, gaze gentle. "You can do scary things. You've created a great life for yourself—a career, raising your sister..."

"Good friends," Molly adds.

"The best friends," Taylor agrees. "The story here isn't you having sex for the first time with somebody famous. Whether you're ready to admit it out loud or not, you had sex with a man you love. That's a big deal."

"I hope you wore the good underwear," Iris says.

I roll my eyes. "He didn't care about my underwear."

"That's what I've been telling her." Piper steps back into the house but closes the door before any of the dogs can enter.

I cross my arms over my chest and lean back against the edge of the counter. "We never talked about my underwear."

Piper flips me the bird. "Because the important part is that Ian Barlowe has real feelings for you, no matter how fake things were at the start."

"Listen to your sister." Molly points at Piper. "She's smarter than her choice of fiancés would lead you to believe. No offense."

"None taken," Piper says with a genuine smile.

"Even if you're right..." I shake my head. "It's too late now. I let him go."

"It's never too late for love," Iris says, a wistfulness in her voice I wouldn't have expected. "We just need to figure out how we're going to fix this."

29

IAN

"Dad, you have to fix things with Sadie."

I reach across the console of the SUV and pat my daughter's thin arm. We touched down at the private airport south of Denver about an hour ago, after being in LA for a week. My daughter and I needed some time away from Colorado to catch a break from the gossip that was sure to follow in the wake of Piper Hart's canceled wedding.

"There's nothing broken, Rivs," I tell her, my voice confident even as my heart lurches like it's taking that first giant plunge on a roller coaster track. "You were there when Sadie and I agreed to pretend date. Maybe things got a little carried away, but we both did our part and now it's over."

"She likes you, Dad." Riva yanks her arm away and growls in frustration. It sounds remarkably like a sound I'd make, which is oddly satisfying. "And you like her, and I like her more than any of the bubbleheads you've dated before now."

"Bubbleheads? Is that necessary?"

"Mom called them bubble butts, but I'm trying to be nice."

I could say something about my ex's propensity to flit from

one on-set romance to another, but I choose to be the bigger person because my daughter needs me to.

Besides, it's not the point. Overhearing Sadie trivialize our relationship left me with a yawning sense of betrayal and the uncomfortable feeling of having been used for my body and fame. But, in the end, she probably did us both a favor. I'm not sure how to be in a real relationship, and I would have screwed things up eventually anyway. If I'd admitted my feelings before knowing hers weren't the same, the humiliation would have made the pain so much worse.

How do I explain that to my daughter without admitting I'm the problem? She probably already knows it, but I desperately want her to see me as someone better. I want to be that better man.

"Sadie and I can still be friends," I tell her, even though I likely ruined that chance by letting anger dictate my actions.

I should never have told her sister or anyone about the terms of our arrangement. I can pretend I did it for Piper, but the truth is I was butthurt over what I heard. Ironic, because if you asked most of the women I've dated, they'd tell you I don't have the capacity for hurt because my heart isn't capable of it.

"I think you'll like the bigger house I'm looking at," I tell Riva. "It's got a barn and lots of land. Enough room for a pool."

"I like our house." Great. Even the pool isn't enough of a carrot to entice my kid. "I like living next to Sadie so I can help her."

I like living next to Sadie, too, but I'm not sure my pride—or my heart—can take being so close to her with how things ended. It's time to break out the big guns. "I talked to your mom about our current living situation."

Her head whips toward me. "I don't want to go to boarding school, Dad. Please. I'll move to whatever house you want. Can we stay in Colorado?"

"Of course we're staying, sweetie. No boarding school. That isn't on the table."

"I overheard you and your agent talking." Her voice is low and careful. "He wants you to move to LA or some other big city because there are more opportunities for work."

My heart squeezes at the worry in her voice. "You only heard part of the conversation, Rivs. I told Phil if Colorado makes you happy, there's no chance of me living anywhere else."

"Really?" She doesn't look convinced. "So what are you going to do for work now that you aren't a quarterback? Mom always said you don't know how to be you if you aren't playing football."

Wow, Monika really has no problem throwing me under the bus and then backing over my body a few dozen times. I guess I brought it on myself by being an absentee father for so many years, but I'm going to prove to both of them I've changed.

"I can be me just fine without football," I lie. The more challenging part might be being me without Sadie in our lives. "Let me figure out the future, kid. But you're my top priority."

"Okay," she whispers with an almost shy smile. One that gives me hope she might believe me.

"Speaking of the future, we should revisit the no-pet rule your mom established."

"Are you serious?" The joy on her face makes me want to buy an entire damn zoo. "Are you going to let me get a dog?"

"Your mom and I discussed it." I nod. "I explained to her that having a dog would be good now that we're settled in Skylark."

The squeal that greets my words could break glass, but it also makes me grin. I hold up a hand before Riva can take off with her plans. I know she has them. "There are some non-negotiable conditions you need to agree to first. As you've learned working with Sadie, dogs are a big responsibility. They need to be trained and exercised every day. You have to be willing to do the bulk of the work."

"I will, Daddy." Killing me with the daddy again. "I'll do it all. Sadie taught me, and she's the best."

No argument from me, because Sadie being the best is an

undisputed fact. I hold up one finger. "When you visit your mom, even if it's for an extended period or she sends the private jet for you, the dog stays with me. No guilt trips or making her feel bad that she's allergic."

"Is she really allergic?" my daughter grumbles.

"Not for you to question," I remind her. "The dog will be yours, but only at my house. Got it?"

I can see that she wants to argue but can't quite stop smiling. "Got it."

"Then let's talk specifics." I gesture to my phone on the console between us. "Check out the last text. There are some puppy pics I think you might like. A golden retriever would be a good starter dog. I found a breeder about an hour and a half from here. A litter will be available around the start of the school year. Champion bloodlines and—"

Riva tosses the phone back to me like it's a poisonous snake. "We have to adopt a dog, Dad." Back to Dad again. "A dog who needs us."

"These puppies need a good home."

"I already know what dog I want, Daddy." Suddenly, the daddy term feels ominous. "Two dogs."

"Whoa there, kiddo. Let's not get ahead of ourselves."

"They need me."

"Who needs you?"

"Princess and Beast. I follow Sadie's sister on Insta, and she posted that Sadie is helping to rehome them."

"Beast isn't a dog, Rivs. He's a chicken with floppy ears."

A horrified gasp greets my words, even though we both know it's true. "That's so mean, Dad. He needs me because I can love him for who he is."

A shot straight to the heart.

"Princess is super easy," she tells me. "She even potties on pee pads in the house."

"Not a selling point," I mutter as visions of a friendly, loyal, good-natured—not to mention good looking—retriever vanish from my mind. "Besides, I thought that dog's owner was obsessed with her."

That was how the whole fake dating deal started. I refrain from reminding either of us of this fact out loud.

"Penelope had to move and couldn't take her." Riva cocks her head. "Princess also comes with her own wardrobe. Penelope gave everything to Sadie."

I roll my eyes. "Um...do I look like a match for a dog who wears dresses?"

My daughter turns in her seat to study me. Her face is illuminated in the afternoon sun coming through the front windshield, the freckles across her nose making her look younger than the young woman she's on the cusp of becoming. I can't get back those years I wasted focusing on myself and my career instead of her, but I'll make the most of every moment going forward, even if it means welcoming a chicken-dog and a pup with a penchant for playing dress up into my life.

"Do you remember when I was into having my hair done and you learned how to do braids?"

It was the year she turned eight. Monika had to do a last-minute press junket, so Riva spent two weeks with me. "I sucked at braids."

"Yeah," she agrees, wrinkling her nose. "But you tried. And when I was tiny, you let me paint your fingernails sparkly pink."

I glance at my giant hands on the steering wheel, thinking about the few and far between weekends when Riva would come to stay with me as a toddler. I had my assistant buy loads of the top-rated toys for preschool-age girls. All my daughter wanted to do was make blanket forts, have tea parties, and take turns painting each other's nails.

I didn't understand it at the time, but now I realize being a good parent isn't about the toys or VIP tickets to Disney. Riva had been trying to connect with me and forge a bond.

I was too stupid and selfish to appreciate it at the time, but I get it now.

"Basically, I'm going to say yes to the pampered pooch and chicken dog because I'd do anything for you."

She flashes a *duh* grin. "Exactly."

The kid is not wrong, and I'm glad she knows it. I want her to feel secure in my love, the way I never did from my dad.

I pull off the exit for Skylark and head in the direction of our neighborhood, dread settling like a boulder in my gut. "To be honest…" I clear my throat, unsure how to broach the subject that needs to be discussed before we get home. "I'm not sure Sadie will let me have the dogs. I know I told you she and I are still friends, but I'm not sure if that's true. There's a decent chance she won't want anything to do with me. I said some things that were not very nice to her in Vail."

"Why?" she asks quietly, and I'm surprised at her calm tone.

I shrug. "I was mad and hurt and I acted like an as—like a jerk. Football gave me an outlet when things got tough in real life. I could work out being angry or frustrated on the field. I'm not good with emotions, kid, but you know that already."

"You do okay."

Those three words feel like the biggest compliment in the world.

"Adopting Beast and Princess will help fix things with Sadie."

I pull onto our street, and sweat beads on my forehead as her house, and mine come into view. I owe her an apology, and I suck at apologizing more than I do at braiding hair.

Thinking about Riva's misinterpretation of the snippet of conversation she overheard between my agent and me makes me pause. Should I have given Sadie a chance to explain her call with her friend. It seemed obvious that she used me based on her words, but maybe I missed a bigger piece of the puzzle. Maybe I'd been looking for an excuse to end things because going all-in felt too risky for my heart, and when her words met my fear, assumptions took over from logic.

"Something tells me it won't be that easy."

"You can sign up for obedience lessons," Riva suggests as we get out of the SUV. "That's a great way to spend time with Sadie."

"Okay, kid." I hold up a hand as I grab our luggage from the back. "Another stipulation—no more matchmaking from you or anyone else."

She purses her lips and glares at me. Apparently poop scooping and exercising a dog are more straightforward parameters to agree to than giving up on Sadie Hart and me.

The truth is I don't want to give up on us either. I've never felt this way. And I might not be the sharpest knife in the drawer, but I'm smart enough to realize how precious that is. How special Sadie is. Even if loving her means opening myself up to a whole world of potential hurt.

"Can I text Sadie right away about Princess and Beast?"

"Let's sleep on it at least one night to make sure you don't change your mind."

"I won't."

"One night."

She sighs dramatically as she turns back to me from the door leading into the laundry room. "First thing tomorrow, so somebody else doesn't adopt them first."

"Highly unlikely, but fine."

"You never know now that Sadie is famous."

She doesn't add an explanation, but I still cringe. I'm not sure if famous is the right word. Possibly infamous in this town based on what I did to her. Right now, I feel like as big of a douche canoe as Bradley Carlson, and that's a rough pill to swallow.

"You're the best, Dad. I love you," she calls over her shoulder and disappears into the house, the door slamming behind her.

She loves me. She said it out loud. Once again, the thought of becoming a zookeeper holds a ridiculous amount of appeal. Still,

I'm agreeing to a dog—two because I'm a pushover. But I'm doing it so she knows I can commit. I'm going to be a good dad. Set limits and rules.

I'm about to hit the button to close the garage door when I hear someone walking up the driveway. My breath catches as I turn, hoping it might be Sadie. I want to see her like I want my next breath, even if she's only here to read me the riot act for ruining her reputation in town.

Instead, her friend Sally stares at me, arms crossed. If looks could kill, I'd be long gone by now. I didn't give Sally or her wife an explanation when I picked up Riva early, but it's clear she knows exactly what happened in Vail.

"You don't have to tell me I screwed up," I say, placing the suitcases on the ground. "I didn't mean for anyone but Piper to hear about the fake dating."

"No one was supposed to know," she says, one Converse-clad foot tapping her temper onto the driveway.

"Did you know about her plan to get me into bed so she could tell her book club about it?"

Sally lifts her aviator sunglasses to the top of her head. "Are you going to whine to me because you think sweet as spun-sugar Sadie Hart used you for your body? Pretty sure The Playmaker nickname was as much inspired by your activities off-field as on."

She's not wrong, but she's not exactly right either. I'm not saying I didn't make mistakes. "I never kissed and told," I tell her, my voice measured. "Let alone fucked and told."

Sally doesn't bat an eye at my crass summation. "She didn't choose you because it made a good story. Don't get me wrong, I'm not a fan of the fact that her virginity was out there for public consumption in that bucket list challenge, but she did it for the right reasons."

I raise an eyebrow. "Such as?"

"She has a friend who might die and who has a long, scary,

unknown journey ahead of her. A friend asked Sadie to face fear alongside her. That's what you're missing here, Ian."

The fact that Sally uses my name, instead of the nickname I'm quickly coming to hate, means something. I cross my arms over my chest, matching her body language. "Explain."

"Sadie may have fooled herself into believing it, but her biggest fear was not the physical act of having sex." Sally takes a step forward and leans in like I need to pay attention. "Her biggest fear is real intimacy. She's never loved anyone who's loved her back unconditionally."

I scrub a hand over my jaw, but it doesn't relieve the tension. "Plenty of people have plenty of sex without being in love," I say with a laugh. "I'm one of them."

"Trust me...I was one of those people too. When I met my wife, it was different, and, more importantly, scary as hell. For the record, Sadie isn't like you and me. She can act like she's never had an opportunity or that she's been friend-zoned to death, but sex is easy to come by. We both know it. Intimacy, not so much. Love is one in a million."

Don't I know it.

She inclines her head. "Have you ever had sex with someone you truly loved?"

"None of your business," I snap, but look away because I don't want her to see the truth in my eyes.

"It's different," she repeats. "It's all Sadie knows. You are all she knows."

Some primal protective beast roars to life inside me at those words. "What if you're wrong?" I can't believe I've exposed my soft underbelly like this. I can't let myself feel this vulnerable. It's like trying to throw a pass outside of the pocket with no protection, wearing nothing but a pair of boxers. A sure way to get pummeled, body and soul.

"What if I'm not?" she asks. "Are you going to take the chance of missing out on something right? Because it feels right, doesn't it?"

"More than I ever expected," I whisper.

And as much as Sadie hurt me, I might have done even worse to her. "People are going to rake her over the coals for the fake dating lie."

"Oh, buddy, you've got a lot to learn about small towns." She shakes her head. "Maybe Amanda and some of the other thirsty women hoping you're up for grabs feel that way. The rest of us love Sadie. She's one of us. She's the best of us."

Sally wags a finger in front of my face. "If you want another chance with her, you'll need to convince the whole town to give you one. It's going to take more than an autographed football or a round of beers. It's going to take you getting real. Can you do that?"

The honest answer? I don't know. Other than football, I've never tried to get real before Riva came to live with me, and Sadie is the person who showed me how to do it.

"I'm not sure I know how to be real." Or win a woman back. I've never had to try that hard. I've never cared about making an effort for anything other than football, and more recently, my daughter. But I want to try for Sadie.

I'm a lot of things, but a coward isn't one of them. If it takes me a thousand years and adopting every reject dog I can get my hands on, I'm going to try to be the man who deserves the love her friend is convinced she has for me.

"You know what every great player needs before they go into the big game?" I ask Sally.

She cocks her head. "A hype man holding an energy drink?"

"A coach," I say. "Welcome to the team."

She stares at my outstretched hand for a long moment then laughs. "Wait until my wife hears about this," she murmurs and gives me a mighty shake.

30

SADIE

I WAKE up early to bake a batch of muffins for Piper before she starts her drive to Kansas City. She's planning to leave before the first of my day school clients arrives, or possibly before any more of my friends stop by unexpectedly.

Penelope was right about the effect of the viral video. I'm booked solid for the next three months and my waiting list is long —both for boarding and training.

I hate that dogs in crisis are the reason my business is flourishing again, but I'm not turning people away. Mona, my former assistant, reached out last night and asked if I needed help, so things must be bad over at Dogapalooza.

My gaze flicks to the window facing Ian's house. The blinds are down, but that doesn't stop me from feeling his presence. I lost too much sleep last night after realizing he and Riva had returned home.

I owe him an apology and an explanation. If my friends have anything to say about it, that convo will lead to me telling him I love him and the two of us will ride off into the sunset together.

Not sure I have the nerve to open my heart with the potential of having it shattered again, but it's important he knows that I wasn't using him for a memorable V-card story. I'm embarrassed I lied to Sloane and owe her an apology as well.

I've always prided myself on accepting myself for who I am, but my behavior in the past few weeks hasn't lived up to that.

A fake relationship seemed harmless when Sally and Trina suggested it, and the idea of boring me being linked to snack-and-a-half Ian was exciting at the start. Then I got to know him—the real him—and I fell hard.

Beyond his public image, he's deeply genuine and unpretentious. He listens and makes me feel seen in a way I haven't felt before. Despite his past in the spotlight, Ian also values the quieter, intimate moments that matter most to me.

He's a devoted dad, and with him I feel safe and cherished. I was careless with his heart, and I'm so sorry for that.

Hurting people—even accidentally—isn't my idea of excitement.

I hear Max's footsteps on the staircase. Princess and Beast have already eaten and been out for the morning, but Max slept in Piper's room. The dog is going to be forlorn when she leaves, but hopefully she won't stay away so long. Or maybe Max and I will take some time off and drive to Kansas City to see her.

I turn to greet her, then blink when I realize she's still wearing pjs, yawning like she had about as much sleep as me last night.

"You're supposed to be leaving early. Change of plans?"

She walks over, grabs a muffin from the wire rack, and pours a large mug of coffee. My sister can't function or speak in the morning until she's had at least a few sips of caffeine. She pours a generous amount of creamer into her cup then gulps down several giant swigs.

"Pump the double-shot brakes, Pip. And take a bite or you'll get the jitters."

She gives me an indulgent smile. "I could drink the whole pot and stay calm as a Tibetan monk. Don't forget that most of my

CNA shifts during nursing school were overnight. Sometimes it felt like I was mainlining coffee."

"Hopefully, those days are behind you. Have you thought about where to look for a new job, a non-hospital position?"

She slides into one of the chairs at the kitchen table and crinkles her nose. "I like working in the hospital."

"Then you and Bradley will have to—"

"I'm going to apply to the county hospital here."

My mouth falls open. "You want to stay in Skylark?"

Max whines at the back door, and I let him out to do his business. Princess and Beast follow him into the yard, so I leave the slider open.

"Would it be too much of an imposition if I stayed with you until I get settled?" she asks with a timid smile. "I can find someone to sublet my place in Kansas City easily enough, but I'm tapped out from wedding expenses."

My mind is whirling with everything there is to unpack from this conversation. I start with the most straightforward question. "Why are you tapped out? When I offered to help, you told me the two of you had it handled."

"The *me* part of we had it handled," she admits, lifting the mug to her mouth.

"Piper, he's a doctor." I shake my head as I drop into the seat across from her. "Besides, I know you have student debt even with Mom's life insurance money and your job."

"Every time I mentioned an expense, he acted like I was spending frivolously. His mom made me feel like a cheapskate when I tried to cut corners. I didn't want to ask you, so I took out a wedding credit card. I figured once we were married, I could pick up a few extra shifts, or he'd be willing to help pay it off because of how great everything went."

I wince at that. "First, of course, you're welcome to stay here. It's your home, Piper." I reach across the table and take her hand. "If you need help, let me—"

"Sadie, stop. I don't want you to rescue me." She yanks her hand away with a pleading look. "Just be my sister, okay?"

Right. This is new me, not trying to fix everything for everybody. "Fine. You can stay here, but you'll either help with groceries and do chores or pay my rent."

The words sound funny coming out of my mouth and Piper laughs. "Way to put your foot down, sis."

"It's a start," I say, and walk around the table to hug her.

"It's a new start for both of us," Piper agrees. "One where I finally learn how to take care of myself, and you let me."

"I like that for both of us," I say.

"Me too," she agrees and hugs me a little tighter. "I'm sorry it took me so long to grow up. And I'm sorry I didn't bring Max to live with me when I graduated. Maybe if I'd had a decent man in my life, even the canine variety, I wouldn't have settled for Bradley."

"Max loves you no matter what. So do I."

She tears off a generous piece of muffin and pops it into her mouth. "Thank you for everything. Not just recently, but everything you sacrificed after Mom died."

"She'd be proud of you for calling off the wedding."

"Mom would have hated Bradley." She grins up at me. "But she would have liked Ian."

"You don't know that."

"Pretty sure I'm right, though." She takes the last bite of muffin and stands. "I'm going to shower, then start figuring out my next chapter."

"Wipe your crumbs first, please."

"Taking your hard-ass era seriously, huh?"

"It's about time."

"Agreed." She looks over her shoulder as she wets a paper towel. "Maybe your book club will let me join, I could do with my own bucket list challenge."

As happy as it makes me that Piper is going to stay in Skylark, I want her to find her own way. She needs that. We both do. "Could be that starting over is enough of an adventure for now."

"Maybe." She winks and begins to wipe the crumbs off the table. "Do you regret making your non-existent sex life a part of your bucket list?"

"No longer non-existent," I remind her. "And, no, I don't regret being with Ian. But I do owe him an apology. Even if it doesn't make a difference, I want him to know our time together meant something to me."

Because, if I'm being honest, it meant everything.

I glance out the kitchen curtains toward his house. "I just need a bit of time to figure out what to say."

Her smile is knowing. "You'll figure it out. He's a good guy. You deserve a good guy. Don't sell yourself short." She tosses the paper towel into the trash. "People make mistakes, but most of them are fixable."

"Hey, Piper?"

She turns at the base of the stairs, Max at her feet. "Hay is for horses."

I smile because that's a bit we did when she was little. "I'm taking Princess and Beast to the farmers market and fun run this afternoon."

"Good for you. I hope someone falls in love with them both."

My hands curl into fists as I work up the nerve to continue. "Ian and Riva will probably be there. Is there any way you'd go with me as moral support? I don't want to face Amanda—or anyone—alone."

Piper inclines her head, shock clear in her hazel eyes. "Are you asking for my help?"

"It's okay if you don't want to." The words spill out in a rush like a mountain stream during the spring runoff. "You probably want to keep a low profile right now. I'll be fine on my—"

She cuts me off with a flip of her wrist. "I'd be honored to be your wingman. Whenever you need it," she says, and relief pours through me. "I've got your back with Amanda and anyone else who thinks about coming for you."

"Thanks, Pip. I'm happy you're staying."

She blows me a kiss and disappears up the stairs.

Glancing out the front window, I see my first client of the day pull into the driveway. I smooth a hand through my hair and head for the garage to make the transfer.

The thought of showing up to an event half the town will turn out for gives me significant intestinal distress, but knowing Piper will be at my side eases the anxiety a bit. God willing, I won't be puking on anyone's shoes or making a run for a porta potty.

I should have let my guard down and allowed people in way before now. But no time like the present to create the future I want. I just wonder if I can convince Ian—who plowed through the walls around my heart like a three-hundred-pound linebacker —to be part of it.

THE FARMERS MARKET is in full swing, with people milling about the park just off Main Street when Piper and I set up chairs near the local Humane Society booth. Things are initially awkward as it's clear everyone has heard about the fiasco in the mountains, but my sister and I are a team. And we're a good one, despite everything that's happened.

As Penelope requested, Princess is wearing her frilliest pink dress, and I even managed to bathe and brush Beast so his coat resembles fur, not feathers.

Several families approach, but no one expresses definite interest in adopting either of the animals. Could be because Beast is audibly farting at regular intervals, and Princess keeps growling low in her throat. Neither of them is exactly making a great first impression.

We're also visited by a number of both of our former

classmates. The consensus is that Piper's better off without Bradley, and I'm selling myself too short thinking that I can't get a man on my own.

It's mildly humiliating, but once the novelty of rehashing the situation wears off, both Piper and I relax. We even talk to one of our mom's old friends who works as an administrator at the hospital. She gives Piper her card with the promise of helping connect her with an open position.

My nerves haven't fully settled because I know the most challenging part is still to come. Ian and Riva are bound to be here for the fun run.

Sure enough, about an hour after we arrive, a group starts to form at one end of the park—elementary school kids and their parents all wearing matching neon yellow shirts with the Skylark Elementary Wolves logo splashed across the front and a list of sponsors, my business included, on the back.

I busy myself adjusting Princess's rhinestone collar, but Piper grabs my arm.

"He's here, and he's looking this way."

I don't need her to alert me to Ian's presence. Moments earlier, goosebumps erupted along my arms and legs, a sure sign he's nearby.

"Does he look like he wants to shank me?" I ask.

"He's wearing sunglasses, so it's hard to tell."

I bark out a laugh. "Very reassuring."

"Oh sorry, is this the point where I blow sunshine up your ass and tell you it's going to be easy and you don't have to publicly castrate yourself and beg for his forgiveness?"

"Something like that. Don't quit your day job to become a professional wingman," I advise.

"Hey."

"Is for horses."

She squeezes my hand. "If falling in love were easy, everyone would do it."

It's the reminder I need. As much as I'm not relishing the whole public humiliation thing, I love Ian. I'm *in love* with him. Hopelessly head-over-heels. Not because of *what* he is—a famous, hot-as-hell ex-football player. But because of *who* he is—someone who makes me feel safe and like a better version of myself. The version I want to be more often.

"I'm going to do this." It's unclear whether the words are for her benefit or mine. "I can do hard things."

"Yes, you can." She starts to take the leashes from my hand.

"Oh, hell, no." I yank them back. "The dogs are coming with me. Canine moral support."

"Um...if the idea is to not look like a fool, maybe don't haul along the ugliest dog in America and one dressed like a cartoon character with an underbite." Piper's eyes widen. "Oh shit, too late. He's coming this way."

"Don't look so terrified." It's hard to keep my gaze straight ahead. Even harder not to run for my car. "You're freaking me out, Pip."

"Because I'm freaking out."

"We're all freaking out," one of the shelter volunteers whispers.

Piper swallows. "He's taking off his sunglasses. Dang, he looks intense."

"Pissed intense?" I crouch down to scratch behind Beast's ears when my knees turn to rubber. He lets one rip, and I'm enveloped in a cloud of dog stank. Perfect.

"Intense like there's seven seconds left in the Super Bowl, we're fourth and goal, and he's going for the win."

"The win," I repeat, trying not to choke as Beast farts again. Princess whines like she's embarrassed for us both. I don't blame her. "What's the win in this scenario?"

"I don't know," Piper snaps. "But stand up, wipe the dog slobber off your jeans, and act normal. Normal for you, anyway."

"Worst wingman ever," I say through gritted teeth. And difficult to manage when my knees are still the consistency of Jell-

O. Somehow, I manage to stand without toppling over and turn in Ian's direction.

Riva is at his side, and both of them look like they're on a mission. Nearly all activity in the market has stopped, and I notice groups of people drifting closer, silently, as they glance from him to me then back at him.

As a woman who doesn't like to be the center of attention, I picked an interesting guy to fall for.

"Hi, Sadie." Riva waves and does her best to ignore the gathering crowd. "My dad has something he wants to say to you." She bites down on her lower lip like she's trying to suppress a smile. "He's been practicing with his coach."

Ian glances down at her. "Subtle, kid."

She shrugs, her grin widening.

"That's great." I sound like a cartoon chipmunk who just took a hit from a helium balloon. Piper pinches my arm. I stifle a yelp then clear my throat. "I have something I want to say to your dad, too."

My voice is shaking, but that's okay. Just because I'm willing to do something hard doesn't mean I'm not terrified. Being brave means being scared but taking action anyway. Which is exactly what I intend to do.

"I'd like to adopt the dogs," Ian blurts out, catching me off guard.

"What dogs?" Those words were last on the list of the things I expected to come out of his mouth.

"Beast and Princess," Riva clarifies. "But that's not what he's been practicing."

"It's one of the things," Ian corrects her. "It's the thing you wanted me to say."

"It's not the only thing I want."

The back and forth is making my head spin even more. "You want to adopt Beast and Princess? I thought you had a no-dog policy." I glance down at the two dogs. Beast is straining on the leash to get to Ian, while Princess is straining to attend to her lady bits around the skirt's tulle fabric.

His eyes crinkle at the corners just the tiniest bit as he offers a soft smile. My heart beats double time in response.

"Things change. This is one of them. I've talked to Riva's mom, and we agree that having a dog—"

"Two," Riva interrupts.

"—at my house is acceptable. Riva's going to be responsible for them. I'll help too, of course, because I'm a Skylark local now."

He looks at the crowd that surrounds us, and it's hard to know whether he's trying to convince himself or me or the people watching us.

"I'm here for the long haul," he adds, nodding toward his daughter and the dogs, "and I'm here for you, Sadie."

I hear a snicker to my left and turn to see Sally, her hand clasped with Trina's, shaking her head. "Not exactly the smooth transition we planned, Playmaker, but go with it."

"What is actually happening?" I ask no one in particular.

"I'm asking you to give me another chance," Ian answers. "Awkwardly, but my heart is in the right place." He takes a step toward me. "No matter how this thing between us started, my heart is with you. I think it always has been."

"Fake news," someone shouts from the back of the crowd.

"Shut your pie hole, Amanda," Piper hollers back.

Ian sighs and runs a hand through his hair. "It's not fake, not for me." His voice is loud and sure and carries across the quiet square. Everyone seems to be waiting for him to say more. I'm right there with them.

He doesn't disappoint.

"I fell for you from the start. I think it might have been that deer leg sticking out of your backpack."

I snort out a laugh. "Or the fact that I called you a creeper to your face?"

"That, too," he agrees, his gaze tender. "My feelings were never pretend. They've only gotten more real the more I've come to know you, Sadie. You've got the biggest heart of anyone I know. You take care of everyone else because it's who you are. I love how you support the people you love—Riva and me most of all. You don't play games, and I'm done chasing a ring or fame. I want real love, and I'm absolutely head over heels in love with you."

There's a whispered murmur in the crowd. I blink back tears as his words wrap around my heart, patching up all the cracks and broken pieces.

"Because she's awesome," Sally says.

"Because you're awesome," Ian repeats. "You make this place feel like home. I want you in my life, if you'll give me another chance."

"Please give him another chance." Riva clasps her hands in prayer position in front of her. "And not just because he's letting me adopt the dogs."

"Because I love you." His gaze is filled with so much tenderness, it makes my heart ache. "Not from pretending, but because of the real you. The one you don't let everyone see. You're strong and kind, and you make me feel like I don't have to be perfect every moment. You're perfect for me, Sadie. I'm going to spend every day proving it if you'll let me."

"Your turn." Piper gives me a gentle shove.

"I love you, too," I whisper, then swallow down the emotion making it difficult to speak. This is important, and I want everyone to hear it. "I love the man you are inside. And how you make me feel like I'm enough just the way I am."

"More than enough," he confirms and takes my hands, giving me the boyish, heart-stopping smile I've come to adore. "You're everything."

I lift our hands and swipe the back of mine over my cheeks. "I'm sorry for what you heard me say to Sloane. It wasn't true. You're the man I wanted to..."

I look around, because there's public humiliation, and then

there's too much information and oversharing. I'm smart enough to know the difference. "To let into my heart. For real and forever."

"So we're done pretending?" he asks as he steps so close the front of him brushes against me, sending sparks zinging along my spine.

"So done."

When Princess starts spinning in a circle, Riva grabs the leash from me and scoops up the dog.

"Okay," she says, waving her hand between her dad and me. "You two do the kissy face stuff quick so we can start the fun run."

"I like a girl who stays on task," Iris says, giving Riva a thumbs up.

"Are you ready for the kissy face stuff?" Ian asks as he cups my face in his hands.

"Oh yeah," I tell him.

And then his mouth is on mine, gentle but demanding, like a silent promise. Like a dream come true.

There's a round of cheering, and he pulls back. "I love you, Sadie," he says again, softly. This time, the words are for me only.

"I love you, too."

The light in his eyes ignites a fire inside me, and I know that as much as Skylark has always been my home, this man is the place my heart belongs, forever and always.

NEXT UP IN The Skylark Series is SOMEONE TO TEMPT, a steamy, opposites-attract, second-chance, brother's best friend romance. Keep reading for a sneak peek of Iris and Jake.

BONUS EPILOGUE

For an exclusive bonus epilogue, join Michelle's newsletter via her website or at the address below. Happy reading!

https://BookHip.com/VXRDSCM

SOMEONE TO TEMPT
SNEAK PEEK

Iris

TO THE OUTSIDE OBSERVER, this might look like any other Tuesday morning at the mayor's office in Skylark, Colorado. It's not. Because the mayor—that's me—is waiting, not so patiently, for the most important meeting of her life to begin.

I straighten an already perfectly tidy stack of papers on my desk and lift an arm to take a sniff. Damn. Nervous sweat is the worst. Digging into the emergency stash of toiletries in the desk drawer, I triumphantly pull out a travel-sized deodorant. But when I flip off the lid, dried out clumps scatter over my navy blue suit.

Ugh. Ocean breeze scented snowfall. I stand up, hoping the crumbs will fall to the ground without incident, but no such luck. My skirt is dotted with the chalky white bits.

And why is it that women are stuck with names like lavender blossom and spring meadow, while guys are living their best deodorant lives with glacier punch and sharknado?

I'd like to glacier punch something at the moment, but there's no time for toiletry ramblings.

I have exactly three minutes until the woman who holds the key to my political future arrives at the mayor's office—my office of the past five months. I need to make a good impression, something that's eluded me with this particular individual. Former U.S. Senator Gloria Johnson makes me more nervous than a group of middle schoolers at their first coed dance, hence the anxiety sweat.

Today I need to wow, connect, and convince her I'll make an excellent state senator, and hope she agrees to back me in the next election. It's an important first step if I want a career in Colorado politics, and I'm not sure I can manage it without her. Not with my limited connections and a family background I'd rather forget.

I rush over to the tiny closet in the corner of the room where I keep a spare outfit for times like this. Fortunately, there's never been a time like this because I'm always prepared.

And now that there is, I'm too nervous to do anything right. The skirt's zipper catches, and my button-down shirt strains across my breasts as I yank it more forcefully.

Two minutes.

Voices float in from the other side of the closed office door. I've got to get this skirt off and the other one on before Jodi Moore, my assistant, walks through the door. She never knocks.

The zipper finally gives, and the silk fabric pools around my ankles. I flip off the dark pumps that match the skirt I was wearing, but not the beige one I'm about to tug on. Gloria won't notice my shoes if I stay behind my desk.

The door clicks open just as I've got the new skirt hitched up to my knees.

"What's going on out there?" I demand.

Jodi stares at me, mouth agape, before pulling the door closed behind her. "You're half-dressed." Somehow she makes it sound like she caught me doing naked cartwheels across the thick rug.

I yank the skirt the rest of the way. "Fully dressed now. What's the deal? Is Gloria here?"

I'm discombobulated. Otherwise, I'd notice the gleam in Jodi's teal green eyes.

"Oh, yes." She preens. *Preens.* "Senator Johnson is here. Along with a half-dozen disgruntled residents."

My head snaps up. "Disgruntled? What are you talking about?"

"I guess they heard about you cutting funding for the community spirit budget."

"I haven't cut anything."

"But you're *planning* on it, and it's not going over well."

"First." I hold up a finger, then curl it back into my fist when I realize I'm trembling. "How does anyone know about that plan? We're still in the draft phase."

Jodi shrugs. "It's a small town."

"Second, I'm not trying to mess with the town's community spirit. I'm all about community spirit."

She gives a disbelieving snort, as if I don't care about this town, when I've spent every waking second trying to make sure it thrives.

I just happens to believe in practical solutions over feel-good fluff. "I'm trying to find a way to fund the library's early learning literacy program since the state cut funding."

"By sacrificing Skylark's reputation as one of the happiest towns in America," she insists.

A couple of online articles give a town a made-up title and people go nuts. It just so happens those people aren't responsible for the town's budget.

"No one and *nothing* is being sacrificed," I counter through gritted teeth.

She pretends to study her nails, and I remember the moment last week when she asked to leave early to have them done to match the outfit she was wearing to the Apple Harvest Parade.

I said no, and this is payback. I'm certain of it.

"Can you schedule a meeting with the spirit committee for next week?" I glance at my watch. "Gloria is particular about punctuality."

Jodi shakes her head with an exaggerated sigh. "How's it going to look if you send away important members of the community? They're concerned about the integrity of the town."

Heat crawls up my neck, but I swallow it down. Jodi is thirty-two, a year younger than me, and has been in her position since her uncle hired her a week after her high-school graduation. Homer Moore spent over a decade as Skylark's mayor, but suffered an unexpected—and fatal—heart attack six months ago. Jodi made a play to be named interim mayor, but the town council appointed me instead.

I love this town, but I'm not a Colorado native and only moved back a year ago when I was hired as Skylark's director of community partnerships. I've tried my best to form a solid working relationship with the assistant I inherited. However, due in large part to her resentment over me getting the job she wanted coupled in larger part with my mother's past relationship with her late father, it all went to shit from the jump.

But I underestimated her. She waited until this moment, when I'm meeting with the woman who could be the linchpin for the career I want, to really throw me under the bus.

"You're right." I finish tucking in my shirt and roll my shoulders. "I should be the one to talk to them. I'll explain it. They'll understand."

Jodi's smile is smug. "Good luck with that."

She doesn't straight up give me the middle finger, but I get the message.

And it's my own fault. My friends from book club told me I should fire Jodi when I became acting mayor, but I didn't want the history and heartache our parents caused to have power over either of us. I'm all about breaking cycles and doing things differently. But now it's come back to bite me in the ass in bigger ways than missing staplers or reports that I have to review with a fine-tooth comb because she's inadvertently–or intentionally–left out key pieces.

Sabotage is one thing, and I looked at rising above it as a personal challenge. Now that she's put my potential connection with Gloria at risk, the gloves are coming off.

I walk past her and open the door. There's a moment of quiet as eight sets of angry eyes focus on me.

Crap. I hope I don't sweat through my shirt and end up with nervous pit stains . I should have picked black instead of pale yellow. My eyes meet Gloria's. She raises a curious brow in my direction, and I offer a bright smile in return.

"I'll be with you in one moment, Mrs. Johnson. I need to ensure these concerned citizens know I'm committed to hearing what they have to say."

Just like I'm committed to kicking my assistant's ass.

Several snorts of disbelief greet my words, but I'm also committed to killing them with kindness. "Can I get anyone a glass of water? Fun-size Snickers? I keep a stash in my—"

"We want answers," Marla Stewart, retired homemaker and chair of the Community Spirit Committee, demands. She takes her job seriously. "We want to know why you're *ruining* this town." *Very* seriously.

I automatically shake my head. "Marla, I'm not ruining anything. I'm trying to balance supporting our busy calendar of community events with other initiatives that need funding."

"The events are what make Skylark special." George Mason, owner of the largest realty company in town, earns a round of nods from the peanut gallery with his comment. "If you have your way, we're going to be known as the place where fun goes to die."

Fantastic. My political legacy is going to be as the mayor who killed fun.

AN HOUR LATER, the barrage of complaints that rained down like golf-ball sized hail have left me shredded inside and out.

"You didn't have to stay for all that," I tell Gloria as I slump forward in one of the chairs at the large conference-room table.

"Where fun goes to die," she murmurs with a grimace.

Gloria Johnson looks like a quintessential grandmother—snow-white hair styled in a neat bob, twinkling blue eyes behind understated glasses, and a face lined with experience. But there's more to her than that. Her years in office were marked by pragmatic decision making and unflinching determination to do what she believes is right.

I make a noncommittal sound in my throat.

"It's a catchy tagline, but not one you want associated with your term as acting mayor, and definitely not one that will get you elected this fall."

Her words pierce the veil of numbness covering me like a shroud. The same one I retreated to as a kid when things got too rough in our house. Shutting down my emotions and disassociating is hardwired into my system, serving me well in a variety of situations. Not this one, unfortunately.

I meet her gaze across the table. "I'm running unopposed."

The undertone of steel in her laugh reminds me that she's more than the president of Skylark's local knitting club. Gloria is not someone to trifle with.

"Honey, if you think someone isn't coming for you after that set-up, you need more than mentoring from me to start your political career. Hop off the starry-eyed trust train and open yours to what's really happening here."

My mouth does this weird open-and-shut thing several times like I'm a fish on dry land gasping for air.

"I have a plan," I tell her, like that makes a bit of difference. "I'm going to spend one elected term as Skylark's mayor then run for state Senate. I'll be thirty-five when I'm elected, and I'll serve a four-year term in the Colorado legislature, which should coincide with Congressman Allen's retirement plans. That congressional seat has always been held by someone from Skylark." I force a smile. "I want to be the next woman to hold it, to follow in your footsteps serving this town."

"I started by filling my late husband's seat when he was diagnosed with ALS," she says, her voice steady. "Matthew Allen was elected because Reggie Moore had to shut down his campaign after the scandal broke. Hard to run on a platform of family values after..." Her voice trails off.

My stomach clenches. "The video of him and my mom leaked." As if the affair wasn't bad enough, the video revealed the former mayor's penchant for *Star Wars* cosplay.

"I'll never hear the pew-pew of an interstellar gun," she says with a shake of her head, "without picturing the two of them."

"Which is why I asked for your help." When Homer, Reggie's brother became mayor after the scandal, the younger Moore served the town tirelessly and with no scandals attached to his name. But now Homer is gone, and things are different for me. I have a past in this town, even if it isn't one I created. "I don't want to be associated with my mom's legacy or her affair with former Mayor Moore."

Mom hasn't been back to Colorado for over a decade, but I know she still considers herself a fun-loving free spirit. Only her version of fun left me and my brother without care or food half the time and made enemies of married women in every town she blew through.

"Skylark can't be the place where fun goes to die, Iris." Gloria steeples her fingers on the polished cherry table. "I also cannot back a candidate who has a reputation for killing community spirit. Do you know why Skylark's leadership first started actively investing in the town's image?"

I do. As a way to distract the town from his brother's scandal with my mother fourteen years ago, newly appointed Mayor Homer Moore began instituting prescribed events to bolster community spirit and build a reputation for wholesome small-town fun.

In the last decade, we've gone from hosting the usual seasonal festivals and an occasional juried art show, to at least one event a month funded by the town for the purpose of bringing a smile to the faces of residents young and old. I'm not a fan of forced fun, but I've attended most of the events, at least in passing, because of my position. Thanks to social media and a bajillion lists ranking small-town life, plus the fascination with romantic movies centered around the very same thing, Skylark has grown in popularity. Our reputation and designation as one of the happiest towns in the country is a source of pride for many residents. But others, like me, have festival fatigue.

"Not every event brings in enough revenue to offset the cost associated with them. Plus, sometimes they prevent us from supporting the people who live here in a meaningful way. That's all I'm trying to do. Isn't that what good politicians do? We take care of our constituents."

She inclines her head to study me. "You're a smart girl. I didn't expect you to show such Pollyanna tendencies."

"I'm not—"

"This isn't Camelot, Iris." She closes her eyes for a minute. "Politics is as much about impressions as intention. You have to get elected before you can do the work, and you aren't going to get elected in a town like Skylark if everyone thinks you're the grim reaper of fun."

"I'm fun," I insist, but the words come out like a snarl.

She cracks a real smile. "Oh yes, that tone will convince people. Figure it out, Iris, and then we'll talk. Is the life of a career politician in the public eye *truly* what you want?"

I frown and force myself not to argue. Of course, it's what I want. Okay, maybe that hasn't always been the case.

But once the members of the town council appointed me interim mayor, I realized this was how I could both *do* good and show that I *am* good. Prove to everyone in town that I'm not my mother. Sure, my biggest role model still subscribes to the belief that sex, drugs, and rock and roll are the only kind of fun worth having, but she was some kind of holdover groupie. Only instead of collecting famous notches on her belt, my mother collected married notches.

"I *am* fun," I tell her again. "And if I need to stay sunup to sundown at every event this town sponsors to prove it, I will."

She lets out what I can only describe as a disappointed sigh, confusing me all the more.

"Isn't that what you want from me?"

"I want you to do something for *you*. Something that lights you up and takes you out of your comfort zone."

Her blue eyes bore into me like she's imparting some great wisdom, but for the life of me I have zero clue as to what lights me up. I think about my book club's bucket list challenge. We're meeting tonight, and I need to be ready to tell them what I'm going to do. I haven't been able to come up with anything that would rival our friend Sadie's choice of a challenge: losing her virginity. How do I compete with that?

My friends would tell me it's not a competition, but...my brain doesn't work that way. I thought about training for an ultramarathon, which isn't nearly as interesting as sex, but it *would* showcase my strength and perseverance to the people in town. We're in Colorado, and the freaky fit outdoorsy types like that kind of crap. But it's not exactly fun, and now it feels like fun is mandatory.

Gloria's right. I don't do fun.

"Speaking of fun..." Gloria glances at her watch. "I need to get ready for my dance class."

I offer a smile because it's not going to help for Gloria to see how freaked out I am about all of this. "I didn't know you were a dancer."

"I'm not, but I love shaking my hips." She does a little wiggle that's surprisingly sensual for a woman in her mid-seventies. "Salsa is my favorite," she says. "Find something you love that doesn't have anything to do with the job or getting ahead. Do it because it makes you happy. You do, after all, live in the town voted one of the happiest in the country."

I hate that stupid slogan, but I keep the smile on my face. "I will, Gloria. I won't let you down."

"This is about *you*, Iris."

I try not to squirm under her steady gaze. I don't like things being about me. I'm not worth the attention. Sure, there are plenty of politicians who crave the spotlight. I want to make this about the town, not me.

I wait a few minutes after she leaves, a cloud of Chanel No 5 lingering in her wake, before following her out of the conference room. Instead of walking back to my office or past Jodi's desk near the main staircase, I rush to the cramped staircase at the end of the hall. The air inside is stuffy, and my heels make the metal steps clang, the sound reverberating as I rush down.

It's like I can't breathe. I can't get the air in, and not because of what happened with the angry community members or Gloria's advice about having fun. It's the betrayal I feel from somebody who I should have known isn't my ally.

I trusted Jodi. I thought we were on the same team, working together for the town. I thought we were doing good things and putting our personal differences aside. It turns out I'm the fool again, thinking I could trust just anyone.

I bust out of the back door of town hall and take deep gulps of the crisp fall air. I will *not* cry. I haven't cried since the day my twin brother got carted off to that camp for juvenile delinquents when we were seventeen. He told me tears are for losers, and I took his words to heart. It gave me something I could control, which I needed badly in the chaos of that summer.

Maybe an occasional hay fever flare up makes my eyes water, but I do not cry. Not when I watch sad movies. Not when my friend Sloane told me at the start of summer that she has cancer.

Not when Sadie and former NFL legend Ian Barlowe announced their engagement. Nada.

I drag in another deep breath and keep my eyes forward as I exit the alley and march toward the crosswalk. I don't have a destination in mind, and my keys are tucked in the bottom drawer of my desk, so I can't truly escape. But I can head for Cover to Cover, the book store Sloane Winslow owns on the other end of downtown.

Since her diagnosis, she's reduced her shifts to part-time, but she's always there on Wednesday mornings because it's the children's reading hour.

It's early enough that there isn't much traffic, so I don't worry about being spotted in my mismatched outfit and red-rimmed eyes. Until I notice one of Jodi's many cousins walking toward me. Oh, hell no.

I pivot and dash across the street, only I don't notice the truck zooming in my direction. I have no idea how I missed it, but brakes squeal, and the vehicle stops inches from my kneecaps.

I know that bumper. I've been pressed against that bumper for a deep, passionate kiss.

My gaze raises to the man behind the wheel. When the hazel eyes that used to haunt my dreams meet mine, it's like looking directly at the sun. My corneas burn and my vision goes hazy at the corners.

I press a hand to the hot hood of the old Chevy truck as Jake Byrne climbs out of it. The cherry on top of a shit show sundae of a day.

He looks different than he did over a decade earlier when he was the most beautiful boy I'd ever met. He's become a man in the intervening years. The thick coat of stubble that covers his jaw makes those gray-green eyes look all the more distracting and his full mouth even more kissable.

Stop that, I command myself.

No thinking about Jake and kissing in the same sentence. We

only shared one soul-shattering—not to mention panty-melting—moment before things went to hell, yet the feel of his arms around me remained seared on my memory for far too long.

Whatever he's doing in Skylark, I want nothing to do with it. With him. He might have turned my life upside down once, but I'm smarter now. If this morning is any indication, I don't need any help getting into trouble. I've got that covered all on my own.

I quickly fix my face and plaster a bland, tight-around-the-edges smile on it. Taking a step back from the car, I lift my hand.

"It's fine," I say, like Jake and I have no history. "Just watch where you're going next time."

He takes two steps toward me but stops and throws up his hand, exasperation rolling off him like a wave. "Are you crazy, Iris, or do you make a habit of jumping in front of moving vehicles?"

That word...crazy. All my emotions—the worry, regret, and self-doubt—coalesce into something different inside me. Something that feels dark and thick like sludge. I lean into that darkness and let it ooze through me. I may not like Jake Byrne, but he's the one person in this town I don't have to be nice to. Might as well take advantage of it.

"Go to hell, Jake." I start to flip him off, but realize that's not a great look for the mayor when there's an audience staring from the sidewalk. Instead, I lean in closer. "Or crawl back under whatever trustafarian rock you slithered out from? Polish the watches in your overpriced collection or count the zeros in your bank account. Whatever guys like you do when you're not busy pretending to be real."

He rears back like I've slapped him, and a swish of guilt creeps up my spine. I shove it down because I don't owe him anything. Jake Byrne doesn't get to breeze back into town—my town—like he owns the place. Like he still has any claim on my heart.

Nope. He doesn't get my sympathy. Not today.

ABOUT THE AUTHOR

USA Today and Top 5 Amazon Bestselling author Michelle Major writes swoon-worthy stories full of heart, heat, and guaranteed happily-ever-afters. When she's not dreaming up romance, you'll find her hiking the trails (or avoiding housework) in her home state of Colorado.

Connect with Michelle
website: michellemajor.com
Instagram: @michellemajorauthor
Facebook: michellemajorbooks